Never

Lost Souls MC Series

Blue Saffire

Perceptive Illusions Publishing

Bayshore, New York

Blue Saffire/Perceptive Illusions Publishing, Inc.
PO BOX 5253
Bayshore, NY 11706
www.BlueSaffire.com

Publisher's Note: This is a work of fiction. Names, characters, places, and incidents are a product of the author's imagination. Locales and public names are sometimes used for atmospheric purposes. Any resemblance to actual people, living or dead, or to businesses, companies, events, institutions, or locales is completely coincidental.

Ordering Information:
Quantity sales. Special discounts are available on quantity purchases by corporations, associations, and others. For details, contact the "Special Sales Department" at the address above.

Never/ Blue Saffire. – 2nd ed.
ISBN 978-1-941924-10-5

Never be afraid to go for what's yours.

–Blue Saffire

Dropping In

Sal

Evanescence's "My Immortal" plays in my ears as I sit lost in the screens before me. The words couldn't speak more to my soul. My mind has been full the last few weeks.

I try to force the coding and work before me to distract me. I reach for my shoulder, the flesh there raw from my trying to wash the past away. It didn't work, it never does.

I still feel filthy. My skin only hurts and serves as a reminder of the pain that radiates within. I close my eyes as the memories try to rush me. My phone rings startling me.

I nearly jump out of my skin. Seeing its King, I rush to answer. The last thing I want to do is alarm him.

I take in a deep breath and forces a smile on my lips before I speak as if he can see me. "Hey," I sing into the phone.

"Hey, baby girl," he replies. "I'm on my way up."

I look at the monitors that have surveillance of the inside and outside of my apartment. Sure, enough I catch sight of King walking into the lobby, toward the old, caged lift. The sound of the lift outside my apartment door reaches me and snaps me into action.

I hang up and go to open my front door. King always calls before he comes up and he never uses the entrance that will bring him straight into the apartment, even though he has full access to.

To be honest, I hardly use that direct entrance myself unless I'm taking my bike out or returning with it. It's safer to come in through the front. My apartment and building are a rare New York gem, but it's still New York.

It's as if King wants to make sure I'm descent or to prevent startling me when he comes by. Either way, I appreciate my stepbrother's thoughtfulness. Stepbrother. King has been more like a blood brother to me from the day our parents moved us into together, maybe more so.

"Hey, what are you doing here?" I say when King saunters toward me as he steps off the ancient elevator.

"I got some shit I need you to look at."

I back up and allow him to step in. I close the door and turn right into the bear hug King has for me. He always smells so nice and it's welcoming. No, comforting. Something I can use today more than he can ever know.

"Cool, do you just need me to look, or should I input any of it?"

"It's all for input. You can shred it all after," he replies.

That's my job. I use my photographic memory to store and encrypt information for the Lost Souls. It's a little known fact. A fact King wants to keep to himself as much as possible.

Sometimes I think he was relieved when I asked to move away somewhere to be alone for a while. Less questions, less eyes. A win, win if you ask me.

"You want something to drink?"

"Yeah, you got any of that beer I left here?"

"Sure do," I say and laugh.

He knows I'm not touching the stuff. I'm not that big on the taste. Especially not the brand he likes. Not to mention, I like to be alert at all times.

I go to the fridge and get him a beer before I go back to my desk where he's placed three large files. This might take a while.

"Give me a few secs to close out this stuff I was working on and I'll start," I say as I quickly finish up the last of the coding and data entry I was working on.

King moves to stand over my shoulder. "Is that the new program?"

"Yeah."

"How's it holding up? You think we'll be able to use for all the chapters across the board?"

I snort. "Did I code this?"

He palms the top of my head and shakes it as he laughs. "The hair cut looks good on you, by the way," he says through his chuckle.

I reach up and touch my newly chopped off main. I thought it would take the eyes off me. I thought it would release the pressure that builds in my skull. It's didn't.

Honestly, I think I get more looks. I've been offered business cards of agents that want me to model or act. Not that I trust any of them. This is New York after all.

"Thanks. I needed a change," I say.

Again, I appreciate King not making a big deal out of my need for change. Leave it to him to be smooth about my cut. I might keep it.

It does make me feel badass some days. I shrug off the thought and close out of the work I just finished. I reach for the first file and start to look through the docs.

"I'll leave you to do your thing. You want something to eat? I'm starving," King says as he moves toward the couch.

"Yeah, I say absently as I flip through the pages."

I'm lost in absorbing what I'm looking at. My mind takes a snapshot of each page, committing it to memory. I smile as an old memory comes to the surface. The day Cage realized I was able to do this.

Cage patted his pockets looking around the garage where he was fixing a bike. I was glued to his side to watch him take it apart and put it back together. I was too small to give any real help, but Cage always allowed me to watch.

"Where'd I put that damn paper?" he grumbled to himself as he held his phone and searched.

"555-6822," I said.

Cage looked down at me and wrinkled his brows. I was shy, so I started to feel nervous. I wasn't sure if I did something wrong, so I repeated the phone number, and this time gave the address too.

"38 Hudson Ave.," I finished as I watch Cage's face.

"What's that, baby girl?"

"The number and address on the paper," I said in almost a whisper.

"How do you know that?"

I point toward his office in the clubhouse, where I'd been sitting on his desk as he barked orders and handled club business. The paper he's looking for was on top of his desk, placed over a stack of other papers. I could see it in my mind as clearly as if I were still sitting there.

"The paper is on your desk. That's what's written on it. I saw it when we were in there," I replied.

Cage grabbed my hand and walked back into the clubhouse. We entered his office and he stop before the desk. He picked up the piece of paper.

"What's the zipcode?"

"29063," I replied.

His brows threaded. "And you're telling me this from looking at this paper while you sat on the desk?"

I nodded. "The paper under that one has a number on the top. Invoice 678094," I answered.

He reached for the other paper. His brows shot up into his hairline as he read the top. He looked back at me with wide blue eyes.

Cage squatted down to get eye level with me. "Can you just remember numbers?"

I shook my head. "No, it's not the numbers. I can see the desk. Like pictures in my head.

"I remember everything on the desk. You have a pen that says Soul Emotions by your mug. The mug says Body and Soul Body Shop.

"You have a picture of Mommy on the right side of the desk, in a wooden frame, but it's only there when she's not around. You put it in the top right drawer when she is. It sits on top of the red folder," I reply, remembering the day Mommy came to pick me up and Cage placed the picture in the drawer as I sat on his desk reading a book.

Cage never let me out of his sight when I went to the clubhouse to watch him fix bikes. I was his shadow. I had several pictures in my brain of the time I spent in his office and the garage.

Cage cupped my little head in his hand and roared with laughter. "I knew you were a genius, baby girl, but this takes the cake."

"Kodax," King calls pulling me from my thoughts.

My smile grows. That's the name Cage gave me when he learned of my talent. Only those close to me know about it.

"What's up?" I murmur.

"I asked if you wanted Chinese or pizza," King says.

"Oh, not pizza. Dude, I got so sick the last time I ate from that one place. I haven't had pizza since. Chinese is cool."

We fall silent again. Only the sound of the shredder beside me and the TV King put on in the living room area playing as background noise. My mind has found peace for now.

My big brother is here. I can breathe.

Gutter

I've hit rock bottom. I don't know whether I'm coming or going. At this point, I don't know if I want to live anymore.

I snort into my beer. Trust, I couldn't even tell anyone how I ended up in this bar in Richmond, Virginia. I got on my bike and rode until I couldn't anymore.

"You want another one, handsome?" the brunette bartender behind the bar asks.

I grunt my response and nod. She's been giving me more attention than any of the other patrons here. I'm not much for talking, but I've kept my responses to her simpler than usual.

I want to be left alone. I'm not interested in whatever she's thinking behind those gray eyes she keeps batting at me. I finish the beer in my hand and put it down as she arrives with the fresh one.

"I've never seen you in here before. Are you just passing through?" she says this time.

"Yeah."

Her smile brightens. "Not much of a talker, are you?"

I give her a pointed look. What the fuck does she think? If I'm not saying shit, isn't it obvious. She lifts her hands as if in surrender.

"All right, cowboy. I can take a hint. Just thought you'd like some fun, no strings attached."

I turn away from her and look toward the door. Right as I do, a dude with blond locs and a biker cut walks in. He looks around the place before he saunters to the bar.

There are other bikers around the bar, but this guy has a presence that draws the eye. He moves like he owns the place and could give two fucks about who has a problem with it.

He takes a seat across the bar from me and like him, I go about minding my business. I drown my attention in the beer before me. I have so many questions for the being who created me.

At the top of the list, what did I do to piss them off? I had to have offered someone to end up with this fucked up life. Why have I never had a place to belong?

"Lord, have mercy on my soul," I mutter as the ache of a lifetime of hurt washes over me.

"You heard what the fuck I said."

The loud words grab my attention. I look across the bar to see some big guy shouting down at the blond dude. The guy with the locs turns slowly to look at the loud mouth. When he stands its painstakingly slow, he towers over the guy and says something I can't hear from here.

The hairs on the back of my neck stand up as I notice five other guys who begin to surround the blond. He's a big dude but he's definitely outnumbered. I don't know what makes me get up.

Maybe I have a death wish and I'm ready to meet my maker in a filthy ass bar over a stupid bar fight that has nothing to do with me. Or it could be this feeling I have, like fate has something waiting for me if I butt in. Either way, when the blond hauls back and throws the first punch as if he's not outnumbered, I smash my beer on the side of a stool and get to work with his ass.

Soon we end up in the middle of about ten guys. I've stabbed a couple before I drop the bottle and go with my bare knuckles. I've just knocked another one out when through the corner of my eye, I see a guy heading for the blond dude with a knife.

"Look out," I bark before I move to block the guy and grab his wrist.

I snap the fucker's wrist with the force of my pent up rage. The blade drops to the ground as he howls and falls to his knees. With a hand on the back of his head, I bring his face into my knee and relish the satisfying crunch of his nose.

"Hey, these motherfuckers run deep in these parts and apparently I've worn out my welcome. If you want to leave here breathing let's go," the blond says as he heads for the door.

I look around and think it over for a split second before I start out the door behind him and jump on my bike. I don't know why, but instead of heading North, I rode South with the guy in the Lost Souls cut. For the first time in a long time, it feels like I'm going in the right direction.

Not Better

Sal

Two years later…

"You sure you're good?" King says over the phone.

I turn from my view of the street to shift my gaze up to the ceiling as I perch on the windowsill. I blow out a breath and roll my eyes shut, knowing he can't see me, or the anguish and exhaustion written on my face. The words are there, but I trap them inside.

They can never come out. Am I good? No. Am I surviving? I guess.

The nightmares still come and go as they please. I think I sleep less because of them, trying to avoid what awaits me in the shadows. Then there's the paranoia, but I can't tell King any of this, because I know the outcome. I can't have that on my conscious.

"Yeah, I'm fine. Just busy," I reply.

King's quiet for a few beats. My brother has this way of speaking without saying a word. You almost feel as if you're being chastised in the rumble of his silence.

"You know I'm here if you need me. When you need me."

It's clear in his voice he wants to push, but he knows me. I'm not going to talk unless I'm ready. Which is most likely why he restrains himself and doesn't force me to cough up my issues the way he would with anyone else, especially our sister, Eva.

"Yes, King, I know. Listen, I'm going to get to work. You need anything else from me?" I reply.

"Just to know you're good. You feel me?"

"I feel you. I'm fine. I'll call in a couple of days to check in."

He snorts. "Yeah, I'll call you." He laughs and hangs up.

I know, I know. I probably will forget to call. I get lost in my work and forget the world, but that's the best thing for me. An idle mind is a playground and all of that.

I look down at the street below. Couples and groups walk by. They make life look so easy.

What I would give to feel that kind of normal again. I pull my knees into my chest and wrap my arms around my legs. The tears begin to burn the backs of my eyes.

My soul hurts. I was robbed... I stop my thoughts short. I'm not going to sit here feeling sorry for myself.

"Time to rebuild. Regroup," I breathe and stand. "Back to work, Sal."

I'm working on a special project for King, so I'll probably be pulling an all nighter. *What's new?*

I push up and head toward my desk. My stomach growls and reminds me I had planned to go for coffee and donuts or something before King's call. I frown.

King had some tension in his voice before he picked up on my own. I can't help wondering if club business is the cause or is something else wearing on him the same as me. I push all that aside.

King is a great prez. Whatever's eating at him, I'm sure he'll figure it out. Getting my part done will help smooth things out.

"Focus," I mutter to myself.

One look around my apartment and I slump my shoulders. This place is starting to weigh in its loneliness. I snatch up my backpack and shove my laptop inside.

I can work from the Vigo's, it's a great restaurant not too far away. Camdan, Vigo's son runs the place and he's always so protective of me when I come in to eat alone.

I hate to be one to stereotype, but I swear Vigo and Rabbi give me a mob vibe. However, they make me feel safe like the brotherhood of the Lost Souls. Rabbi and a few of his guys have walked me home a time or two. Something I only allowed after King and I ate at Vigo's together and I got the feeling their kindness wasn't a coincidence.

"Food," I hum as I think of the delicious sauce they make.

However, my heart is just happy we won't be feeling lonely. Yes, I'm lonely. Heartbreakingly so.

Will this ever get better?

Gutter

"Forty-eight, forty-nine."

Sweat drips down my chest and face as I force one more sit up. It's going to be another one of those nights. I'm not going to get any sleep. Each time I close my eyes guilt, disgust, and torment rushed me.

My phone rings and I bare my teeth at it. If this is Terry again, I'm going to hurl the damn thing across the living room. Although I know he's not the trigger for all of this, I want to blame my cousin for my rising demons.

I cut ties a long time ago. I had to. Whenever, Terry and I are in each other's lives nothing good comes to us.

I'm a Lost Soul so not checking to see who's calling isn't an option. I reluctantly reach for the device resting on the coffee table I built with my own hands. One of the things I've found that actually brings me some peace.

"Fuck," I hiss when Terry's number flashes on my screen.

The peace I've been trying to find all night goes out of the window. I refuse to allow him to pull me back in. My soul tells me he's going to rub raw these old wounds I'm doing my best to ignore.

"Not now." I send the call to voicemail and stare into the empty space.

I came to Seattle to check on my property and make a drop for the club. I thought I'd take my time, clear my head and shove these demons back into their closet before I head home. *Home.*

No matter what state I'm in, I've yet to find that. South Carolina is as close as I've come. However, it's still not there. This place has none of the comfort it should. Another property, another vacant space if you ask me.

The phone rings again. I growl at it, but when I glance at the screen some of the tension lifts from my chest. Picking up, I pinch the bridge of my nose, trying to release the pressure sitting there.

"What do you need, brother?" I answer.

"Nothing, just checking on you. Diggs said you took a trip. You taking a trip means your head's fucking with you," Grim replies. "What's up? You need to talk?"

"It's club business. I'm fine," I say tightly, only frustrating myself.

I know my brother means well. Grim and Reap pulled me in when I first arrived at the Lost Souls' compound with King two years ago. They made me feel like I belonged. No questions asked.

"You and I know that's bullshit. But I'll allow you your space. I know what it's like to have demons on your back. I'm just offering an ear."

"I know. Look, I'm dealing with it."

"Do what you need to do. We here if you need, you feel me, brother?"

I pause for a moment. Grim is a one crazy motherfucker. If anyone would understand the crazy going on in my head, it would be him.

I shake the thought away. I'm not about to open this box. It needs to stay locked forever. No, this isn't getting any better, but talking about it isn't going to change a thing.

"Yeah, I feel you," I reply instead of taking the offering of a listening ear.

The line goes dead and I'm suddenly tired. Tired of life, tired of running from shadows. Tired.

CHAPTER TWO

My Bike

Sal

"Have a good one," the barista says as I take my coffee and head out.

I lift my cup in thanks and nod my head at her. She's always so cheery in the morning. I don't know how.

My laptop weighs me down with the reminder of work. I got distracted at Vigo's. Rabbi and Vigo sat with me to tell old stories while I ate until my heart's content. I need to catch up on the lost time.

Initially I'd considered working from the coffee shop. However, something urges me to head back home, so I turn for the exit. I like my life simple.

It's the reason I almost didn't take the job King offered me when I came to him about wanting to get away. King is different with me than he is with my older sister.

Had it been Eva to come to him saying she needed to get away, he may have questioned her motives. Not so much with me. I ask, and King finds a solution we both could bear with.

A small breeze hits my face as the sun starts to peek through the buildings. It's supposed to be a hot one later. I will forever be amazed at how the buildings here in New York keep the city so cool on a scorching day.

I take a sip of my drink and stroll back to my loft. Rolling my shoulders, I crack my neck to the side. I let daybreak without so much as blinking. Day is night and night is day to me, most times.

I happen to be on one of my twenty-four-hour sleepless runs. Nothing out of the norm. It's the life of a hacker like me. I've never lived by the hours of others.

Actually, I'm glad I was finally able to get lost in my work and not my thoughts. Once I double check everything.... My thoughts trail off the moment I step off the lift.

An eerie feeling comes over me. Something is off. I slowly move toward my front door.

It's slightly jarred open. I listen for sound coming from inside, but nothing greets my ears. Deep down inside, I know I shouldn't, but the part of me who refuses to be a victim pushes me to reach into my pocket for my teaser as I hold tightly to my can of mace in my other hand.

Slowly, I easy the door open and slip into the apartment. A gasp leaves my lips as my tossed apartment comes into view. I'm frozen in place until I notice the vacant space my bike once resided in.

"My bike," I cry out. "They took my fucking bike."

Anger replaces panic. I rush through the apartment quickly. Something is wrong about this. Wrong enough for me to grab a few burner phones and some other things I might need before taking off. My instincts are screaming for me not to stick around.

"Time to get the hell out of here," I mutter once I have all I need, not bothering to waste time.

If this is tied to the club and someone has figured out what I do for the Lost Souls, I could be in danger. I know more about the club than most, but no one knows I do.

At least, we thought no one knew. This is just bullshit. I loved this loft and my bike.

I'll get somewhere safe and then I can call King.

***

I bounce my leg nervously as I huddle in the corner of the back seat of the bus I'm riding on. I've gotten as far away from the apartment as I can. I don't believe I'm being followed, but I can't be sure.

"Pick up, pick up, pick up," I chant as the other line rings.

The nearly packed bus doesn't give me too much reassurance. It feels like someone's going to rat me out to whoever broke into my place at any moment now. I counted my blessings to at least get a seat alone.

No one wants to sit next to the smelly bathroom after all.

"Hey, darlin'. What's up?"

The relief I have when King answers is palpable. God, I hadn't realized I was holding my breath after that last chant. I rush through my words as I steal a quick breath.

"King, someone broke into my place. They stole my fucking bike. Cage gave me that bike."

"Wait. What the fuck? Where are you?"

With a quick glance outside the window, I recall the random ticket I purchased. It was what I could afford with the cash in my get away bag.

"I'm on a bus heading for D.C. I took off as soon as I noticed the break in. I didn't know if they were still around. I grabbed what I needed and ran."

"Get off the bus at the next available stop and get on a plane. I want you to head for lady, make a few stops don't go straight."

"King, come on, I can't take this there," I huffed in impatience.

There's a huge pit in my stomach as I listen to King bark orders. Not many people know Lady is King's grandmother's nickname or where she can be found. She's always been good to me and Eva, treating us like her own. I know exactly where King wants me to go. Yet, I'm still hesitant.

"Have I ever stirred you wrong? I'll get to you before you get there, but if anyone is following you, they'll get a whole lot of *Lost*, you feel me," he growled into the phone.

"Yeah, I feel you." I sigh. "I'm dumping this phone. I have three others. I'll text you when I'm headed the right way."

"Good, I'll send you the name of the Soul I'm sending. Stay low. If you run into trouble, call me ASAP."

"Okay, okay. I got it."

"It's going to be okay. I'm gonna get you home, kid."

"I know."

Gutter

I swing out but only connect with air. I'm surrounded. Jeers and taunts fill the air. The room recks of sweat, alcohol, stale perfume and cologne.

My skin starts to claw. I swing again and again. I'll fight my way out if I have to.

"Fuck," I bellow as my phone wakes me. I didn't know I'd finally passed out.

When I pick up the phone King's name lights up the screen. I take in a claiming breath before I answer. The nightmare still clinging to my skin and thoughts.

"Hello," I huff as I shake off the rest of shadows.

"Don't head back just yet. I need you to pick up a package for me. Hang tight and I'll send you all the information you need."

"All right. Got it."

"Keep your phone close. I'll have more details for you soon."

He ends the call and I release a heavy breath. Getting up, I stretch and try to clear my head. Deciding a shower might do the trick, I head for the bathroom to be ready when the text arrives with my next instructions.

By the time I step out and get my jeans and boots on, my phone alerts me to a text. I reach for the nightstand as I sit on the edge of the bed and pick the phone up. It's from King.

I sit looking at my phone with a frown. When King first said he had a package for me to pick up, I thought I'd be hauling arms or something. Not a person.

Prez knows he can count on me for anything but picking up some dude on the back of my fucking bike. What the fuck? That shit ain't happening.

Maybe I'm miss reading the text and Sal has the package I need to pick up. Good thing I have a truck here. I hadn't planned to drive it back home, but I will now. In any case, it will be best to take the truck since I don't know how large the load will be.

And if it is a person.... Hell, honestly, I have a problem with anyone riding at my back, but if Prez needs something, I'm there for him. He had my back, when I had nowhere to go.

I wouldn't even have a dime to my name if it weren't for King. I found the Lost Souls at the lowest point in my life and King was there to help me through a lot of my bullshit.

"Shit." I blow out a breath and run my hand through my hair.

I won't pretend that I'm not still a whole lot of fucked up. You don't just bounce back from the shit I have been through. My days of riding around carefree have long ago moved on. As a matter of fact, I don't think they ever existed.

I'm only twenty-five, but some days I feel so much older. Life just started beating on me and never stopped. I know I'm broken, but that's what makes me, me.

"Son of a bitch," I mutter and get moving as my thoughts continue to spin.

King once offered me the office of Enforcer, but I told him, no. I don't think I'd come back from the dark places being an Enforcer would take me. Sergeant in arms suits me just fine.

Not to mention, I'm a bonafide Squad member. That role comes with its own brand of crazy. You have to be damaged to a point, to even be considered to be a Squad member. That part was easy for me, as was the need to be loyal.

Yeah, it's loyalty that's has me head to this job. The words run through my head as I look at the text again.

After shaking off the feeling that this isn't going to be an ordinary or easy job, I get to my feet and pull on a white T-shirt and my cut. This is the way I'm most comfortable.

Putting on suits and showing up to my office has become an adjustment for me. Suits reminds me too much of back then, where I come from and who I used to be. Once again, I'm grateful to the Lost Souls for helping me turn my life around.

I now own one half of one of the top security firms in the Southeast and we plan to expand Southwest and up North. I employ a number of the Lost Souls, something I never imagined doing. Me, having people who listen and follow me. I'd once been so lost I couldn't trust following myself.

I'm making myself and the club a hell of a lot of money. It hasn't changed me though. Not in the way most folks change, when they start making enough to fund a small country or two. I guess that's because I'm no stranger to money and the things people do to get it, keep it, or show it off.

Fuck, I wasn't broke when King found me. Still, I was on my way there with the life I was living, but it would have taken a least a few more years to get there. I didn't care about money then and even now it doesn't drive me. There's one thing that drives me.

I love to ride and get lost on the road. It's how I keep my head clear of all the shit in it. I look longingly at my bike as I load it onto the back of my truck and secure it.

It's been one of those weeks when my past is riding me hard and a good ride is in order to chase the demons away. I guess that'll have to wait. Once I get this package to King and after checking in at the clubhouse, I'll take off again for a few days.

Another text comes through and as I look at it I scrunch up my face once more. King has sent me the location and now I'm sure this is a person and not an actual package. I'm not too far from the pickup. With a grunt, I head to the bus station.

This guy better not get on my fucking nerves all the way to South Carolina.

CHAPTER THREE

Hidden

Sal

I got off the first bus just like King told me too, catching the first plane I could to Vegas and then took a plane to Oregon, before the six-hour bus ride to Seattle, where Lady lives. Once the bus to Seattle stops at my final destination, I shove a piece of gum in my mouth as I reach into my bag and pull out a little cam. It was one of the few things I thought to grab before I left my place, along with a few phones and a couple of devices.

Thank God for my hidden stash. I can always get clothes. I'm not big on fashion anyway. When I step off the bus, I pull the wad of gum out of my mouth and stuck it to the back of the cam. Without anyone noticing, I fix the cam to the trashcan facing the parking lot and keep moving.

"Would you mind sparing some change?" A man shoves his cup in my face.

I sidestep him and mumble. "Sorry. I'm tapped."

In New York, I usually empty my pocket of all the change I have. This once I have to think ahead and I'm limited on resources. I rush into the station and head for the bathroom.

Me: I'm here.

I wait for King's response as I wash my hands and look into the mirror at my tired face. My phone chimes, causing me to jump. I shake my head.

King: Gutter. On the way.

Gutter? I have photos of every member of the Lost Souls in my database on my tablet. The database I created for the entire organization, upon King's request. It only takes a second to pull an image and profile up.

Me: Isn't he from the SC chapter?

I'm confused by this. There's no way I'm waiting here in this bus station for hours or days for that matter, for someone to come get me. I thought King would send someone from a local chapter.

King: I have it covered. It won't be long.

Me: Are you sure?

I want for a reply that never comes. When King is done with a conversation he's done. Of course, in his mind he made himself clear. I sigh in frustration.

About fifteen minutes pass and I cannot believe I'm hiding out in this nasty bathroom, waiting to be rescued. All I wanted was a good cup of coffee, so I could finish going through the financials King had sent over yesterday. I walked to the coffee shop to get some fresh air instead of making coffee in the apartment.

I would just like to know who I pissed off to have them trash my place and take my bike. Did they take the bike so I couldn't go anywhere far? Aggravated with my thoughts, I blow out a breath and watch the screen on my mini device.

Another five minutes pass as I watch and wait. Just when I pull out my phone to try King again, a large pickup truck pulls into the lot. I scowl at the screen because the black monster truck is blocking my view of everything else in the lot.

I grab my bag and get ready to go and move the cam. I pause when I see the huge guy that gets out of the truck is wearing a cut. It's him. I've never seen him in person, but I know this is Gutter. *Wow.*

The Pickup

Gutter

I pull up to the bus station and hop out of my truck to scan the place. I see a few women wrestling with their children and some lanky guy, staring down at his phone. When the guy looks up, his eyes widen. Avoiding eye contact with me, he looks back down quickly.

I snort. That's not my guy. I go to do another sweep of the people buzzing around the station, wondering if I should move inside. My gaze moves past a little redhead that's drooling all over herself as she ogles me.

Her daddy should've taught her better than to look for fun with men like me. I'm not interested either way. I haven't been interested in a real live woman in years.

Not after what I've been through. I tend to steer clear of women and men for that matter. I've heard the rumors around the club that I'm a faggot.

I've never tried to correct them because I just don't give a fuck. However, I'm not gay. My cousin, Terry, now he's gay as the day is long. What happened to us broke him in ways I fight to forget. He got it a hell of a lot worse than I did. Terry decided to turn to men for comfort from our past. I stay away from people when it comes to sex, *period*.

I groan inwardly, when I catch the redhead out the corner of my eye, gaining the confidence to approach me. I don't have time for this shit. As my annoyance starts to rise, someone else pulls my attention from behind red.

It's like my chest is blown out as my gaze lands on her. She's fucking gorgeous. For the first time in years, my cock stirs to life, twitching behind my jeans.

The first thing that grabs my attention is her hair cut. The sides of her hair are cut short into a low fade. At the top, she has just enough hair to stand up in a little shark fin. The fact that she doesn't have enough hair to obstruct her face only draws emphasis to her long as fuck lashes.

Her chocolate skin glows, making the details of her haircut that much more stunning to her face. Those lips... I've never wanted to kiss a woman more in my life. I lower my glance to her full breasts stretching the hell out of the tank top she's wearing under the leather jacket her mounds have shoved open.

Her curvy legs are incased in a pair of black leather riding pants that should take away from her figure, but only mold to her long legs in the most inviting way. Her small feet are covered in a pair of badass black rider boots to complete her look. She's tall. She has to be at least five eight, five nine.

Something inside me rears up, loving the fact that while she's pretty tall, I still tower over her at six five and a half. If I ever wanted a woman to fit in my arms, she would be the one. When her chocolate brown eyes lock on mine, I have to reach out to place a hand on the side of my truck before my knees give out.

Fucking gorgeous.

Sal

Damn, he's big. Pictures don't do him any justice. I feel breathless as I move toward him with purpose. We need to get out of here, fast, but that isn't all that's moving my legs.

I'm drawn to this man like something is connecting me to all six feet and change of him. I'm five eight and a half feet tall and he still makes me feel small. Anyone in their right mind would pick up on the vibes this guy gives off and would stay away from him.

I guess it's safe to say I lost my mind a long time ago, when I became damaged. So, like a moth, I'm moving right to the flame.

It is all I can do not to run right into his arms. I turn and head for the passenger side of the truck instead. His dark eyes follow me.

At least, I think they're dark. His lashes are so long. Gutter would be pretty if he wasn't so rugged. The long dark lashes, his full pink lips, and slightly pointed nose, soften his face.

Then you have the scuff on his sharp jaw and the harder planes of his face that say all sexy male and masculine appeal. Although, I think even with a clean morning's shave, he would still have that tough edge.

There is just something about him that screams, *look at me. I should be in movies or on the cover of magazines. I'm gorgeous.*

When I reach for the handle of the passenger door, he lifts a brow at me. I tilt my head to the side. I get ready to ask him if he was expecting someone else, when a redhead walks up to his side and practically throws her boobs on to his arm.

"Hey," she breathes next to him.

He reluctantly pulls his gaze away from me to look at her. I cover my mouth to keep from bursting into laughter when he flings her off his arm and takes a step away. The snarl on his face is hilarious.

"Babe, we really need to hit the road," I call out as I reach for the door.

Gutter turns back to me again. His eyes narrowed. "Okay, Sal," he raises a questioning brow.

I smirk and give him a small nod. His eyes roam over me and he nods back. With that, I open the door and climb up into the huge truck. Gutter gets in as well, not even looking back to see the pouty, disappointed look on the redhead's face. It's priceless. She shoots me a dirty glare, once Gutter starts the truck.

He looks over at me again, taking me in like I'm his next meal. I try not to suck in my breath, when I get a good look at his eyes. They're not dark at all. Not in color at least. They're a mix of blue and gray, tipping his face more on the side of pretty, I decide. He is breathtaking, even with the faint scar that runs from the base of his neck and disappears behind his ear.

"You're Sal," he grunts in a low, sexy voice.

"The one and only," I say and frown, when my voice comes out all breathy.

He knits his brows, while studying my face, but he doesn't reply right away. Then he does and it almost brings a smile to my face. Something that's hard to do for any man nowadays. Well, with the exception of King or Mix.

"You don't look like a Sal to me," he says gruffly.

"Actually, it's Salalia, family calls me Sal for short. I've never liked my name." I shrug.

"Salalia," he says, and I swear, a grin form on his lips.

With that, he throws the truck in gear and backs out of the space. I look longingly over my shoulder at his bike on the truck bed. It's a custom with a sick paint job. I want a better look, but that will have to wait.

I pull out one of my last three burner phones and text King to let him know I'm with Gutter. A minute later, Gutter's phone starts to ring. He grunts at the screen after he pulls it from his cut.

"I've got her, Prez," he says as he answers the phone, placing it on speaker.

"Good, that's my baby sister, Gutter. I don't think I need to say more, but I will anyway. Kill anyone that looks at her wrong and ask questions later. Get her here safe," King replies.

"Not a question, Prez," Gutter says and glances over at me. There's something like recognition in his eyes. He turns back to the road and ends the call. I snort to myself. He's just as short as King, if not more so. No nonsense, to the point.

"I thought you looked like Eva," he says, almost to himself. "Never knew there were more of you."

"Just me," I mutter back.

"God bless, King." He snorts.

I turn to glare at the side of his face, but I don't say anything. I'm too tired to get into it with this gorgeous grump. The coffee and adrenaline are wearing off and my body is crashing.

Gutter

She isn't just gorgeous; she smells fucking amazing. Like cotton candy and pineapples and all types of things that are sweet and delicious to have on your tongue. I know from seeing firsthand how crazy King gets over his sister, Eva. That adds one more reason why I shouldn't have a reaction to the girl sitting across from me in my truck.

I peek over at her for the millionth time. She's just as beautiful in her sleep. The way her long lashes fan across her high cheekbones makes her look like a doll. A chocolate doll I want to taste so fucking bad, my head is buzzing.

The drive home is going to take about two days. We haven't been driving long, but I'm exhausted from keeping late nights. I needed to take care of some repairs on my place and there's always my own mental torture.

Some nights, I don't sleep at all. When I start to feel caged in, it's worse. This is one of those times.

I pull into a bed and breakfast I've trusted a few times. From King's words, I know I need to watch our backs. There's never much that needs to be said between me and the prez. I get him and he gets me.

I read between the lines. Baby girl is in some type of trouble and it's my job to get her home safe. It's what I do, but I can't do that if I'm not alert. Before it gets too late, I want to attempt to get a few hours of shut eye and then get back on the road before daybreak.

Even though the bed and breakfast is off road, I drive around the back of the place to park out of sight. I cut the engine and turn to sleeping beauty beside me, frowning as I think of the best way to wake her up.

"Are you just going to stare at me?" she asks sleepily, before cracking open an eye.

I snort as she opens both eyes and looks around. She stiffens as the unfamiliar and sparse surroundings come into view. Her gaze turns cold and she looks at me. The fear in her eyes jumps out at me. It's an emotion I never want her to have around me.

From her expression, her brain seems to be calculating. I witness the survivor within. She's getting ready for action. Just knowing what I'm witnessing in her eyes rubs me raw.

I open my door and start out of the truck. When I'm halfway out of the cage, I turn to look over my shoulder.

"We could both use some sleep. We'll get a room and be back on the road first thing," I grumble, stepping all the way out of the truck.

I slam the door harder than I mean to, but I already understand that look in her eyes. She's been hurt before, which makes me wonder if that's what she's running from now. My blood is boiling in my veins. If I know that look like I know I do, I'm ready to explode.

Sal slides out of the truck with that backpack of hers cradle tightly in her arms. I take in a breath to calm my temper. As we enter the B & B, the young clerk who's usually behind the counter is there. Her eyes widen as they land on me. It's been a while since I've been this way.

The Lost Souls have been keeping me busy lately. I usually stop here on more personal trips. I don't think Sal would take too kindly to some of the dives I've stopped at on Club business.

"Hey there," the clerk says breathily as she roams her gaze over me the way she always does. She bites her lip and smiles. "Long time, no see. I was hoping you would stop by soon."

I grunt and reach for the sign-in book. I never give this girl the impression something will ever happen between us and that's not going to change today. *Fuck*, especially not today.

I can feel Sal's eyes on the both of us. Not many things make me nervous, but the way she's burning a hole in the side of my skull has me hyperaware of everything around me. I want to tell her she's the only one that even remotely turns me on, but I just focus on my task so we can get our room.

I pull out cash and count out the usual, tossing it onto the counter. We need to speed this up. The young clerk takes the money. I know she has told me her name more than once, I just never bothered to remember it. After counting the money, she looks at Sal and frowns.

"This is for one room," the girl states the obvious.

Sal stiffen beside me once again, but this time when I look at her, her eyes are blazing with fury. She moves closer to me and places her small hand on my chest. I swear my cock loses his mind and goes hard as a fucking rock.

"Is that a problem?" Sal says possessively and the shit turns me the fuck on even more.

"I... I... well, are you guys married or something?" the clerk says, with an annoyed pout.

I get ready to growl at the little twit, when Sal steps into me even more and runs her fingers into the short strands at the nape of my neck. I flinch, not used to being touched like that. Not ever wanting to be touch like that, *until now.*

I look down into Sal's eyes and she smiles and winks at me. On instinct, I place my hands on her hips and it's like coming home. She fits my huge palms perfectly.

"Actually, I just became his old lady. Just as good as being married. Isn't that right, baby?" Sal taunts.

Hearing those words and her claim makes something snap in my fucked up head. All at once, I see my name tatted on her smooth brown skin. I envision my cut on her shoulders. Images of Sal writhing beneath me consumes me so viciously, I think they're real.

I cup her face between my hands and crush her full lips with mine. Her gasp of surprise leaves room for my tongue and growl of possession. I devour her mouth nipping and sucking at her lips as she wraps her arms around my neck.

My hard cock throbs against my jeans, painfully as it stabs into her belly. With each of her sexy whimpers, I'm lost more and more. Each sound tells my brain that she's mine, that I need to take her.

I break the kiss only to grunt at the clerk. "Key, now."

She hurries to pass me the key to our room. I grab Sal's backpack in one hand and lift her onto my waist with the other. Swiftly, I head toward our room.

We lock eyes the entire way up the stairs. My blue-gray eyes telling her everything I plan to do to her when I get her behind closed doors. For the first time, in—no make that ever—I want to fuck and I want to fuck hard.

Halt

Sal

I'm shivering from that kiss and the intense look he's giving me now, but it's a good shiver. I only wanted to fuck with that dumb bitch at the desk. I didn't know Gutter would take it so far, but once his lips met mine, I was gone.

I never thought I would want a man the way I want Gutter in this moment. Being in his arms, I feel so small and safe. I'm not a small girl, so this is a hard feeling to come by for me, but Gutter carries me to our room as if I weigh nothing.

Just to think, when I first woke to the unfamiliar surroundings, my first instinct was to panic. I didn't mean to show so much, but I know he saw it. I was even going to fuss about sharing a room at first.

Now, all I can think about as my juices soak my panties, is having this man's big hard body pressed to mine. As I cling to his shoulders, I can feel the strength coiled within his body.

Gutter maneuvers me and the key to our room, pushing the door in and kicking it closed once inside. Dropping my bag to the side of the door, he turns my back to the door and pushes me up against it.

Once again, he devours me whole with hungry kisses. He unbuttons the front of my pants and slides his rough hand into the front of my panties. He growls, when his fingers find my soaked slit.

My mind is in a tailspin. I try to fight back the memories that are battling to come to the forefront. I want to only focus on his big, callused hand that's cupping my mound.

He's just cupping my heat. His fingers haven't penetrated me. As if, he can feel the panic that wants to rise within and he's giving me time to adjust and relax. He moves his lips to my neck and sucks on my flesh, but he still doesn't push a finger inside me.

It almost feels more intimate than if he were to. Instead of freaking me out, it feels comforting, almost like he's cherishing the treasure within his palm. That's when he slides his two fingers through my outer lips, soaking his fingertips and teasing my seam.

I moan and shudder, but everything stops. It's like the air is sucked out of the room. Gutter pulls his lips from my neck and he looks into my eyes. His eyes are narrowed and look so dark. Not in color, but there's something in his past that has left a dark side, lurking at the surface of this man's soul.

Just as quickly as he pinned me to the door, he sets me on my feet. He rubs his thumb against his bottom lip as his eyes remain on me. His chest is heaving. I know he's as effected as I am.

So, I'm surprised when he shakes his head, as if to clear it. He turns, pulling his cut off and tossing it on a chair as he heads to the open door of the bathroom. Without looking back at me, he calls over his shoulder.

"Sorry, Salalia, I can't do this. You can have the bed, just toss a pillow on the floor," he mumbles, then slams the bathroom door shut. I hate my real name, but somehow, him using it softens the blow just a little.

Does he know I'm damaged? Am I not good enough? What did I do wrong? Is it too much to ask for him to teach me?

Gutter

I just couldn't do it. As good as she feels, as good as she tastes, and as much as I want to be inside of her, I couldn't. The images that have haunted me all of my life wouldn't go away so I could focus on her. I tried, fuck, I tried like hell to stay in the moment, in the room.

Then she moaned at the same exact time as the voices in my head, and I couldn't. I couldn't ruin that perfect angel out there with my dark past and my insane thoughts. She had no business being so wet for a man like me.

I had to hightail my ass into this bathroom for her protection. I needed a shower. I now stand under the spray, with my hard as fuck cock in my hand. I haven't jacked off in years.

A part of me once thought my dick was broken and I would never want sex. Now, I have my fingers in my mouth sucking her juices from them, while I pump with the other hand. I can't get her eyes out of my head.

I grunt and growl as my release hits me hard and sprays all over the shower wall. I slump against the tile. *Fuck*, my head is so fucked up. For the first time, in a long time, I loathe myself. It took me so long to figure out none of it was my fault. However, at this moment, I just feel dirty and disgusting, just like I did back then.

"You don't deserve her," I murmur.

Sal deserves better than me. I'd never forgive myself for destroying something as beautiful as her. What I thought I saw in her eyes earlier was only me projecting my past onto her. Me, wishing I found someone as fucked up as me.

I pull my shit together and step out of the shower. Placing a towel around my waist, I take a breath before collecting my clothes I folded neatly before getting in the shower out of habit.

When I step into the bedroom and the room is dim, but the first thing I notice is Sal. She's sitting in the middle of the bed in only her T-shirt, with her knees pulled into her chest. She's shaking and her lips are trembling. Then she looks up at me with those big brown eyes.

I'm thrown back in time, when I see the look on her face. I don't see Sal, I only see Terry, my cousin and his sad gold and blue eyes. I'm filled with such anger and helplessness.

There's nothing I can do. I can barely protect myself, but I manage. I manage to keep what happened to Terry from happening to me and I feel sick that I couldn't save him.

My body starts to tremble as fury rips through me. Then, I'm brought back to the present by her softly spoken words. I'm gutted by them because I know I'm going to be ripped to pieces because for the first time I'm finally going to share with someone other than Terry what happened to me. I have to share because I can't allow her to think this shit is on her.

"Am I not good enough?" she whispers. "Di... did I do something wrong? Why'd you stop? I... I didn't want you to stop. I... I... I think I can handle your touch."

I close my eyes. So, I wasn't projecting. One fucked up soul is about to meet another.

I walk over to sit on the foot of the bed, placing my clothes at my feet. I take a breath and start to speak. "It's not you, it's me. What I'm about to tell you, I have never told a soul.

"I don't know if I can take you like you deserve. I've never been with a woman for my own pleasure. But... I'm going to tell you this because the idea of you being my old lady sounds so fucking good coming off your lips.

"If you don't think you can handle a fucked up man like me, then I need you to say it now, darlin'. Because once I tell you my secrets, you're mine. This Lost Soul plays for keeps," I say and turn to look her deep in those big brown eyes. "You feel me?"

Bare Bones

Sal

Do I feel him? Oh, I feel him in every cell of my body. Even as he sits at the foot of the bed, not touching me at all, I can feel him. His eyes are cutting through to my soul.

I want to be his and it excites and scares the fuck out of me all at once. I wait for my flight instinct to kick in, but it never happens. I'm rooted to this bed and don't plan to move.

"I feel you," I whisper as I look him back in his eyes.

That dark look returns to his orbs as he reaches for my ankle and pulls me to him. I yelp in surprise, but I don't fight him. Gutter plucks me up from the bed by my waist and drops me into his lap. His arms go around my back, and he simply stares at me for a moment.

I bite my lip, feeling my bare crotch meet the heat of his lap. His hard member presses up between my cheeks with his towel as the only barrier between us. I had to take my panties off along with my pants. They were soaked through from our earlier encounter.

"One promise, Salalia. After I bare my bones, you will do the same. I see it. I know you're bearing a cross of your own. You will lay that one on me. I will carry it for you, after I hand you my shit," he says gruffly.

I nod my head and draw out a breath. "All right."

He cups my face and runs his finger over my bottom lip, when I allow it to pop free from my mouth. He closes his eyes and takes a deep breath. I notice his once rock hard erection softens.

"My birth given name is, Pierson Jeremy Bridges, the third. My father was Pierson Bridges, the second, of the Crestwood Bridges. I come from the kind of money that runs deep and moves the world around it." He pauses as his jaw works. Turmoil flashes in his eyes.

"My father and mother were amazing. They loved me and Terry with everything they had. Terry is my cousin. We are two days apart. His mother died in childbirth and his father committed suicide a few nights after.

"My parents raised him like he was my brother. We were as close as twins. We sort of looked like twins too," Gutter snorts and a faint smile touches his lips. Then his face turns grim once again. "Our looks would be our downfall in the end."

"My mother, she…" He trials off and shakes his head. "She was killed in a car accident, when I was nine. My father was a mess after. Some days, I don't even think he would shower. He threw himself into his work and on one of his business trips, he met his second wife."

Gutter's haunted eyes lift and lock onto mine. "Baby girl, when I tell you I lived the nightmare version of Cinderella, I did, no exaggeration. My dad married Melody within two months, and he died of a heart attack two months later. He left everything in her name, including custody of Terry and me and our trust funds.

"The woman was pure evil. She paraded the two of us around, bragging on how lucky she was to have two boys who were so beautiful. She would throw these parties with all of her sick friends who would come to ogle the two of us.

"Melody intentionally grew our hair out, so we'd appealed to everyone with our fair looks." Gutter clenches his jaw so hard, I think it might break. "It started with the women. They would make us pet them, then it graduated to more touching and intimacy. I lost my virginity at thirteen. The woman had to be in her late thirties."

He shakes his head and continues. "I pissed Melody off, when I started to fill out. I wasn't as soft and feminine as she could pass Terry off for. When we turned seventeen, the men were tired of just looking and touching here and there.

"Melody promised them a taste. I still can't get that night out of my head. I thought it would be like always. I would pleasure one of her horny friends, while her husband or boyfriend watched. Then, I would be left alone after. Only, things were different this time. The husband wanted to be alone with me.

"After his wife got off, he told her to leave. That motherfucker climbed in the bed and tried to force himself on me. Like I said, I had filled out. I was no small seventeen-year-old. I nearly beat the life out of that son of a bitch."

He turns away from me, but he keeps talking. "What I didn't know was that Melody had promised that monster and one other, they could break me and Terry in that night. I didn't know, while I was fighting to keep that shit from happening to me, Terry was down the hall being..." His words trail off and he becomes silent.

"Later that night, Terry came crawling into my bed. He broke down sobbing and told me everything. We were just close like that. We told each other everything. I couldn't let us go through that shit anymore. I already knew Melody was going to find a way to punish me for what I'd done.

"We grabbed what we could take and left that night. I'm not proud of the shit we had to do to survive in the beginning, but it was our choice to do it. It wasn't being forced on us.

"I got lucky. One of the bouncers at a club I stripped at, made me on my age. His name was Kirk. He took me in and got me into security. I tried to help Terry, but he was too fucked up back then. We both were, but he got into drugs and a bunch of other shit. I couldn't save him without him pulling me into all of that shit.

"I had to let him go. I failed him for the second time." He runs his hand over the scar that flows from his neck behind his ear. "I tried. I really did, before I had to wash my hands of him. I ended up in the hospital cut up.

"Some guy Terry was caught up with beat his ass and when I showed up, the fucker was ready with his boys. They jumped me. It was the only way they could take me down. I took at least three of them down with me, before one of them sliced me open.

"Terry showed up at the hospital once, after. High out of his fucking mind, screaming at me for beating up his boyfriend. I was done.

"When I got out of the hospital, I had nothing and no one. Terry really fucked shit up for the both of us. Kirk thought I was involved in some shit, so I lost my job and my place," Gutter huffs.

He has a haunted look in his eyes. It's clear he's somewhere else, lost in the thoughts of the past. My heart aches for him.

"I roamed the street for a while before some old dude found me to tell me Melody had met with a barrel of a gun. He'd been searching for me and Terry for some time. Apparently, she caught the blowback from that ass whipping I handed out.

"I don't know what broke me more. The fact that we didn't have to be out on the street, doing all the shit we did. Or that after all we went through, we were still fucked up no matter how much money we had waiting for us.

"I didn't want to go back there. I left the house for Terry to do whatever he wanted. He eventually got his shit together, but things changed so much between us.

"I bought my bike and just got lost. I didn't worry about money. Hell, I blew so much of it, not giving a fuck. I went wherever the wind blew me. Then I walked into some bar one night and watched a bunch of guys surround some blond dude with dreads.

"I don't know what made me get involved, but I did. I've been a Lost Soul since. King says I helped save his life, but he's the one who saved me. He helped me put my skills and what money I had left to use." He shrugs, then turns back to me.

"I'm all kinds of fucked up in the head, Salalia. I didn't stop because of you. I stopped because I have these voices in my head that are constantly reminding me of my past. You're too beautiful for me to soil you with my filthy past."

Clear Things Up

Gutter

She looks at me with a pained expression and scoffs at my last words. "Your filthy past? You have no idea what I'm running from. I'm not talking about the reason King sent you for me. I'm talking about what sent me running to live all alone in New York in the first place."

Her eyes fill with tears, but she blinks them away. She drawers in a breath and shudders. "I can't believe I'm about to tell you this. I have never told anyone. Not King, not even Eva.

"Computers and gadgets have always been more interesting to me than people. I spent so many hours working on my next great idea. My teachers called me a prodigy.

"My first year in college, I had one professor who took a little extra interest in me. I soaked it up. He had access to publications, labs, and technology no one else had. To a geek like me, he was a god."

She pauses and her lips tremble. I get the feeling she's reliving the memory. "He offered me a spot on a developmental team that went to London for the summer. I was so naïve. I didn't see what was going on.

"Once we were in London, something conveniently happened to my apartments. There were five others, and everything went smoothly for them. My professor promised it would be straightened out in a matter of days. He offered to let me stay at his flat for that time.

"I... I didn't think... he had a wife. She was due to join him a few weeks after we arrived. I never paid attention to the way he looked at me. I dismissed his occasional flirting. I ignored his light touches. I missed it all, until it was too late," her words come out brokenly as the tears spill over onto her cheeks.

"He was a gentleman the first two nights. We stayed up late each night, drinking wine and laughing like old friends. I had no reason not to feel safe. That all change the third night.

"I had gone out with some of the other students to sightsee. I came in a little late and... he'd been drinking. He was in a jealous rage. He accused me of sleeping with one of the male students. I can still hear him shouting, calling me a whore.

"He went on and on about how I had led him on to get a spot on the team. How I was just there to whore around for the summer. I was stunned. No one had ever talked to me that way," Sal chokes. She stops talking and swallows hard.

"One minute, I was trying to pack my things to leave. The next, I was on my back blinking away tears as he breathed his hot breath in my face. I felt so stupid lying there. While it was happening, I could see everything I had missed before.

"The next morning, I was informed that all of my paperwork fell through and I would have to return home, while it was straightened out. I came home, but I didn't go back to school.

"I made up some bullshit to tell King and asked him to get me away. I knew King would kill him. I wanted him dead, but

I didn't want King to go to jail because of me." She folds her arms across her middle.

"I can't stand the touch of a man. You're the first I have allowed to touch me. I was a young naïve virgin when I went to London. I came back something... someone else. So, you can't make me filthy with your past, Gutter. I'm already dirty," she whispers the end.

I growl and I growl deep. I cup her sweet face in my hands and look her in the eyes. "It took me a long time to see what those motherfuckers did wasn't my fault. The shit I chose was the shit I chose, but the things forced on us, baby... that shit ain't on us.

"You're not dirty, Salalia," I say through clenched teeth. "And I don't ever want to hear you say that shit again."

Before I can say another word, her lips are pressed to mine and her fingers are locked in my hair. I reach for her hips and deepen the kiss as my cock comes back to life. I had gone soft the moment I thought of my past.

The hunger I had for Sal earlier, comes back with a vengeance. I kiss her hard and ravenously. I lift her shirt over her head and try my best to push my demons to the back of my mind.

I want this. I want her. I squeeze my eyes shut as the voices in my head rise. I guess that's the wrong fucking thing to do. Sweat breaks out on my forehead as images of the women and their men fill my vision.

I pull my lips away from Sal's and place my forehead to hers. "Fuck," I grunt.

She cups my face with her small hands. "Look at me, Pierson," she whispers.

My eyes fly open at the sound of my real name. It has been so long since I've heard it. Melody had pet names for us. She wouldn't call me and Terry by our names. I remember my mom being the last woman to call me Pierson.

"It's okay. We don't have to rush. I'm just as scared as you are. We can take our time. I'm yours, just as I promised, so we have all the time in the world."

I nod and reach to wipe her tears from her cheeks. We're one fucked up pair, two lost souls for real, but she's right. We can take our time. I don't want to hurt her with my demons and lack of control of my shit. I pinch her chin and bring her face to mine to softly kiss her lips.

"I'm sorry, baby. Just give me a little time. I want you. I just need to deal with the shit in my head," I say.

"You and me both." She gives me a shy smile. "Don't be sorry."

I move back on the bed, bringing her body with mine. I lie down and cradle her against my chest. "Salalia."

"Yes, Pierson." She releases a tiny laugh.

"I want his name. It's not a request, baby girl. I want his name and you're going to give it to me," I say with finality.

"Yeah, I figured that." She sighs, but says no more.

We don't say anything else as the room falls silent except for our breathing. That crazy ass fucker, Grim, has been trying to get me to meditate for months. I was resistant at first, but knowing him and Reap the way I do, I figure if it works for them, then it could work for me.

Grim and Reap have done and seen some shit as club Enforcers and in their brief military careers. I'm willing to try anything that may have chased away their demons. I've been working at it in the last month or so, and right now seems like one of the best times to try it.

I focus on clearing my mind, allowing Sal's breathing to guide me to clear thoughts. Her soft body against mine pulls me deeper into the peace I'm chasing. When I inhale, her sweet scent becomes a lullaby.

All the bullshit evaporates, and I am here in this room. For the first time, in a long time, I am in the moment, something that is very hard for a man like me.

Sal shifts to my side and snuggles in close. My peace isn't broken with the move. Instead, I start to lazily run my hands up and down her side as if she's my anchor, tethering me to the here and now. Her warm brown skin is the softest I've ever touched.

This is the most peaceful I've ever felt. I stare up at the ceiling and my mind drifts to how this could be my life. A woman who's mine by my side.

It's only when Sal giggles that I bring my gaze from the ceiling and look down at her.

"What?" I grunt as she turns that beautiful face up at me. "What's so funny?"

"Well, first, you're tickling me." She giggles again and squirms against my side.

I still my hand and lift a brow at her. She gives me a breathtaking smile, then she lowers her lashes and bites her lip. I reach for her face, lifting her chin so her eyes meet mine.

She takes the cue and responds. "I've never been this horny. I mean, I'm really turned on by just being in your arms," she says softly.

The blood in my veins catches fire. I slip my hand to the back of her neck and drag her up to my lips. The kiss is every bit as hungry as the others from earlier, maybe more so. I want to devour her whole.

She whimpers into my mouth. I swallow the sound like my last meal. She tastes so good and refreshing. Salalia tastes like the home I've never known.

She draws back much too soon, breaking the kiss. She looks me in the eyes. There is passion mixed with caution in her gaze. I'm sure she sees the same within my own eyes.

"Maybe we could start with where we're both comfortable," Sal whispers, as her eyes drop down to my cock standing at attention. She drags her gaze back up to mine as she licks her lips. "If it's too much for either of us we can stop, but maybe we can start off slow. Just do something to take the edge off."

I nearly growl but draw it back in before it escapes my chest. I want a taste of her so bad, I'm ready to come out of my skin. I nod my head, not sure of what words will sound like at the moment and not wanting to scare her off.

Sal looks at my mouth and this time I lick my own lips. I finally find my voice and say to her. "Come sit on my face, baby girl."

Sal hesitates for a few seconds, long enough for me to consider she may not be ready for this much. Then, she lifts to her knees and crawls up to straddle my face. I lock my hands on her thighs, before she can settle in. Lifting my face, I inhale her sweetness and take my first lick.

I groan deep in my throat. She tastes better than I could ever have imagined. I'm gentle, letting her get used to my touch and easy strokes. When she starts to rock her hips against my face, I let my restraint slip a little.

My head is still clear, thank fuck, because I don't ever want to stop eating her pussy. The scent of leather clings to her thighs, and I don't know why it turns me on so much. It makes me want to have her on the back of my bike with my brand on her, in the worse way.

"Mmm," I moan into her sweet heat, as I buck my hips up off the bed at the feel of her first lick of the tip of my cock.

I nearly come on the spot. When she wraps her lips around the crown and slide down slowly, I roll my eyes in my head. I clench my jaw to keep from embarrassing myself.

When I have control of my body once again, I return to eating her pussy with vigor as she humps the shit out of my face. I slip two fingers inside her, finding that sweet spot. Circling my tongue around her clit, I work her toward the edge.

When I know I have her right there, I clamp down on her nub and suck, hard.

My cock pop from her lips and she cries out into the room. Her whole body trembles with her release. She slumps to the side.

I'm sure her legs are jelly. Sal covers her face as she tries to catch her breath. I watch her roll onto her back and stare up at the ceiling, blinking.

I still taste her on my lips. I lick them, wanting more. Slowly, I climb over to her, moving between her thighs as I scoot her body down the mattress, before I settle my big body between her long brown legs.

Before she can catch up to what I have planned, I have my mouth on her pussy lapping at her juices and sucking her pussy lips into my mouth. First the right lip, then the left, before I twirl my tongue into her heat.

I grunt and groan into her as my mouth fills with her juices. She tastes so good. I close my eyes to savor her flavor, *wrong move*, once again. As soon as I close my eyes, Sal moans into the room and I'm thrown back in time.

My body tenses as the first of the images assaults me. I grip the covers, trying to shove the memories back. It doesn't help. I'm drowning and drowning fast.

"Gutter," Sal calls my name, just barely breaking through the raging voices and visions. "Gutter, babe, look at me. Come on, babe. It's me. Your baby, Salalia." My eyes fly open and I look up at her. "No one else is here. No one can hurt us. It's me and you. Just keep your eyes on me."

My mind reels back. *Did she just say she's my baby? What is this woman doing to me?* My need to claim her possesses me.

I climb her body and crush my lips to hers. Her juices are still clinging to my face. Sal stuns me when she licks them from my chin and lips. I groan into her mouth.

We reconnect our lips. I reach for my aching cock and line myself up with her entrance and pause as I look into her eyes. As hard as it will be, I will stop if she wants me to. We lock gazes and there's something unspoken that passes between us. I nod my understanding, while I slide slowly into her tight heaven.

This is right. I feel it with everything in me. The look of trust in her eyes proves it. I couldn't ask for more.

Feeling her trust and trusting her, goes a long way to balm my aching soul. Her entire body arches into me. I wrap my arm around her back and hold her to me as I move in and out of her, creating a safe place for both of us. She's so slick and tight. I nip at her full lips as my name falls off of them.

"My baby," I mutter. She was so right. She is mine. No one can change that or take it away, and no one will ever keep me from enjoying her in this way ever again. "My Salalia. Mine forever. I'm never letting you go."

"Good, because I won't leave you," she whispers back.

I capture her lips, but neither of us closes our eyes. I don't think we can. Not yet.

I move in and out of her with care, until her heels dig into my ass, urging me to move deeper. I give her what she wants rocking into her long, hard, and deep.

I'm completely lost. I was once drowning in my past, but now I'm drowning in my woman. The woman I want to be my future. I just pray I don't fuck this up.

Sal

I have never experienced anything like it. It's like Gutter is sucking the life out of me through my core. I wanted to finish what I started earlier, but I couldn't stay upright on my shaky legs. I didn't expect him to go down on me again.

When he freaked, I felt the moment I was losing him. My thoughts scrambled for a way to bring him back. I knew we could do this, please each other and slay our demons. All we had to do was try.

I just wasn't expecting this. I didn't expect Gutter to make love to me. It maybe a little rough as he holds me to him and rocks into me hard and deep, but he's making love to me. That's the only way I can describe this.

I pull my legs back and open wider for him. He moans and cups one of my ass cheeks in his huge palm. His warm hand sends a shock of electricity through me. I look deep into his eyes and nearly fall apart. I never thought I would experience this or would even want to.

So much has changed in such a short amount of time. I know we said we would take things slow, but I know neither of us would've been satisfied with anything less.

"Baby girl, I need you to get there," he grunts as he squeezes my ass and drags his thick dick through my folds and over my nub. "Give it to me, baby. I'm gonna come."

"Please," I whimper, not knowing what I'm begging for.

He loosens his hold on me, reaching between us. He cups one of my breasts and dips his head. Keeping his eyes on me, he latches his lips onto my nipple and sucks. Apparently, one of us knows just what I need.

I come apart. My juices gush around him. Not too long after, two more strokes and he spills into me with a heavy grunt of my name.

We cling to each other as we catch our breath. After a few moments, Gutter cups my face in one hand and searches my eyes. "Thank you, baby," he murmurs. All he doesn't say crosses his face and pass through his eyes.

CHAPTER EIGHT

Reinforcements

King
South Carolina...

I count to one hundred for the millionth time. Gutter or Sal should have reached out to me by now. Like I told Brick last night, I haven't spoken to them, since they first linked up.

Normally, I wouldn't be wound this tight, but this is my sister. My baby sister at that. Sal has been through some shit.

She thinks I don't know, but I've seen it in her eyes. Sal is just different from Eva. I know when and how to push both of them.

The look I saw in Sal's eyes told me it wasn't the time to push her. She'll come to me when she's ready for me to fix whatever it is. It's her way, when she's ready to deal with something she commits to the action.

I just want to know she's safe. I don't know what's really going on. There's always a chance I brought this bullshit to her door.

"I've given them until morning," I grumble against Misty's belly. "You and Brick said to give them until morning. Where the fuck are they?"

Misty sighs. "I don't know. I don't have a bad feeling, but maybe sending out some reinforcements isn't a bad idea."

"You're fucking right, I'm sending out reinforcements. Neither of them has answered a fucking phone in hours." I sit up and run my hand through my dreads. "I have enough on my plate. Some fucked up shit is going on around here. I can feel the disloyalty in the air."

Misty sits up and looks at me with wide eyes. "You think someone set Sal up?" she gasps, reaching for her little belly. "A brother from the club?"

"That's what we're going to find out. Something ain't right, something hasn't been right in a long, long time."

Misty licks her lips and nods. "Yeah, I guess you're right. Remember you thought someone was tailing us a few months back? Shit, King. This is the last thing we need."

"We… nah, baby girl, there's no we. I will take care of all of this. You take care of my baby." I narrow my eyes to make my point.

"King," she whines.

"No," I say firmly. "I need to call Grim and Reap. They'll be able to meet up with Gutter and Sal the fastest. They can fly to them. You get some rest." I lean forward and kiss her temple.

"I love you," she whispers in that sweet voice.

"I love you too, baby."

Who We Are

Grim

Grim and Reap in South Carolina...

"Colin," Reap moans as I slam her back into the wall and squeeze her little face with one hand. She's the only one I let call me by my given name.

It's been that way since we were kids. Back then everyone called me Sticks, because I was all sticks and bones. When I got to high school everyone called me CJ. When Cage brought me into the fold, he's the one who named me Grim.

Shit, I earned the name. I was a grim son of a bitch and anyone who fucked with me, learned quickly I had no problem beating the life out of them. Reap has been by my side through it all. It's hard to believe I once tried to only see her as one of the guys.

My Erica has always been my heart and we have always been inseparable. If I'm beating someone's ass, she's right there with me, whether I want it or not. It has always been that way. That's why Cage started calling her Reaper. She hated that name and had him shorten it to Reap.

I think her little crazy ass is the only one in the world who had the balls to tell Cage what he would and wouldn't call her. That's what I fucking love about her. Reap says what's on her mind, no matter what.

She digs her nails into my back and I growl. I pull away from the wall and slam her against the one across from it. We're in the living room in our apartment. The place looks like a fucking war zone.

Reap has been bitching at me all morning. When I decided to just ignore her, she started trying to whip my ass. Our fights always get heated and turn into the hottest fucking sex ever.

"Colin, stop being a pussy and fuck me already," she snarls.

I grin and dig my nails into her ass. I have the leather mini skirt she's wearing pushed up to her waist. Her purple thong is ripped to shreds on the other side of the room, along with her tank top.

The cups of her bra are pulled down under her perky breasts. I grunt again, releasing her face and leaning in to bite down on her smooth brown neck. I love to watch her toffee colored skin wrapped around mine. I am in heaven when she wraps her arms around my neck and grabs a hand full of my long blond hair. She knows I love that shit too.

"Reap," I groan.

"So, you're not mad at me anymore?" she purrs in my ear. She knows I only call her Erica when I'm pissed the fuck off.

"You're the one with the problem with me," I snort. "Say you're sorry and I'll fuck this pretty pussy."

She glares at me through narrowed light brown eyes. There not hazel or anything like that, but a light whiskey brown that draw you in. Her eyes are one of the sexiest things about her. They're oval and large with incredibly long dark lashes.

When Reap looks at you, I swear, you can see your life play over in her eyes. It's like she can look into anyone's depths and read the truth. Her eyes have this soulfulness about them that's haunting.

I lift my head and turn toward her cheek. My mouth is open, so my hot breath fans against her skin. Her nipples turn hard as rocks against my bare chest.

"I'm not apologizing for shit, Grim. I'm tired of cleaning up after your stinky ass," she hisses.

"I wasn't stinky five seconds ago, when you commanded, I fuck you." I chuckle.

"That's cause your big ass hasn't worked out yet. All I ask is that you put your gym clothes in the hamper I bought," she says, with a little pout no one else in the world will ever see. She's too tough for that shit. This is who Erica is with me and me only.

"Fine, baby, I'll put the fucking clothes in the hamper. I'll fix that shelf in the closet too," I relent, giving into all of her demands that started this in the first place. I then lick the side of her face.

Without further argument, I thrust into her soaked opening. I know she's ready for me. I ate her tight pussy, while I had her pinned to a wall across the room. We have been wrestling and having the world's hottest foreplay for long enough.

We fuck rough. It's one of the reasons Reap is perfect for me. She knows all of my crazy shit. She can handle the brute caged within. I don't have to pretend for her, and I don't have to hold back if I don't want to. I'm the same for her.

"Grim," she cries out as I move in and out of her.

I grunt and bite her chin as I hit her favorite spot over and over again. I grind my hips. She thrusts her head back against the wall. If this were anyone other than Reap, I would be concerned about how hard I'm pounding into her. The hard slapping sound of her back hitting the wall would probably cause me to pause.

However, this *is* Reap, and I know she's loving this shit. I bend my knees more and pull her down onto my cock by her ass. I fucking love her hot pussy wrapped around me.

"Shit, baby, I don't think I'm going to last. You've got to come for me," I say through clenched teeth, when my balls start to tingle.

"Fuck you, Grim. You better not come. I'm not fucking kidding," she hisses at me.

I groan and cover her mouth with mine. I fight off my release, but she isn't in the mood to play fair. She clamps her tight pussy around my dick, not once, but twice.

I rip my mouth from hers and growl. Roughly, I pull out and set her on her feet. Reap looks up at me from her five three frame and growls back at me.

She's fucking adorable. At least, to me she is. Reap may be small, but she scares the shit out of most men.

I slap her ass, then grab her waist and turn her around. "Hands on the wall," I hiss in her ear.

Her little ass turns her head and glares at me, but she does as I say. I slap her ass again, when she turns her head back around. Digging my fingers into her full ass, I spread her cheeks and plunge right in.

"Shit, Colin," she sighs out.

"Fuck, baby, you know I love watching your ass on my cock. Make it bounce for me," I grunt.

"Yes," Reap moans and gives me a show. Her toffee brown skin swallows my thick pink cock, and the sight is glorious.

We are going at it for another ten minutes, when my phone rings in my jeans that are still wrapped around one ankle. Reap reaches for my wrist and digs her fingers in. She turns to look me in the eyes.

"Don't. You. Fucking. Dare," she snarls.

I lift a brow at her. She knows when that ringtone comes through, I'm answering with no questions. It's the prez.

I'm one of the Lost Souls enforcers. Fuck that, Reap and I are the most trusted club enforcers and two squad members. We're part of the foundation. Reap may not be a patched in brother, but she might as well be. When Prez calls me, he knows he's calling Reap too.

I reach around for her clit and pick up the pace. I'm close as it is. I can feel that she is too. I get us there in a matter of three more strokes, then I collapse to the floor, pulling Reap down onto my lap.

I fish the phone out and manage to answer it right before it goes to voicemail. "Hey, Prez," I'm able to pant out.

King scoffs on the other end. "I should've known," he grumbles to himself. "I need you. Suit up and head out. Gutter is heading this way with Sal, but I have a feeling they're gonna need back up. Break out the toys."

With that, the Prez ends the call. I have my instructions and I know he will text me the rest. It's the way things are done. I don't need to ask questions. I have walked into fire for King and he knows I'll do it again and again.

I kiss the side of Reap's head. "Playtime, baby girl. Load up," I rumble.

"Well, today must be my lucky day. A great fuck and I get to play with guns. Wooo whoo," Reap chirps. "Let the church bells ring, my guns about to sing."

I throw my head back and roar with laughter. My woman is a fucking lunatic, but I wouldn't have it any other way. She's right, though.

If someone is coming for Gutter and Sal, they're about to meet the Grim Reaper in the form of a five three, toffee, murderous vixen and six seven, unhinged beast.

Someone's luck has just ran out.

CHAPTER TEN

Time to Move

Gutter

Sal giggles as her moans fill my ears, while I push in and out of her. I grunt against her neck as I kiss and suck on her sweet skin, causing her to moan and giggle some more. I'm in heaven as the shower rains down around us, causing our skin to become slick with the down pour of water against our heated flesh.

I marvel at how good she feels on my hard rod. Sal is so wet and tight. I could spend the rest of the day with her pinned to this shower wall. We were supposed to be showering together to save time and get out of here before sunrise.

I don't think that's going to happen. Now that I have had Sal, I want nothing but her. I love how her slick heat welcomes me deep, it's like I'm chasing something, and it can only be found within her warm walls.

"Shit, baby," I groan as her walls tighten around me.

I lick and kiss her neck, causing her to moan and giggle once again. She's ticklish around that sensitive spot on her neck, but it turns her on when I lick or kiss that same spot. I bite down on that exact place and I feel her explode around me.

"Gutter," she cries out as her body jerks against mine.

I pick up the pace, going from the slow agonizing grind, I'd been torturing us both with, to a pounding pace. I'm trying to catch my own release as her pussy comes all over me. I'm so close. I rest my forehead to her cheek and stare down at where our bodies are joined.

It's that connection that's chasing my demons away and I'm in awe of it. When her tight little pussy begins to come around me again, I'm done for. I growl and look up into her beautiful brown eyes. Sal looks at me with the same awe I have of her.

"You feel so good," I groan, before calling her name and spilling my hot seed inside of her.

Sal strokes my wet hair as we catch our breath. I capture her lips and suck at her swollen lower one. I know we need to get going, but I'm reluctant to pull out of her heat. I don't want this feeling to end. As long as she's here in my arms, she's safe.

"We should probably get going," she says sweetly. "King is going to want to hear from us soon."

The real world comes crashing in with her words. I haven't thought about King in hours. I especially haven't thought about how he would feel about me fucking his little sister. This is a problem, because I'm not giving Sal up.

I grunt and pull out, staggering back a step. I steady Sal on her feet and grab the body wash to finish what I had started in the first place. I had only meant to wash my woman, but one touch and I had to have her.

This is so out of character for me, but it feels right. Taking care of Sal feels right, like my job. I'm supposed to take care of her in every way. My hands on her body are meant to be. My arms around her at night is law. Nothing can change the fact that this is my woman.

"What are you thinking about?" Sal asks as she cups my jaw. She runs her finger along my scar.

"Nothing," I murmur.

"Uhh-uhh, not going to happen, Pierson. You have to talk to me," she says as she moves her head to catch my eyes.

I place a soft kiss on her lips. "King isn't going to like this. That's going to be a problem," I grumble.

Sal snorts. "King can mind his own business. I don't tell him who to date and he won't be telling me who my man can be," she sasses. She then looks up at me through her lashes and gives me a shy smile. "Besides, I already belong to you. Ain't shit he can do about that now."

I back her into the shower wall and grab her by the face, tipping it up for me. I dip my head and devour her lips. "You got that fucking right," I grunt, when I release her lips.

Sal looks up at me and grins. We have to get out of this shower before we don't make it to South Carolina for another three days. Sal is right, King will be looking for us to check in.

I back up and pull her under the spray to rinse her off. She ducks her head to the side, so that her short, sexy hair doesn't get wet. My lips curl into a smile. She warned me before we got in here, not to get her hair wet.

I don't know why, but it's the simple things with Sal that make me feel human. I've never learned about someone else in a relationship. I like knowing that I'm learning about her and will get to learn more. I look forward to it.

I cut the water off and pull the curtain back before stepping out first. I reach for a towel then turn to dry Sal off, before wrapping the towel around her and lifting her from the shower.

Her sweet laugh fills my ears again as she wraps her arms around my neck and buries her face in it. Her legs go around my waist. I turn to carry us out of the bathroom.

"Get dressed, baby, we need to get going," I say against her temple. Reluctantly, I release her so she can do as I say.

I find my own clothes and tug them on. When I reach for my phone from my jeans, I frown, finding the thing has died.

No wonder King hasn't called to chew my ass out for not checking in sooner.

"Hey, what's wrong?" Sal asks as she looks over at my frowning face.

"Phone's died, I forgot to charge it last night," I reply.

"No worries, we can charge it in the truck. I'll text King from my burner." She pulls a cell from her backpack. "Shit," she groans and bites her lip. "Mine is dead too."

"Let's go," I say, feeling on edge. I want out of this bed and breakfast. We've been sitting too long.

I get this unsettling feeling in my belly. My instincts have always served me well. We need to get out of here, *now*. I grab Sal's backpack and her wrist. She's still trying to pull on one of her boots.

"Gutter, what the hell?" she pants while hopping beside me.

"We need to go, now," is all I say.

I don't stop until we're out at my truck. I took care of the room in cash last night, so we don't need to stop for anything. I help Sal inside and round the bed to get in the driver's side.

We're on the road, before Sal can get settled into the seat. Her stare burns at the side of my face. I get us onto the highway and make sure we're not being followed, before I turn my focus to her questioning eyes.

"I don't believe in coincidences, baby girl, and I always follow my gut. We were there too long. It was time to go. I don't know what's chasing you or what King has me protecting you from, but I will follow my gut every time, especially to keep you safe," I turn to her and say.

Sal licks her lips and nods. "Then there's something you should know about me," she starts. "I'm not sure who broke into my place, but I think it has something to do with the club."

"Wait, someone broke into your place?" I snarl.

"Yeah, they tossed my place and stole my bike," she seethes. "I took off right away. King told me to head this way and he would have someone he could trust pick me up."

I nod my head and grunt.

I look to my phone Sal has been charging. It's well over time to check in. I snatch it up and dial King. The phone only rings once, before King picks up growling.

"Where the fuck have you been? I've called your ass a hundred times and sent you texts. Where's my sister?" King sneers.

"I'm right here, King. Our phones died. We stopped to get some sleep," Sal explains. "Neither of us thought to charge our phones."

"Well, this ain't the time for that shit. We've got trouble," King hisses.

"What kind of trouble?" I grit through my teeth.

"The kind that has Grim and Reap on their way. They've been trying to get a lock on your fucking phone. They're going to flank you in. Gutter, I need you to keep your shit charged. In the meantime, get somewhere safe. Stop moving as much as you can."

I wrinkle my brows. I hate the idea of being sitting ducks, but if it's what the prez wants. I purse my lips and grunt.

"I'll skirt Oregon and Nevada. It'll be better than just sitting," I offer. If push comes to shove, I have a plan.

King is silent for a moment. "Yeah, all right. Just keep your eyes open out there. We'll be on lockdown here. I want to know as soon as you hit the fucking state, Brother. When you get eyes on Grim and Reap, hit me and let me know you have back up," King orders and hangs up without another word.

"Shit just got real," Sal blows out a breath and sags in her seat.

"Fuck, yeah," I reply.

If Grim and Reap are on the way, they sure as fuck have. I tighten my grip on the steering wheel and run my tongue over my teeth. Someone is about to learn why they call me Gutter.

Sal

Gutter has been silent for the last few hours. I've been lost in my thoughts too, but I'm starting to become on edge with all of this silence. It's bad enough that I am worried now.

King couldn't and wouldn't go into detail about what's going on over the phone, but the mention of Grim and Reap has my skin itching. Erica is straight crazy, and she's crazy about Colin. Where you find one, you find the other.

Grim and Reap leave a lasting impression. I know Erica better than most. She was the one who wrote to me while I was away at school. She would fill me in on everything I was missing. Erica was the only one who knew how homesick I truly was when I was younger.

I know a few of Reap's secrets and she knows most of mine. It's the reason I'm freaking out. I know what Grim and Reap are capable of. Shit is about to hit the fucking fan.

"You don't have to worry. I would never let anything happen to you. I'm sure Grim and Reap are just a precaution. You're King's sister. He's going to do everything in his power to protect you," Gutter says out of the blue.

"Yeah, I know," I reply absently. "I just wish I knew more about what's really going on. Erica and Colin are just…" I can't find the words.

He actually chuckles. I look over to him to see if that's what I'm truly hearing. Sure, enough there's a small smile on his lips.

"Yeah, I know what you mean, but you're sitting next to a carbon copy of them, baby girl. You don't have to worry about getting home safe," he says.

I don't know if that's supposed to make me feel better or not. I look over at Gutter and narrow my eyes. I guess I could see him doing some of the things Reap has told me she has done, heck, some of the things I've seen her and Grim do.

I shake my head and sink into the seat. I might as well settle in. This is going to be a long ride, with or without the new company that's on the way. I can only hope it's a peaceful one.

On the Road

Gutter

"We only have two bottles left," Sal says into the quietness as she reaches for two waters and hands me one.

"Thanks. We'll stop soon."

We've been on the road for a few hours. Our phones being off really fucked things up. Grim couldn't locate us right away. However, once I was able to text him, he got a lock on us.

We lost a lot of time at that B&B, but I'm grateful for the rest. I need to be focused. Sal's life is in danger.

I'm itching to get back to South Carolina to figure out what the fuck is going on. I'd drive the two days through if it weren't for King's orders. Instead, we've been driving aimlessly, waiting for our reinforcements.

I know this shit has to be big because King has trusted me to handle shit on my own before. However, I've never had one of his baby sisters in my care. While the silence has been comfortable, I want to get to know Sal better.

Problem is, I haven't been able to relax. I have so many questions about the break in and who's after her. She's been lost in thought, so I don't want to bombard her with all the shit going through my head.

Traffic comes to a standstill allowing me a chance to look over in her direction. Her eyes are on me, searching my gaze as I lock mine with hers.

Reach for her face and brushing my hand across her cheek, it occurs to me I'm not the only one who's curious. The questions seem to scream from her brown depths. I'm not surprised by the one that leaves her mouth as she parts her lips.

"You became a prospect two years ago. What brought you to the Lost Souls? South Carolina's chapter specifically," she says.

Inhaling deeply, I turn my gaze back to the road ahead. My first instinct is to be guarded and change the subject, but this is Sal. She's already giving me so much of herself in such a short time.

"I was wandering through life, stopped at a bar one night and jumped into some blond guy's fight. Not sure why." I shrug. "After, when we left the bar, my gut told me to follow him. I've been a Lost Soul since."

"King," she whispers, the awe in her voice causes me to turn back to her. "The blond guy."

I nod. A smile crosses her face, and she shakes her head. My heart twists at the sight. She's so beautiful when she smiles.

"King is like Dad that way. They find us wanders and give us a place."

"Yet, I've never seen you around the clubhouse in the last two years I've been around," he says.

I shrug. "I don't ask King for much. South Carlina is my home, but I needed to get away."

I can understand that more than she knows. I take this opportunity to change the subject. Finding the opening I've been looking for.

"Want to tell me what happened at your place?"

She frowns and hurt covers her face. The soured look almost makes me regret the question instantly. However, my desire for answers wins out.

"They stole my fucking bike. Cage bought me that bike. I wasn't even big enough to ride, but he bought it for me and promised when I was big enough, he would teach me how to ride it." She pauses to take a breath, so much pain plays across her face.

She looks down into her lap. Wanting to take away that pain, I cup the back of her neck and start to massage it. It feels like an odd action at first, but her warm smooth skin is inviting and makes me want to touch her more.

She continues after a few beats. "That never happened, but King was there when I was ready. He taught me."

"You're into bikes I'm guessing," I muse aloud before I can catch myself.

She gives a small laugh. "Yeah, I've always had a thing for cars and bikes. When I was around, I spent all my time with Cage and Mix, learning everything I could about them. Cage saw the way my face lit up the first time I saw my bike and he bought it right there on the spot."

"Yeah, I heard a lot about the guy. He sounds like he was something special."

Sal turns to me and beams like only a proud daughter can. "Cage was the only father I've ever known, and he was the best a kid could ask for—"

She cuts off and her eyes shine with tears. A horn blares behind me, causing me to look forward again. I mutter a curse when I find only about a few feet of movement before me, but the moment is already lost.

Sal

I'm glad I shut up when I did. The fact of the matter is, Gutter is technically a stranger and I'm not sure how much King wants him to know about me.

I turn to glance at Gutter's gorgeous face. I haven't talked about Mom or Cage in a long time. Something about sharing with this man beside me makes the memories hurt less.

"You would have loved Cage," I say and scoot over to rest my head on Gutter's shoulder.

He kisses the top of my head and wraps his arm around me. I can't help but smile. It's the safest I've felt in a long time.

"Do you mind if I ask what you were doing so far from South Carolina? My arrival was short notice. You had to be pretty close," I say after a while, when the silence starts to feel heavy.

"I have a place back in Seattle. Planned to send a few days there after some club business."

"Did I interrupt your stay?"

"Not really, I don't know how much longer I was going to be there."

I turn my face up to look at him. He glances down with those Blue-gray eyes. Years seem to have taken over his face within the seconds.

"Do you ever feel like it's getting old?"

"What's that?"

"Running."

He lifts a brow, a shocked expression coming to his face. At first, I don't think he's going to answer. I've pushed too far too fast.

"It's been old since it started. I've just never had the time to stop and think about it. Too busy running to find peace," he replies, his expression turning thoughtful.

My stomach chooses this exact moment to grumble. We both laugh. I cover my face in embarrassment.

"I'll get off the next exit and feed you. I can't have you reporting me to the prez."

"We wouldn't want that now, would we?" I tease back.
And just like that, we fall into silence again.

We Need a Stretch

Gutter

I look over through my lashes to see Sal sweating bullets. It's hot. The AC seems to be blowing hot air as the sun bakes us through the glass.

We've been in Nevada for a while. The few stops along the way still haven't been enough to eat up any real time. At this rate we're about to roast.

"We're pulling over. You need to change into something cooler," I say.

"I don't have anything cooler. I grabbed the important things I needed. That didn't include clothing," she says, with the lift of her shoulders.

"Fine, we'll stop somewhere to get you something. You're soaked. We need water again while we're at it," I say more as a thought to myself.

Sal sighs. "Maybe it would be better to stop somewhere and blend in for a while. It's going to be a long ride home. My legs are cramping. I've been traveling for days." She winces as she rubs her legs. "Another shower would be nice at this point."

I grunt and blow out a breath. She's right. We have been in the truck for hours and it's nearly a two-day drive to South Carolina. Shit, I could stand to stretch my legs.

"Come on, it's Vegas. We can find something to do for a bit," Sal says with that pretty smile of hers. She wiggles her brows. "Let's have a little fun."

That smile alone could talk me into a world of trouble. I think it over. I have a few connections in Vegas. We could relax a bit more if we go someplace, I'm comfortable with.

I look at a drenched Sal and grunt. I need to get her out of this heat for a while. I'd feel safer if I could get us supplies without having her out in plain sight. I rub my forehead, but I know I've made a decision already as she bats those lashes at me.

Sal

"Please," I plea.

I don't know what has gotten into me. Maybe it's the heat. The Vegas scene isn't my thing, or at least it wouldn't have been yesterday. It's crowded and I can't even remember the last time I allowed myself to cut loose and party. I stopped making friends a long time ago.

All I know is I want to stop riding around aimlessly and I want out of this truck. At the same time, something about the atmosphere outside is drawing me in. I look at Gutter, wondering what it would be like if we met like a normal couple.

A couple who doesn't have the baggage we have. I wonder what that couple would be doing here in Vegas. Gutter hasn't said much to me and I believe it's because he's focused on my safety, but I want to forget it all for just a little while.

If we have to be stuck in limbo waiting, why can't we do it while having fun. I don't know why I think being in one of these casinos will be safer or any less restricting. I just need out of my head and this confining seat. Sitting here, I feel like I'm doing nothing. I need to do something, before I lose my mind.

I watch the look that crosses Gutter's eyes as he grunts in response to my request and pulls out his phone. He shoots off a text, before tossing his phone on the dash and turning the truck in the opposite direction from where we were headed.

I turn to look out the window. We pass by the strip and all of its attractions, causing my heart to sink a little. I was hoping we could do something fun in one of the casinos.

His phone buzzes and he picks it up and grunts to himself, before tossing it back. When he turns into the driveway under the huge guitar, my smile comes back. I turn to Gutter and beam.

"Yes," I squeal.

I don't know why I'm so excited. There's something about the thought of seeing Gutter in a casino, trying to relax that has me giddy.

We hop out of the truck and Gutter is right at my side. One of the doormen walks right up to him. They lean into each other, the doorman whispering something, while Gutter nods in reply.

Gutter murmurs something back as they shake hands. He then reaches for my hand, turning to me. "We can go up to the room and shower first. Then I'll go for water and a few things from the store," he says in that curt tone of his.

"Okay." I beam up at him.

I'm taken back by the smile in his eyes, though it doesn't show on his lips. I'm used to his type of gruffness. I've grown up around it all my life. Just because a man doesn't smile openly, doesn't mean he doesn't have a secret smile for those he cares for.

Cage had those secret smiles for his girls. Remembering those smiles makes my chest ache. It's been so long since I

allowed myself to think of Mom or Dad. Something about
Gutter has me all in my feelings today.

I lace my fingers with his and follow him inside. I lift a brow
as we move into the hotel and casino, but Gutter bypasses the
registration desk. It's clear he knows the place well as we turn a
corner between slot machines, restaurants, and shops.

I'm wide eyed while we make our way to a row of elevators.
Gutter jabs the button and the doors to the car, right in front of
us open. He leads us into the elevator and places a card into the
slot, before pressing for the tenth floor.

I look at him curiously, wondering where the card came
from. Then it dawns on me the doorman must have handed it
to him. Gutter gives me a knowing smile and pulls me into his
arms.

I'm still sweaty and sticky. My clothes are clinging to me,
but the hotel is cool, bringing some much needed relief. He runs
his nose through the sweat at my temple, then kisses the same
spot.

I wince, grossed out, but he doesn't seem to mind at all as he
inhales. He tightens his arms around me, and we bask in the
moment as the elevator carries us up. When the bell chimes, we
exit the car, and he leads us to the left.

We walk for what seems like forever, until we reach the doors
at the end of the hall. He opens the door to a huge suite. I break
into a smile, when I take in the pool table, bar, and the amazing
view. I wasn't expecting this at all.

"This place is amazing," I say, making my way further into
the room.

"It's all ours until Grim and Reap get here. You can shower
or whatever. I'm going to get us some clothes and a few things.
Don't leave this room and don't open the door for anyone. You
feel me?" He breathes in my ear as he walks up behind me.

My feet have taken me to the balcony as the room has me
entranced. The view is too enticing to ignore. I lean back into
him and release a long breath.

"Yeah, I feel you," I say.

I could stay like this forever. If only this were my life. As if reading my mind, Gutter gives me a squeeze.

"When this is all over, we'll make time to come really enjoy this place and anywhere else you want to go," he says and his voice rumbles through me.

I turn in his arms and look up at him. "I would like that. A lot." I smile.

He pecks my lips. "All you have to do is say the word." He slaps my ass. "Now, go cool off. I'll be right back."

I give him a soft kiss in return, before heading to the bathroom. When I look over my shoulder, I find him watching me intently. I wink at him, feeling lighter than I've felt in a very long time. His lips turn up slightly in one corner, warming my heart.

I step into the bathroom and gasp, when I turn on the light. The bathroom is as gorgeous as the rest of the suite. The polished marble, shining fixtures, stunning sconces on the walls, and the large mirrors, only add to the size of the bathroom.

I once dreamed of having a beautiful home that looks like this. When things like that mattered to me. I don't think I ever had a dream of a husband and kids of my own, but I wanted the beautiful home at least. Some place to call my own.

I catch sight of myself in the mirror and wince. My face shines with perspiration. My shirt clings to me and is soaked at the same time.

The shower is calling my name. I sigh and start to peel my clothes off. I turn and eye the lock on the door.

Old habits die hard. I double back and lock it, before stripping completely. Once out of my panties and bra, I move to the shower.

The water is heaven sent the moment it cascades down my back. I sigh in relief, placing my head against the shower wall. I don't know where it comes from, but the dams break, and I begin to cry.

I think my brain is finally catching up with everything that has happened in the last few days. My place, my bike, the weight of my revelation to Gutter, and his to me. Most of all, finally having someone know and understand the burdens I've been carrying.

I sniffle and wipe my tears away. I have to get my head clear. I don't want Gutter to see me like this. I want to forget everything that's waiting for us out there. I want to take this time to be normal for once in my life.

Yeah, I know that won't be easy with my huge scary boyfriend, but I want to try. For once, I don't want to live in a box. I want to peek outside for a little while. Why not take the chance to do it now?

My mind starts to turn toward things I'd like to put off for now, but the nagging won't let me disregard it. There's something I need to look into. Something I've started to remember, from a week ago.

I shrug it off, promising myself I'll look into it tonight. It's unlike me, but that's what I'm shooting for, unlike me. For now, I want to see what the world of Vegas has to offer.

A giggle bubbles on my lips, when I realize Gutter is out shopping for something for me to wear. I may not be into fashion, but I'm pretty sure I should be nervous about what he plans to bring back.

Helpful Friends

Gutter

I rub my forehead, looking around at all the different shit in this place. I groan inwardly, what was I thinking. I should've waited for Sal to pick her own shit.

I dropped off the water and snacks I bought upstairs, before coming back down to look for something to wear for both of us. I peeked into Sal's backpack and she seriously has nothing but a computer and some other tech bullshit. Not a stitch of clothing.

I'd been confident in my mission, until walking into this place. I'm not ashamed to say I called for help. I peek down at my help.

Stormy is someone I trust. She and her brother were two of few who I called friends, before becoming a Lost Soul. The little Latina has a flare about her.

She always tells it like it is. Stormy is also fiercely protective of her brother. If Ramon accepts you then you have Stormy on your side. Trust me, there are times you definitely want Stormy on your side.

She grins up at me and I relax just a little. When her grin turns into a full out beaming smile, I tense up all over again. I'm regretting calling for help already.

"You're adorable, Papi," Stormy chirps. "Can't wait to meet this Chicca that has you all twisted up."

I groan and roll my eyes. "Can you just help me out here? She should be out of the shower by now."

"Fine, fine, but you two are having dinner with me and Ramon tonight, babes. No excuses."

I grunt and nod. "We'll be on the road for a while so she should have something comfortable and cool to wear," I say, watching Stormy move to the racks.

"Okay, no problem," she says, while she starts to pull items.

"Fuck," I growl and run a hand through my hair.

Stormy looks up at me and furrows her brows. "What's up, hon? I got this."

"I forgot to ask for her size," I mumble.

That grin is back on Stormy's lips. "I saw you guys on the monitors when you entered the resort. Trust me, I've got this. She's gorgeous, by the way."

I nod and grunt. "Thanks."

She chuckles. "You're welcome. It's good to see you like this. Last time you were here, you were still licking those old brooding wounds." Her face softens. "You're a beautiful man, inside and out. I've always wanted the best for you."

"You're not so bad yourself, darlin'." I give a small smile.

"Just not your type, I see." She winks. "Don't worry, I won't hold it against you. You're sexy as hell, but not my type either."

I actually laugh. Stormy is one of few who can make that happen. I shake my head and point at the leather skirt in her hands.

"Oh, hell, no. Fuck, no," I hiss.

"Oh, come on. She has to have something to wear tonight. I know those legs of hers are going to look smoking hot in this," she says as I continue to shake my head.

"Not that," I grunt.

"Yes, this. You asked for my help. This is my help. Don't worry, Papi. I plan to have you looking hot as well." She wiggles her brows.

"I'll be fine the way I am," I mutter.

She cocks her hip to the side, placing her hand on the other. "You're not getting into the club like that. No exceptions to the rules. Not even for you," she says with narrowed eyes. "You said your lady wants the experience. You will give her the full experience, Gutter."

I growl and ball my fists, but I know she's right. I want to do this right for Sal. Fuck, this is going to be a long fucking night. Grim and Reap need to get their asses here, now.

A New Sal

Sal

Wrapped in a robe, I step out of the bathroom to the sound of voices. I'd decided to get in the tub for a deep soak after my shower. I was so relaxed; I almost fell asleep in there.

"The Lost Souls have a chapter here. I don't see why you haven't moved down here with us," someone purrs in a female voice.

The hairs on the back of my neck stand up. I'm taken aback for a second. I tighten the belt on my robe and move toward the conversation just as Gutter grunts his reply.

"My family is in South Carolina. You guys are always welcome to come there and expand your business."

"Ramon will never leave Vegas. Believe me, I've tried, repeatedly. I guess we'll never get out of this desert." The woman sighs.

When Gutter and the other speaker come into view, I find a small woman tucked into the couch, across from the chair

Gutter is sprawled in. It looks as if the couch is swallowing her whole, she's so tiny. She's gorgeous.

Although I can hear a hint of Latin in her accent, her skin is only a few shades lighter than mine. When she turns her big brown gaze to land on me, I nearly gasp. She's stunning, a tiny, but wide nose, big eyes, full lips, and her hair frames her face just right.

She has a shoulder length bob that brushes her collarbone in the front. Her artfully tossed bangs are dyed a light shade of gray, while the rest of her hair is a pretty teal ombre. I look to Gutter to see if his eyes are glued to the tiny beauty the way mine want to be.

Only as my gaze meet his, he only has eyes for me. Gutter raises from his seat and moves toward me with purpose. He tugs me into his arms and kisses the top of my head.

It's as if he needs the contact to calm himself or to give him reassurance of my safety. I know the feeling. I hadn't realized how much I needed his touch, until he wraps his arms around me.

"I had no idea what to get you," Gutter murmurs and I swear his cheeks look like they have a little blush. "Stormy helped me out. If the stuff doesn't fit, we can return it."

"It will fit. I know what I'm doing," the little woman, I assume to be Stormy, calls out as she stands from the couch. She grabs a few bags and walks over to us. "Come on, gorgeous. We'll have him on his knees, when I'm done."

She looks up at a frowning Gutter and wink. Gutter grunts, causing Stormy to throw her head back and laugh. Her laugh is infectious. I bite my lip, stifling my own until I see the unease on Gutter's face.

I burst into laughter. Gutter narrows his eyes at me, but a small smile tugs the side of his lips, just a bit. My heart stops. I would love to see what that full smile looks like.

Stormy has my hand in hers, pulling me back to the bedroom I'd came from. There's something very warm about this little woman. I feel so at ease with her, which is so not the norm for me.

"You have to tell me what you did to that man out there to have him wrapped around your finger," she sings, setting the bags down by the bed.

She hands me one. "Here, this one has undergarments in it."

I open my mouth to ask how she knows my size. My things were all locked in the bathroom with me. Stormy holds her hand up to halt my words.

"It's what I do. Everything will fit. I have yet to get a client's measurements wrong after just one glance." She winks.

I peek into the bag at the sexy lacey sets resting inside. Sure enough, it's all in my size. I'm more than impressed. I pluck out a bra and panties set and head over to the bathroom.

Once inside, I tug on the set and place the robe back over it. A knock comes at the bathroom door. When I crack it open, a smiling Stormy shoves her arm inside, handing me more garments. I wrap my fingers around the clothes she hands me.

"Thanks," I whisper, before closing the door back.

I eye the items in my hands. It's a black T-shirt and black leather skirt. I shrug, placing them on the countertop to come out of my robe. I pull on the top first. It's cute.

Not really me, but cute. I wouldn't normally wear a shirt that reveals my midriff. Gutter comes to mind and I smile at my reflection in the mirror. This is something a girl my age would normally wear. It's time I live life like a twenty-year-old. A twenty-year-old with a boyfriend.

I love the glow on my brown cheeks. I look happy for once. Deciding that it can only get better from here, I reach for the skirt and pull it on. The smile drops from my lips as I zip up the back of the skirt. My gaze skims over me, from head to toe.

Yeah, this is totally not me. There's no one here, but I already feel all eyes on me. I tug at the hem of the skirt that hits my mid-thigh. I groan and roll my eyes.

I turn to go out into the bedroom to see what else Stormy has. *Baby steps*, I think to myself. Only, the moment I step into the room, Stormy's face has me second guessing myself.

Her mouth pops open, her big eyes light up, and a huge smile lights her face. She claps her hands together. I stumble to a stop, crossing my right foot over my left, fidgeting my toes together.

"I knew that skirt would be hot on those long legs, but wow. Your skin is amazing all over," she gushes.

"I... I don't think this is me," I say softly.

She pouts her lips. "You look so hot. Gutter is going to lose his shit, but if you really don't feel comfortable, I'll get you something different. I just didn't peg you for some of the other party dress options."

I think over her words. Yeah, I'm not going to wear some of the party dresses I've seen girls my age wear. However, I've always been true to me. Gutter or no Gutter, I don't think I'm willing to change that too much now, even if I want to please him.

"Yeah, Stormy, I don't know. Is there some type of compromise? Something in between?" I ask, biting my lip.

Her face beams and she snaps her fingers. "Are you against heels?" she asks with bright eyes.

I laugh and shake my head. "My sister can't walk in heels to save her life, but I used to play in my mom's all the time." I smile at the memory.

"All right, Chicca, give me ten minutes. I'll be right back," she says as she plucks up a pair of sexy army boots.

I'm guessing those were her plan for this outfit. I wiggle out of the pleated leather skirt and perch on the edge of the bed. I start to chew on my lip as the feeling of being a damaged prude sets in.

It's Gutter's voice just outside the door that settles me. "Is she all right? I thought she'd like those boots."

Stormy gives a musical laugh. "I think she does from the look on her face. She can save them for another time. I have something else in mind for tonight," she says. "No worries, I understand you both now. I'll be right back. You stay out of that room." There's warning in her voice.

Something tells me Stormy may be small, but she's not one to be messed with. Gutter mutters something I can't make out. I giggle from my perch inside the room.

I look down at my gold sparkly toes. It's my one guilty pleasure. When I'm stressed, I like to get my toes painted. I'd gone for a pedicure the day before my apartment was broken into, which leads me in the direction of my nagging thoughts.

Now that my head is clearing, some things aren't adding up. It's clear that whoever broke into my place was looking for something, but why take my bike? That's the part that doesn't make sense.

Sighing, I shake my head, promising myself I will look into all this after we have some fun here. Again, not me, but I have a feeling we will be face to face with all of this trouble soon enough. For now, I just want to be.

I'm still chewing on my lip, lost in thought, when Stormy returns with shoes and something else dangling from her hands. I tilt my head and furrow my brows. This doesn't look much bigger than the skirt she'd given me earlier.

"Don't give me that look. You said compromise." She drops the shoes down next to my feet and holds up a pair of leather short shorts and fishnet stockings. "This is compromise, Gorgeous."

My eyes go wide and I stare wordlessly. "Really," I finally huff out.

Stormy wiggles her brows. "Really."

I shake my head and snatch the shorts and stockings from her, while side eyeing her. The smile she gives me makes it hard to be mad at her for long. I think I'm going to learn to like this woman a lot.

I smooth on the stockings first, before wiggling into the shorts and stepping into to the heels. They're gold sparkly peep toe heels that match my toes perfectly. The stockings are seamless, and the holes are big enough to show off my painted toenails.

I grin and wiggle my toes. Well, she got the shoes right at least. I move into the view of the mirror and blink.

"Damn," I hear rasped from behind me.

I turn to see Gutter practically salivating. His eyes are glued to my long legs. I have to admit. I like the shorts. I feel more comfortable in them than that tiny skirt. It helps that my legs aren't completely bare either.

"Didn't I tell you to wait for us to come out," Stormy hisses.

"I wanted to make sure she's okay. You didn't even give me a chance to introduce you." Gutter frowns.

"Oh, please. Salalia and I are like old friends already." She waves him off. "Give us thirty minutes."

I groan. "Please call me, Sal."

Stormy winks. "Gotcha."

"You all right in here, baby girl?" Gutter asks huskily. His eyes still glued to my legs.

"Yeah, I'm good." I smile at him.

He licks his lips and nods, before bringing his eyes up to mine. The lust is heavy in them. It makes me wonder what his reaction to the skirt would have been.

Just as I have the thought, he moves his eyes to the bed, where the discarded skirt lies. I can see the sigh of relief that leaves his chest. He nods to the skirt, then turns to Stormy, lifting a brow.

"Told you that wasn't going to fly. Don't even make any sense you trying to get someone killed," he says.

As Stormy bursts into laughter, it dawns on me Gutter just showed his first sign of humor in front of more than just me since I've been with him. I'm watching him open up in front of my eyes. I beam, starting to have some real hope for this evening.

"I'm ready to hit the town," I chime.

"Not yet," Stormy says in mock horror. "I'm going to take that natural glow and set you ablaze, honey."

I smile and nod. I feel like we're releasing a new side of me. I want to get this show on the road. I plan to have as much fun as I can, before Grim and Reap show up to bring us back to reality.

CHAPTER FIFTEEN

Give and Take

Gutter

Sal is pretty without all the extra, but tonight. I almost swallowed my tongue, when I stepped out of the bathroom to find her sitting on the bed waiting for me. I'd jumped in the shower to get myself ready, while Stormy worked on Sal's makeup.

I didn't think my cock could get any harder than it was when I first walked in to find Sal in those little shorts and heels. Those chocolate brown legs are a work of art. I'm still trying to wrap my head around the fact that she belongs to me.

Every brown, silky, smooth inch of her is mine. I don't know how I'm supposed to stay focused all night with her looking the way she does. Then there are those smiles.

I have no doubt about it. I'm falling in love with her. At first, what drew me to her was simply the knowledge that we were kindred spirits. We're both broken and trying to find our way. Now, I see more in my feelings for Sal.

She's gorgeous, sweet, and loving. Stormy doesn't take to everyone. To watch her pull Sal in like a little sister has put my mind at ease in a way I hadn't known I needed.

Ramon and Stormy talked me out of a lot of stupid shit in my past. I respect their opinion.

"You sure you want to stick with this old grump?" Ramon says in his gravelly tone to Sal at my side.

"Yeah, I think I'm staying right where I am," Sal says, with a wide smile on her face as she looks up at me.

Ramon places a hand over his chest and groans. "I'm a wounded, divorced man. Couldn't you humor my last request?" He pouts like a kid.

I roll my eyes, sit back in my seat, and fold my arms across my chest. "Other than the fact that I plan to take your life for hitting on my woman, what makes this your last request?" I ask, amused.

"Ah, my friend. My wife may be a bitter bitch who I can't wait to divorce, but she has always been a great lay. I will die of inadequate sex, when the divorce is final." Ramon sighs.

"Gross, disgusting. I can't believe you're still sleeping with her. I told you that shit is going to come back and bite you," Stormy mutters and slides closer to me, away from her brother.

I grunt and shake my head. Ramon's wife isn't one of my favorite people. She's one of the reasons I never chose to settle here before becoming a Lost Soul. I catch a chill just thinking about her.

"Don't you worry your pretty little head, *hermana*. I'm in the doghouse once again. For what, this time, I truly don't know. I guess we're both ready to move on." Ramon shrugs and lifts his brandy to his lips.

Stormy narrows her eyes at him. "Humph," she huffs.

"Ah, it's no matter. I think it's time for a change. How do you like it there in South Carolina, friend?" Ramon asks looking at me.

I stare back at him in surprise. I never thought I'd see the day Ramon would consider leaving Nevada. There's shock written all over Stormy's face too.

"It's home." I lift a shoulder.

"Man of few words." Ramon directs his words toward Sal and winks.

"Fine with me, saves me from having to listen too much," she replies.

I chuckle, reaching out to tug her into me. I kiss the top of her head and inhale. This all is so out of place for me, but it feels right.

"Well, dinner was amazing in your company. I will be calling it an early night. I have an early morning," Ramon says, then his smile falls, and he looks me in the eyes. "If you need anything and I do mean anything, we are at your disposal."

"Thanks." I nod.

"Hermana, let our friends enjoy the rest of their night," Ramon says to Stormy, giving her a pointed look.

She frowns, but she's already in motion to leave the table. She moves to embrace Sal, whispering something in her ear. Sal laughs, but nods at whatever has been said to her.

"Don't be a stranger, handsome," Stormy throws my way with a wink.

"You either," I murmur. "Looks like you may be able to come for a visit."

"You bet your ass, babes," she sings and blows a kiss over her shoulder.

"I like them," Sal says beside me.

I look into her eyes and grunt. My friends are already forgotten. I've wanted to be alone with Sal for far too long.

I cup the back of her neck, drawing her in. My soul soothes the moment I capture her lips with mine. It's a slow passionate kiss that has my own toes curling.

I sound like a pussy, but I don't give a shit. That's what this girl does to me. I break the kiss and place my forehead to hers.

"I know all your deep dark secrets, but I want to know you. Tell me about Salalia," I whisper.

She smirks, kissing the corner of my mouth. "Let's make a deal. I'll tell you something about me, after you comply with my request. One new bit of information with each completed request," she laughs.

I think on that for a minute. If it were anyone else, I'd say no. For Sal, I think I'd do just about anything. I gently kiss her lips and grunt my assent.

Her squeal of delight makes my heart feel like it's about to burst out of my chest. A smile tugs at my lips and her face seems to brighten even more. She looks up at the ceiling, tapping her full, gold painted lips.

The music seems to turn up a notch and that's when I notice something in her eyes change. I groan, because I know her request before she even makes it. I can't dance for shit, but I won't deny her anything she asks for.

Sal

I don't seriously think Gutter will oblige me, but I decide to ask him anyway. What could it hurt? If he says no, I'll come up with something else.

"Will you dance with me?" I look up into his eyes pleadingly.

To my surprise, he's already lifting out of his seat. My mouth pops open—might I add, not for the first time tonight. I almost slipped in a puddle of my own drool, when he stepped out of the bathroom in a pair of well-fitting slacks, cowboy boots, and a white dress shirt.

I didn't even mind that he had placed his cut on over the dress shirt. Stormy, on the other hand, looked like she wanted to kill him. They fussed a bit about it.

Eventually, Stormy won. I don't know what she whispered to Gutter, but whatever it was caused him to look at me with determination, while shrugging out of his cut, and leaving it behind in our room.

It didn't bother me that he wore it. In fact, it's something I'm more than used to. I think he looked sexy.

The way his muscles played beneath his crisp white shirt, how he rolled the sleeves up to just over his elbows. Oh, and don't let me get started on how those thighs flex beneath those slacks. Gutter is just hot.

Smoking hot and all mine, cut or not. I keep that thought in my mind as we move to the dance floor. I don't miss all of his admirers.

Male and female, but he only has eyes for me. He keeps a tight hold on my hand and my waist as we make our way through the small crowd. The place is packed, but respectably so.

We have more than enough room to claim our own little bubble on the dance floor. When Gutter finds a corner on the floor he stops and pulls my back into him.

He slides his fingers across my belly, before settling them on my waist. His warm breath is at the back of my neck. I can also feel him growing against my backside.

The song playing is a fast one, however, Gutter rocks slowly to our own beat. I'm not complaining. I didn't even think he would agree. I love being out here in his arms.

I start to sway my hips to try to guide our rhythm a little, but he just won't be moving to this beat. I laugh and turn in his embrace, throwing my arms around his neck. His gaze locks with mine and once again, moving to the music doesn't matter at all.

"What did Stormy say to get you out of your cut?" I ask.

His eyes become hard, but he's quick to reply. "She reminded me that the last thing I wanted to do was draw attention while you're with me. Your safety comes first."

"Oh." I nod. I wish I didn't ask. This was supposed to be a night free of all of that shit.

"You owe me some information, darlin'. Spill," he says, bringing me right back into our little bubble.

I already have what I plan to tell him. It's a memory I hold dear. There aren't many of those I can still recall, without a sting in my heart.

"I used to love to dance. Eva, Misty, Erica, and I, we would blast music in the back of the clubhouse and dance for hours. Cage started calling it the teen room. We were the only ones allowed in there, when we were around," I say as I beam at the memory.

Gutter wrinkles brows. "Erica? Are you talking about Reap?" he asks.

"Yup, the one and only." I bob my head as my smile grows.

He smirks. "I don't think I can even imagine her dancing or doing anything girly. Fuck, I can't imagine her doing anything without Grim." He chuckles. It's nice.

"Who said Grim wasn't there?"

He gives a knowing expression and tilts his head.

"But you never spend a lot of time around the club? I figure I would have seen you by now if you had," he muses.

"I've been in boarding school for as long as I can remember. I stop coming home after mom and Cage…" I cut my words off, as a lump knots in my throat.

"Yeah, I'm sorry about that," he says.

I shrug. "Cage realized I was bored in school—I mean, super bored, just surviving. However, he knew I loved to take things apart.

"He talked Mom into sending me to boarding school to get a better education that would stimulate me and my interests. It's because of Cage I'm no ordinary computer geek—"

I cut off again, this may not be something I should share. The truth is I could shut the globe down. Yup, I'm that dangerous, which scared the shit out of my teachers.

At least, until they saw I didn't bother anyone, I kept to myself and did my part. I think Cage always wanted me to work for the Lost Souls, just like I'm doing.

I swallow past my thoughts and continue. "Losing my parents was one of the hardest times of my life, but I made it through," I drop my chin and say softly.

Gutter reaches to place his fingers beneath my chin. He places a soft kiss on my lips, then my nose. I blink away tears as my eyes connect with his.

"I'll do everything I can to bring you brighter days from here on out. I don't know how to do this shit, but I'm going to die trying to get it right," he says gruffly.

"You're doing just fine. Or at least I think you are." I smirk.

He wrinkles his brows. I watch as a question forms on his lips. I shake my head and cover his mouth with my fingertip. I love the way his eyes light up. The blue comes out to play more when he laughs.

"So, about that next request. How about we get out of here and go see about a Ferris wheel?"

He releases something between a grunt and a groan, but I take it for a yes as he wraps his arm around me and starts off the dance floor.

Up High

Sal

We take a cab up to the strip, right over to the Linq. I almost squeal like a little girl, when the High Roller comes into view. The night is turning out amazing.

Gutter tucks me under his arm as we start for the entrance of the Ferris Wheel. I shouldn't be surprised when we ride up the escalator and reach a waiting line. I smile when the photo area comes into view.

There's a group making silly faces as their picture is taken. One look at Gutter and he leads me right over. A single nod from him and the picture guy waves us over, ahead of the others waiting.

Gutter guides me over and we take our photo. A few people give us looks, trying to figure out who the hell we are. The photographer takes a few pictures before smiling.

"Perfect," he says as he looks down at his camera.

I expect to wait in line to get in a bubble for the ride, but once again, Gutter walks straight to the front of the line. People move aside for us, but there are a few drunken murmurs.

I guess one good look at Gutter—even without his cut—brings the slurred grumbles to a hush. I draw my brows inward as Gutter leans in to whisper in the attendant's ear. She beams up at him, nodding her head.

Gutter squeezes my waist as I stiffen at his side ready to snatch this chick over the chain separating us. I'm getting real tired of these chicks flirting with my man right in my face. Gutter hands over a few bills that Miss. Smiley tucks into her pocket.

The next Ferris car arrives, and the attendant opens the little chain for us to pass. We move forward to the open bubble, stepping inside. The door closes behind us. I look at Gutter questioningly.

I thought we'd be riding with others. He looks down at me and his eyes light up. It's dark outside, but the bubble we're in has its own lighting. The screens around us show the ascending altitude as the car moves up.

In all honesty, I don't even know why I wanted to do this. I'm afraid of heights. My ears burn with embarrassment as I realize I just may freak out on this thing.

"What's wrong, baby girl?" Gutter asks, his brows knitting as my distress covers my face.

I suck my lip into my mouth before answering. This is so embarrassing. The bubble stops and I squeeze my eyes shut. My breath comes out with a whoosh.

"I'm afraid of heights," I whisper.

The space is silent for a few minutes, except for my breathing and the monitors on the walls. They warn us we will stop from time to time and not to be alarmed. Gutter runs both his hands down my sides, around to my backside. I'm vaguely aware of the music playing around us.

He squeezes my ass, causing me to open my eyes. There's an intense look on his face. He searches my gaze, before he nods to himself.

"I want you to focus on me and me only. Nothing else exists, you feel me." He commands.

"Yeah, I feel you." I nod.

And I do feel him as he kneads my ass. He dips his head capturing my lips. The groan that comes from deep in the back of his throat enters my mouth, calling to my nipples that start to strain against my bra and T-shirt. I close my eyes once again as I allow his touch to be everything I need.

Absentmindedly, I wrap my arms around his neck and lose myself in his kiss. The warmth of his tongue meeting mine, sends heat throughout my body. I bleed into his arms as if I'm trying to bleed into him to become one.

I'm transported from our bubble in the sky to a place all of our own. He reaches one hand between us to unfasten my shorts. I squeeze his length through his slacks, pulling a deep growl from his chest.

"You're missing the view," he says as the voice on the screen tells us we've reached four hundred and twenty feet.

Gutter spins me and pulls my back to his front. He shoves his hand into my shorts and stockings, while his lips meet my ear. I shiver as his warm breath fans against my skin.

"You have nothing to ever fear when you're in my arms. I will protect you from any and everything," he says huskily.

I moan as he skims my seam with his long fingers. When I open my eyes to the world outside our bubble, it's amazing. We have a view of everything. I feel safe in his arms, safe enough to forget we've come to a halt again as we're suspended way up in the sky.

"I'm going to make you come for me, baby girl," he whispers hotly. "You keep your eyes open. Enjoy that view, while I take you over."

He shoves two fingers into my heat, gently tapping my heeled foot with his booted one to get me to spread my legs more. I obey the silent command, giving him better access to my honey. I'm so wet, his fingers slide in and out of me with ease, only to suck him back in.

As I unravel, I blink at the view outside, but I'm not comprehending it. Lost, I flicker my gaze back down to his large hand shoved in my shorts. I don't know why the sight turns me on so much.

Gutter groans in my ear. "That's it, Salalia. This pussy only gets wet for me. Just like my cock only throbs and aches for you. Ride my fingers, baby. Let that juicy pussy come for me."

"Gutter," I cry out.

He grunts against my neck, before sucking it into his mouth. I roll my head to the side to give him better access. My hips move to their own rhythm, chasing the pleasure that's just within my reach.

He shifts his fingers, finding the right spot, causing my eyes to cross. I bite my lip to keep from screaming. My legs start to tremble beneath me.

"Come on, baby girl. I feel it. Come for me," he hisses. He reaches for my clit with his thumb and uses his other fingers to rub me to ruin.

"Holy—" The rest of my words are captured by Gutter's mouth as he covers mine. His tongue plunging into my wet cavern.

He places his hand around my throat, squeezing gently. I whimper into his mouth, causing him to release my neck and drag his palm down to my collarbone, then my breast. He squeezes my mound over my T-shirt. It must not be enough for him or he senses I need more. He glides his hand down to my exposed skin, then up under my shirt.

He pulls the cup of my bra down before reaching for my nipple and rolling it between his fingers. It's exactly what I need. I moan into his mouth and start to shake against his chest.

I come so hard, my legs turn to jelly, my heels teeter, and I sag back into him. Gutter pulls his hand from my shorts and brings his fingers to my lips. I suck his digits into my mouth, savoring my flavor on his salty fingertips.

He pops his fingers free from my lips and raises them to his own, sucking off whatever I've left behind. I smile lazily up at him. The pod has stopped again, the bright lights surrounding us, give his gorgeous face an ethereal glow.

The sound of his belt releasing fills my ears. In the next moment, my shorts are shoved down my hips, pooling around my ankles. Gutter wraps an arm around me, backing up until the backs of his legs hit the bench seat in the bubble.

He sits, bringing me down onto his lap. Reaching for my chin, he then cups my face and brings it back to his. I grind in his lap, while he devours my lips.

The tearing of my stockings between my legs fills the air. I'm ready to be rid of anything preventing him from being inside me. Reaching one arm around my waist, he goes to lift me, but I have other plans.

I turn to straddle his hips, pushing my panties aside, and ease down on his waiting, pulsing, length. He's so hard as he impales me, I nearly drool on myself. I wrap my fingers around the back of his neck.

It feels so good, he's so deep. I throw my head back and arch into him. He reaches for my waist, slowing my pace and guiding me up and down.

"Being inside you is the best feeling in the world," he grunts.

I feel the same way, but when I go to say it, I only manage to drool on my lip. When I make a slurping sound to bring the moisture back into my mouth, Gutter's blue grays focuses in on my lips.

He licks his own, before licking my lower one. I run my fingers up through the short hairs on the back of his head to the longer strands on top and hold on tight.

He moves his hands under my shirt, freeing one of my breasts from its confines. He cups both mounds in his big hands, flicking my nipples with his thumbs. I start to ride him like my life depends on it.

The bubble has started to move again, but I'm lost to the man beneath me. I can't say much for the view and the city below. It's just a beautiful back drop to a beautiful moment— as Gutter groans my name and looks at me tenderly—that's the only word that comes to mind, *beautiful.*

I continue to ride him as my pussy soaks him underneath me. The ride stops again, but that doesn't faze me. I keep bouncing and crying out for more.

When we start to move again, the voice on the screens begins to countdown our ascent to the very top. All at once, I start to reach my ascent as well. The screens flashes images of fireworks and our target height of five hundred and fifty feet. It goes wild and so does my body.

I scream out as I ride through my climax. Gutter grasps the skin at my back and digs his fingers into my flesh. His tight grip causes my walls to clench around his shaft harder.

"I'm coming," Gutter breathes in my ear just before I feel his hot seed explode inside me.

"Fuck," I hiss as the aftershocks hit me.

I sag into him, my chest heaving against his. I finally focus my eyes on the sight around us. It's gorgeous. I giggle to myself as the slot machine music from the on-screen celebration registers in my ears.

Yeah, I would say I just hit the jackpot. I bury my face into Gutter's neck and inhale him. When I lift my head again to look around us, my face flames. I didn't think once about the people in the other bubbles being able to see us.

Gutter reaches to pull his pants back up his hips and fastens them. With little effort, he lifts me and moves to retrieve my shorts. Returning to the bench, still holding me tightly, he places me back in his lap.

He dresses me with care, like I'm a little precious doll in his lap. When he's done, he looks up into my eyes and we lock on each other. I take in all the emotions and thoughts running through his eyes.

I figure now is as good a time as any to reveal the next pieces of myself to this gorgeous man. I cup his cheek and kiss his lips. He reaches up and brushes his thumb over my lower lip.

This is a big one for me. One that's been a well-kept secret as far as I know. It's what makes me unique and valuable to the Lost Souls.

"I have a photographic memory." I smirk. "I will remember this forever. It's like my brain has taken pictures of every moment."

He nods. "I'll remember it forever, but my brain isn't half as pretty or brilliant as yours," he murmurs. "That must have been helpful in school."

"It was. I could see my notes in my head. I would write them on postcards, sometimes in different colors. I would be able to see the notes in my mind and recall all the information." I laugh.

His brows furrow as he takes in my words. His face changes, but I'm not sure what has brought on the change until he speaks. His words turn my body cold.

"You're Kodak," he states more than askes. "Fuck."

He runs a hand through his hair. I completely blanch. My heart starts to pound. I lift from his lap and take a step back.

"Where did you hear that name?" I whisper as I wrap my arms around my middle.

He rubs his forehead and purses his lips. He releases a heavy breath and looks into my eyes. I see the moment something clicks into place for him.

"How much do you know about the Squad?"

I swallow hard. "It's the one thing I don't have full access to. I never needed to know their identities. King thought it better if I didn't. However, I know about the Squad and what they mean to the club," I reply and lick my dry lips. "Everyone knows that."

Gutter groans and closes his eyes. He releases another deep breath. My chest tightens with the onset of a panic attack.

As I said before, there are few people who know I work for the Lost Souls. Those that do know, know me by the name Kodak. Fear that my identity has gotten out consumes me.

The look on Gutter's face isn't helping one bit. He seems to be thinking his words out a little too carefully for my liking. I can't help but berate myself for being so stupid.

What do I know about this guy? Clearly there has been some breach of security. How do I know it hasn't come from him or someone he's working with?

I've started to fall in love with him and never asked any real questions. My heart never had a chance for questions. It has felt like its belonged to him forever. Like finding someone lost, after years of searching. Yet, something isn't right, and I fear he's about to shatter my entire world.

"There are twelve Squad members," Gutter starts. All emotion and expression have left his face. "You have to be some kind of fucked up to be recruited. Squad members have a different kind of loyalty to the Lost Souls.

"If you're Squad, you're always ready and willing to get elbows deep in blood for your brothers and anything they hold dear. Squad stands ready to jump in front of any bullet meant for our prez."

He takes a pause, wrinkling his brows. "Do you know what marks a Squad member?"

I lick my lips again and give a short nod. "The winged reaper with the sword," I reply softly.

"Have you seen my naked back?" he asks, his expression finally revealing an emotion. Pensive.

I pull a face as confusion swirls. "Gutter can we stay focu…" My words trail off as he stands and unbuttons his shirt and shrugs it off. "Sugar is the only one that can and will ink one of these. I asked to have mine done a little different."

I gasp when he turns his back to me. That first night, when he had his back to me after his shower, the lighting was dim. I'd been too into my feelings to pay attention and I can't recall him having his back to me the next morning. I was too busy enjoying the pleasure he gave me before we had to race off.

I can't believe this is the first time I'm paying attention to his bare back, but there it is, as clear as day. A winged reaper.

Only Gutter's reaper is kneeling on one knee, with both hands wrapped around the sword standing before him. The reapers head is uncovered, revealing half a face and half a skull. The face looks just like Gutter's. The detailing is amazing.

I move in closer to touch his ink covered flesh with my fingertips. The weight of this all hits me slowly. A lot slower than I'm used to. I mean, this is like watching a bomb go off in your face, and not being able to do anything about it.

My fingers tremble as I trace the lines of the replica of the face I'm beginning to fall in love with. It looks as if a photograph was imprinted into his skin. I know Sugar does amazing work, but this… this takes the cake on so many levels.

It's so realistic. The dark look in Gutter's eyes, the slight sneer of his lips. I even feel like the eyes are looking into my soul. The fact that the skull side has a matching haunting blue-gray eye, causes a chill to run through me.

There is something in the eyes on this tat. It's the same look I catch when I stare into the eyes of two other Squad members I know of. I move my eyes and fingers to the wings, fanning out from the Reaper's back. It's so clear to me now what Gutter is trying to tell me. I jerk back as his revelation hits me hard.

"Holy shit, you have to be kidding me," I gasp.

"I don't kid about the Squad, baby girl," he says as he turns back toward me. "I had no idea Kodak was a girl, less on my girl, you're on the list of top priorities for us. Whatever you do for the club, you're one bad motherfucker," he says and looks at me through a seemingly new gaze.

"No one is to know that I'm the Lost Souls' accountant. I run the money for all the chapters. I also run the database on all of you and your finances, all assets and resources run through me.

"The whole system you guys have been running the club and your personal money through, I built it. If someone has found this out, it could cause me problems. That's why I took off from my place. Not many people have access to this knowledge," I huff.

"Motherfucker, I just don't get why King didn't tell me I was coming for you," he bites out and pulls a hand down his face.

I lift a brow and grin. "I think you would take better care of his sister than you would his accountant and systems manager," I try to tease.

"No, baby girl." He shakes his head. "King is smart. He knows something, there are ears around that he's being cautious of. Seems to me, you think so too. You've dump two phones since we've been together."

I shrug. "I always operate with caution, but you're right, I have a few suspicions I want to look into when we get back to the room."

He narrows his eyes at me. "We're going back," he says firmly cutting off all protests I may have.

Forgotten Shadow

Pop

"Those motherfuckers should have made sure I was dead when they had the chance to. I've been waiting a long time." I lick my lips tasting my revenge in the air.

"I'm going to destroy everything that son of a bitch ever loved. I hope he's stroking out, knowing I'm coming for him and everything he loves."

"I have nothing to do with this... beef." Juan Castro waves his hand at me. "You do what I ask, and I will hand you what you're seeking. I need the Lost Souls system of operations. I want to know how King does it. Get me that information and I will deal with everything personally."

"Fine, I don't give a fuck about that. As long as I get my hands on King, the boy, and those girls you'll get everything you want. That motherfucker, Mix will watch as it all comes crumbling down around him and then, I'm going to take his fucking head," I snarl.

Juan shrugs and leans forward in his seat. "You fuck this up and you die. You will not get a second chance with me. You have slithered on your belly to get to me. Don't make me regret giving you legs to stand on," Juan says as he looks through me with his cold eyes.

I want to spit in his face. Juan wouldn't be where he is if it weren't for men like my grandfather. It was the hard work, blood, sweat, and tears of my Cuban ancestors that allowed him the power he has now.

I hold my tongue though. I'm too close to what I want to split this piece of shit's wig now. I'm tired of people thinking they're better than me. I grit my teeth and lean forward in my seat to mirror him.

"I will deliver. You just make sure you do," I grit out.

He throws his head back and laughs. He looks at one of his men and fires off rapid Spanish. My blood boils further. This motherfucker must think I'm stupid.

"You can threaten my life in whatever language you like. Just make sure you follow through in the right one when you come for me," I snarl.

Juan tilts his head to the side and narrows his eyes at me. "And what language would that be?" he finally says, after a few beats.

"The only one spoken in hell, motherfucker. Do or die."

"You will die. And I will be the one doing. This, I can promise you. I speak the language proficiently. This you will see." With those words, Juan stands, glaring back at me.

He buttons his suit jacket and turns to leave the dank motel room, along with his men. I crack my neck. I've been trying to hold my temper with that son of a bitch for months.

"Fuck," I mutter.

"Well, that just went all types of wrong." Comes from behind me.

I turn to find my little brother leaning in the bathroom doorway. He'd been hiding out in there in case I needed back up. I sigh and shake my head.

"Shut the fuck up," I snap. "What do you have for me?"

"Nothing, King still doesn't trust me," Wax says. "I came across that New York info by accident. I thought I was dead when I tried to put everything back where I got it from."

"Stop your fucking whining. I told you Trixie would have your back. I need more information. The boys are still trying to find the little bitch. She slipped them. How did those fuckers get dropped on and who the fuck got the drop on them?"

I have nothing but incompetence around me. They had one job, just one. How do you fuck up something so simple? If I had the girl, I could've ended this without Juan talking to me like shit.

Wax rubs his forehead. "You're going to get us both killed," he huffs.

"Cut your fucking whining and man up," I hiss. Sometimes, I can't believe he's my little brother. His little ass is bitch made if I've ever seen it. I guess that's from his mama's side. "Fuck!"

I need real men around me. If I'm going to pull this off, I have to get some men with brains and spines around here. He's right, they're all going to get themselves killed.

"Listen," Wax starts.

"No, you listen. I need more. I need some shit I can sink my teeth into. You feel me? Bring me something I can use or don't bring your ass back here."

"Fuck, man," Wax groans. "I got it."

"And another thing. Find out exactly what King has that that fucker Juan wants. What the fuck is it about the Lost Souls' system of operations? I need some leverage. I'm not liking where this shit is going," I demand as my thoughts start to spin. "It's time all these motherfuckers feel me."

"And Misty?" Wax asks nervously.

My jaw tightens. My heart squeezes. I loved that little girl from the day she was born. It burns my soul to know she calls that motherfucker, Mix, her daddy.

Yet, I'm no fool. My old lady was a whore. I still don't know if Misty was ever my baby girl in the first place. It's something that has burned me for years. I think Wax is right, it's time I know the truth.

"I need answers. Then, I'll know what to do with her. For now, make sure she's safe. I want to know if anything funny happens around her. If things are as they should be, we're getting her out of there," I say and bring a cigarette to my lips to light.

"Pop," Wax says nervously. "This shit goes south—"

"You leave all that to me. Just get me what I need, Wax," I bite out, getting up to leave the room.

Wax

My brother is going to get me killed. I don't want this shit. I've been trying to figure out a way to get out of this, since he showed up on my doorstep with his mad ass idea.

I love being a Lost Soul. It's my home. I was on my way up from a prospect when Pop brought his ass around. I hadn't seen him in years. He split when I was still wiping my nose on my sleeve, wishing I could be cool like my big bro.

Now, I wish he would disappear again. He's nothing like the brothers I've gained at the club. Pop can't see pass this vengeance he wants so bad.

It doesn't even make sense. Who has a hard on for a man that's in the grave—and to loath Mix. Well, Pop would lose his shit if he knew I look up to Mix more than I do him.

I wish I never brought him that information. I didn't know it was connected to Sal. I had no idea who the fuck Kodak was.

Now, I'm fucked. King is going to have me skinned alive for this.

I thought if I gave Pop something, he would leave me the fuck alone. I handed him family on a platter, and I don't know how the fuck I plan to fix this or if I'll live to get a chance to try.

What hurts most is that Sal is like a sister to me. She stood up for me a few times when we were younger. She, Eva, Reap, Grim, Jacky, and Misty were there when kids around the neighborhood first started whipping my ass. Now look what I've done.

I run my hand through my hair as my phone rings and pulls me from my musing. I look down and groan as the name of the incoming call flashes at me. I know this is about to be some shit.

I release a deep breath and answer. "Rodney, bro, what's up?" I say as smoothly as I can.

"Where the fuck are you? King ordered a lockdown. We need all hands on deck. Some shit is going down," he says into the phone. The excitement in his voice causes me to roll my eyes.

Rodney is always close to the drama, listening and watching for what he can learn. His ass will be drunk soon enough, spilling his guts. It's one of the reasons I've gotten close to him, even though I don't care much for him. He's lucky he gets a pass because of his uncle, Mix.

I've tried to figure out a way to pin this shit on Rodney. It may be my best way out of this. Mix will beat his ass personally, but I don't think he'll let anyone kill him. At least, I've been hoping he won't. I have an enough blood on my hands because of Pop.

"Fuck, I'm on my way," I grunt into the phone.

"Hey, where the fuck are you anyway?" Rodney asks, I can hear the curiosity in his voice turn up a few notches. "I've been trying to reach you for two days. Prez called everyone in yesterday."

This isn't good. A curious Rodney is a problem. I think quickly, needing to respond before his suspicion rises anymore. I close my eyes and rattle off the first thing that comes to mind.

"Hooked up with some chick. I'm on my way," I reply and hang up before he can question me any further.

I move to throw my leg over my ride. I knock my phone against my forehead. I have to get out of this fucking mess.

Shit, Cage was like an uncle to me. He took care of me when Pop first disappeared. The Lost Souls are my family. I owe them more than this.

CHAPTER EIGHTEEN

Digging

Sal

We make our way back to the hotel and through the casino lobby. I look at the slot machines and blackjack tables longingly as we pass them. I wasn't ready for our night of normal to end.

I sigh as we get into the elevator. Gutter hasn't said a word since we got into a cab to head back to our hotel. I can see his thoughts moving in his head. I'm not sure what all he's thinking. I just know he's lost in whatever it is.

His phone buzzes as we ride up to our floor. He pulls the device out and grunts at the message. He replies as he pulls me closer into his embrace. It's a possessive and protective hold.

I look up into his face, trying to read him, but his eyes give nothing away. It's as if he has checked out. I can totally see him as one of the Squad. It's that look that has me almost certain I know who a few other Squad members are.

We step off the elevator and head to our room. I stiffen as we get closer to the doors and voices float out from inside.

Gutter doesn't seem to be alarmed at all, so I relax just a bit as I follow him into the suite.

I relax completely as Grim and Reap come into view. Reap sits in Grim's lap with a frown on her face. These two are always together, but always fussing at one and other for something.

Grim has an amused look on his face as Reap looks like she's about to lash out at him. Gutter shakes his head, wrapping me in his arms to pull me in front of him. That seems to break right through whatever Grim and Reap were fussing about.

Both their heads whip in our direction. Erica raises a brow as she looks between Gutter and me. Grim groans and pulls a hand down his face. He looks right at Gutter.

"Please tell me Prez knows about this," he says.

Gutter shrugs. "Not yet. Haven't had time to talk about it."

"Ah, shit. I'm going to have to kill you." Reap chuckles.

"Nope, King's going to do this one himself." Grim snorts.

"Too bad. You two look so cute together." Reap smirks.

"Erica, I'm a grown ass woman," I hiss. "King will have to just get over it."

"Easier said, doll. That man is going to lose his shit." She winks at me.

Reap hops her little self up from Grim's lap and moves over to pull me into a hug. As I hug her tightly, it hits me. I miss my old friend more than I knew. Gutter releases his hold on me as Erica and I embrace for a few beats longer.

He moves to Grim, and they lock heads together and begin to murmur to one and other. I pull away from Reap, trying to listen in on their plans. The dark looks on their faces sends a chill through me.

"What's going on with you? Something happened to your place," Reap says at my side, softly, but seriously.

"Yeah, someone broke in, but I honestly don't know much. I think I may have run too quickly. I should've paid more attention to details," I say in frustration. "Something else is going on here."

Reap nods. "Yeah, but we both know you did pay attention. Just relax and pull up everything you remember. What did you see, what did your brain record?"

I lick my lips and nod. She's right. I furrow my brows as I move to retrieve my backpack. Images of my apartment and things I hadn't realized I catalogued pop up in my head. I plop down in the nearest chair and flip open my laptop.

If whoever broke into my place was truly looking for my laptop, they would've had a time getting pass my screensaver and still they would've been lost. My desktop is false. There's another password that opens to the real desktop and my hidden files.

I open the file on the false desktop to get into my computer. Within seconds, I have the picture I'm looking for up on my screen. I start to hack my way into the database I need, while Reap looks on.

Lately, I've been getting this feeling like I'm being watched or something. I've been paranoid, since coming back to the States from London, but this was different. I remember a strange guy about a week ago, hanging around my building.

I paid it no mind at first, but I'd discretely taken a picture of him, after feeling like I'd seen him one too many times and not just in front of my building.

I didn't want to alarm King with my paranoia and I'd been distracted with work. I'd taken the picture and forgotten about it after not seeing the guy for in the following days.

"Who's that?" Reap asks as she moves her face closer to the screen. "Where have I seen him before?"

She says the last part more to herself than to me. I don't stop to reply. Things are clicking into place.

"You guys should get over here. She's doing her thing. This may help," Reap calls out.

Grim and Gutter move to stand around me as Reap sits on the armrest of the chair. I'm in my zone, focused on the task before me. I tune out everyone as my brain puts all the pieces together for me.

This man in the picture. I've seen him in the supermarket, standing by the fresh fish. I remember the woman who stood to his right, waiting for her order. She was staring at him with lust in her eyes.

I remember it because she had a toddler with her. The little boy was in the cart whining. A tall dark-haired man came along as she was handed her order. He calmed the child and kissed her on the cheek.

The man in the picture ignored her the whole time, trying to seem inconspicuous. I remember feeling like I was being watched that day. That was months before I started noticing him around my apartment building.

Now, my brain won't stop showing me all the places he has appeared. I'm freaking out because I'm always so cautious. I can't believe I've seen this man sniffing around for months and only registered him in my subconscious.

Reap snaps her fingers. "I knew I saw this motherfucker before," she blurts out.

At that moment, I get a match for the picture on the FBI's database, I've just hacked. I download what I need swiftly and back my way right out of their system.

"Did you just do what I think you did?" Gutter asks as he narrows his eyes at me.

"I plead the fifth," I say with a small non-apologetic smile.

He smirks at me and shakes his head. "We need to ask and answer some more questions later," he says and gives me a wink that blows my mind.

It's unexpected and sexy as hell. Somehow, the gesture softens his face and makes him... real. Gutter is so gorgeous and larger than life. It's the little things that make him real and down to earth. Something tells me not many people get that about him or at least he doesn't show it to many.

"So, where you know this fucker from?" Grim asks Reap as he stabs a finger at my screen.

"I ran into him that time I went to see Sal at school. He was outside her dorm. He looked suspect to me then. He tried to approach me, asking if I came to see a friend. He was pissed when I blew him off. Called me out my name," Reap sneers and looks up at Grim through her lashes. "You saved his life. I was going to carve his ass up, but you rode up and started barking that we had places to be." Reap shrugs as she pulls a lollipop from her pocket and pops it into her mouth.

Nope, she didn't just mention cutting anyone up. Not at all.

"Where'd this pic come from?" Grim quizzes.

"I took it recently outside my building, when I noticed that he'd been around a lot of places I've been," I say as a shiver runs down my spine.

Gutter plucks the laptop from my lap and walks over to the couch to sit. He pulls his phone out and starts to make a call. I sit with my mouth hanging open. I had more I planned to look up.

I feel my cheeks burn. I try not to lash out at him. I know he wants to protect me, but I have more digging I need to do. I need that laptop.

I narrow my eyes as I watch him on his phone. Something tells me when it comes to my safety, Gutter is always going to be high handed. I grunt to myself and fold my arms over my chest, while my fingers itch to get to the bottom of this. I'm not used to sitting around when there's something I should or could be doing.

"Oh, forget whatever you are thinking. The way he held onto you when you guys walked in, he'll have this shit sewn up before we hit the road." Reap chuckles as if reading my mind.

"I wasn't done," I huff. Gutter looks up from my computer screen right into my eyes. "I thought it was someone after Club business that broke into my place. Now that I think about it, something was off. I don't think there was only one intruder. I think there were two different parties," I explain.

"What do you mean?" Grim asks.

"The place was tossed differently in the bedroom. The person or persons who were in there were more passionate about it. They weren't just looking for something. They had a different motive." I shrug and pause to think.

"I was so pissed off about my bike, I hadn't given it much attention before. The living room looked more like someone needed to find something and fast. Do you get what I mean?"

"Yeah, I understand." Gutter nods.

He murmurs something into his phone then hangs up. He makes another quick call before he hands my computer back over. I sigh and go for the next thing I'd planned to look into.

I have cameras in my apartment. With all the adrenaline pumping in my system and my flight reflex kicking in, I never thought to check them. My first thought was to get somewhere safe.

I pull up the time around the break in and fast-forward, until the intruders come into sight. The guy from the picture turns up at my front door, just as I thought. My heart starts to race.

I still don't know who he is. He does look familiar. I just don't know where I can place him from yet.

Gutter makes his way over to watch the screen as well. I can feel the rage coming off of the three of them standing around me. I'm pissed too. The cameras switch to inside the apartment. The guy moves straight to my bedroom. I turn my head when he starts to go through my things, sniffing at them.

"What the fuck is he doing?" Grim growls.

I peek at the screen to see the man has climbed into my bed. Suddenly, something must piss him off. He jumps up and starts to trash the place.

My room is ruined in seconds and he rushes from the apartment. Only a few seconds later, two other guys arrive at the door and pry their way in. They toss the rest of my place. It's one of them who lowers the gate and hops on my bike, headed for the back elevator.

I'm pissed all over again. That bitch ass stole my bike. I want to smash his head in for it.

"That one is mine. Cage gave you that bike. I'm going to fuck him up for even thinking about taking that shit," Reap seethes.

Gutter and Grim lock heads again. They're talking too low for me to hear. Reap moves into the conversation as well. I don't feel welcomed to do so, so I stay put.

After squinting at them and straining to hear for a few minutes, I give up and turn back to the screen in front of me. This is my world, me and my computer. I look closely for clues that may help me figure out who the other two in my apartment were.

I chance a peak at the three in the room with me, when nothing jumps out at me. Gutter looks at his phone as it buzzes. He taps the screen to open something and sits as he reads. His face changes with the more he reads.

At some point, he stops reading and places a call. I watch him speak through tight lips. I swear, his face turns all kinds of red.

"Tell me what the fuck I'm looking at," he demands into the phone.

The growl that rumbles in his chest as he listens chills me. I feel myself curl into my own body. The room is thick with a new tension.

The growl only gets louder as he continues to listen. If his anger could take on life it would be dancing in front of him. Without a word, he ends the call.

Gutter looks at me and I truly believe his head is about to explode. He stands silently. I know he intends for me to follow him without needing his directive.

This isn't good. Not good at all. I don't know what's on that phone, but it may be enough to get someone killed.

Gutter

I haven't felt this kind of rage in years. My guys are some of the best in security. Sal made it a lot easier with her skills, I've never seen anyone hack into the FBI database that fast.

I try to breathe, without running out of this hotel headed straight for the targets of my ire. You just can't make shit like this up. *Identical cousins.* That motherfucker who raped Salalia wasn't her professor. I don't even know how to tell her all of this.

Still stewing, I close the door to the bedroom and lead Sal over to the bed. I sit, pulling her into my lap. For a moment, I stare at her gorgeous face and try to find the words that are going to turn her world upside down.

I don't know how to make them pretty or hurt less. I know this is going to open a hole we thought we just plugged up. I close my eyes and breathe, before opening them again and locking on hers. This is how she got through to me, looking into my soul.

"Your professor, the one you told me about. He has an identical cousin," I say slowly and watch her flinch. I wrap my arms around her tighter. "I don't believe it was actually your professor that... you know."

"What?" Sal whispers. "What are you talking about?"

"They found your professor hanging in his loft in London, not too long after you returned home. He'd been hanging there for a few weeks." I pause and rub my forehead.

"Somehow, his cousin... the fucker traded identities with the professor. He then returned in his place. The authorities have been looking for him for years. Philip Spencer is wanted for identity theft, counterfeiting, rape, stalking, extortion, and a ton of other crimes," I explain.

Sal's lips start to tremble and her whole body quakes. "I don't understand. What does that have to do with the man in the picture and my apartment?"

"Here is where it gets crazy. The man we're seeing in the pictures works for Philip or at times he could be Philip Spencer. It's who Philip wants everyone to see.

"At times it's a disguise, one of many, but the asshole has two sets of fingerprints. Which leads me and my guys to think there are two people here, not one. Marvin Hoover, that's the name in the FBI database, but I think it's bullshit. I want to send over all the footage you have to my guys. They have the photos.

"Your professor, Donald Spencer, *was* the man you trusted. After what Philip did to you, he killed Donald and hung him, made it look like a suicide. Donald's wife came forward and told the American authorities that something was foul back in London.

"Turns out she was right. Philip and his buddy followed you and Donald to Europe. Philip managed to pretend to be Donald before Donald's wife turned up and he had to disappear." I stop there not wanting to freak her out any further.

If you ask me, Philip returned to the States looking for Sal. The fuck has some sick hard on for her. Donald's wife, Abigail told authorities that Philip spent a lot of time going to the college campus, harassing his cousin.

He would trick the staff and students into thinking he was Donald at times. Even before the incident that led to her husband's death. Something tells me Philip orchestrated everything about Sal's accommodations.

Abigail said her husband threatened on more than one occasion to report him if he didn't stop. He never got to make good on his threats. I have a few threats of my own, no make that promises.

"But if he hung him…, how did he return in his place… I… that's crazy."

"I want to say ego. He could've used one of his disguises or aliases, but he didn't. It's like he's taunting the authorities. It's how they made the connection once Abigail reported her suspicions," I reply.

"What do they want with me?" Sal says through a trembling voice.

"I don't know, but I do know they're not getting it. Listen to me," I say and pinch her chin between my fingertips. "There are a lot of motherfuckers who have signed their death certificates by coming for you. I will find them all and put each one to ground. You have my word."

My heart breaks as she nods her pretty head and a tear slips free. I reach for her shoes and pull them from her feet. We aren't going anywhere until the morning. Grim and I have a few things to get in order. Until then, she can rest. I'm here now.

I slide back on the bed, bringing her body with me. With a kiss to her forehead, I cradle Salalia with all that I am. She will never want for safety as long as I have breath in my body.

Nightmares

Sal

I wake up gasping for air and clawing at the sheets. Strong hands reach for one of my shoulders and I start swinging. I plan to fight this time. I'm not going down without a fight.

"Fuck," is growled as my vision and my head start to clear. "Baby, it's me. You had a bad dream, it's me. Your man."

I instantly relax at the sound of Gutter's voice. The bedside lamp comes on and his back comes into view. I don't know why but seeing that winged Reaper on his back settles me. It brings on a calm I've never known before.

When Gutter turns to face me, I gasp. His lip is split. I rush to climb into his lap and cup his face. I didn't mean to hurt him.

"I'm so sorry," I pout. "I—"

He cuts me off with the shake of his head. "You were having a bad dream. I know you didn't mean it." He runs a hand over my short hair. "Are you okay? Do you want to talk about what you were dreaming about?"

The images from the dream hit me full force. I shiver and sink into his heat. I squeeze my eyes shut, wanting to force the nightmare away. It doesn't work. I start to shake, causing Gutter to rub my back.

"It's okay. I'm right here. Nothing can hurt you. You don't have to talk about it," he purrs, next to my ear.

Hearing his words makes me want to tell him. I know he will find a way to comfort me. I tuck my face in his neck and start to speak.

"It was the same old nightmare, but different. This time there were two of them. One pinning me down and the other." I gasp and sniffle. "I think its knowing that he's out there, looking for me. It has triggered the nightmares to change."

"I understand. Damn, baby, do I understand. I have all kinds of triggers, but I always have to remind myself that I'm bigger, stronger, and none of that shit can touch me again."

"It's the same for you, baby. You're stronger, you have people around who are going to protect you, and none of that shit will ever touch you again," he rumbles into my hair.

"I know I'm stronger. I'm a hell of a lot smarter and wiser." I pause and blink back tears. "It's just... I get so angry with myself. I was strong then, when it happened. I could have done more; I could have fought harder."

"Stop," he says gently, but firmly. "You did what your brain allowed at that time. You did what you could to survive. I won't let you beat yourself up over going into survival mode. Not when you're sitting here in my arms breathing."

"I shot my first gun when I was eight," I say with a grin.

I decide to share more about myself to lighten the mood. Gutter lifts a brow at me. The nightmare begins to fall away as he tightens his arms around me. I place a soft kiss on his cut lip.

"I know there is a story behind this one." He chuckles.

"Of course." I laugh.

Gutter settles back down on the bed, taking me with him. He's in his boxer briefs, but I still have on my shorts and T-shirt. I smile. Pierson understands me. I appreciate him not undressing me.

"Mom and Cage were just friends, but he was sweet on mom. I've always been shy. Not as shy as Eva, but still shy," I say as I settle my face against his broad, warm chest. I snort and continue.

"Some kid on our street was talking shit about his daddy teaching him to shoot. Then he threatened me and Eva. I knew Mama had a gun in the house, so I went looking for it.

"Cage happened to be over, fixing something for Mama. He found me with the gun in my hands." I stop and smile at the memory. Cage was my hero.

"He looked down at me and said. 'You know how to use that thing?' I looked up at him with wide eyes. I was sure he was about to tan my hide.

"I shook my head and said, 'No, Sir.' Cage nodded and pushed off the doorjamb. He picked me up and carried me out back. He explained how the gun worked, even showed me how to break it down and put it back together.

"Then he let me shoot it. I was so in awe and petrified of the damn thing. When Cage asked why I needed it, I told him. He took the gun back in the house, then took me down to Jimmy Crooks' house.

"Cage called him and his daddy outside. I don't know what he whispered to Jimmy's daddy, but his face was white as a sheet after. He started whipping Jimmy's ass before they got back into the house." I laugh at the memory.

"Cage sounds like an amazing man. I wish I'd gotten to know him." Gutter chuckles.

"Yeah, he was. Only father I ever knew. Mama loved him so much. We all did. He was larger than life and would take the shirt off his back for you." I wipe away a tear.

"Tell me something that doesn't make you cry, baby," Gutter whispers.

I take a moment to think. It's hard at first, but I smile when something clicks. I look up at him with a beaming smile.

"I love you," I say and hold my breath.

Fire lights his eyes. It sets my entire body aflame. He cups the side of my face, not saying a word. Gently, he caresses my skin with his fingertips. His eyes say more than his words ever could.

I release a ragged breath as a chill runs up my spine. He moves his hand under my chin and lift my face to his. He moves his lips to meet mine tenderly. It's our softest, gentlest kiss yet, but missing none of the heat.

I taste a hint of salt and copper from his busted lip, but it doesn't stop either of us. He groans into my mouth, when I gently flick my tongue over the wound. I purr with glee as he growls and deepens the kiss slightly.

Gutter kisses me thoroughly, while he smoothly pushes me onto my back. When he breaks the kiss, he looks me right in the eyes. I look up at him, in awe of the emotions I see in his. Then he does me in with his words.

"When a man loves a woman, he shows her with his life. He worships her mind, body, and soul. As a boy that's what I saw my father do with my mama. That was the only time I knew true love, until now.

"I'm not a whole man, baby, but what I am, is in love with you and I keep falling the longer I'm around you. The rust is falling from my heart and I can feel it beat again. Salalia, I'm not whole, but tonight I think I have enough of a man in me to worship you the way a man in love should," he says, before taking my lips in a loving kiss that speaks volumes of worship and reverence.

He drags lips from mine, down to my chin. I moan and writhe beneath him as he flicks his tongue out over my skin.

He's in no rush. This is going to be slow; I can feel it. Even the fire within is burning slowly.

I inhale Gutter and his loving touch. I take in every subtle caress, every warm breath, every soft groan, before I exhale all the unwanted stuff. The past, my losses, hurts, and pain. When I inhale again, it's like my entire body opens up anew.

I feel him everywhere. Gutter kisses his way down my center, from the base of my throat to between of my breasts. He reaches beneath me to release my bra.

Without hesitation, I wiggle the straps off and pull the fabric free from my T-shirt. A gasp leaves my mouth, when he moves to nip one of my tightened peaks through the fabric. The mix of sensations shoot straight to the happy place in my core.

I draw strength from his touch. I've never truly felt sexy until this moment. His words were clear and resonated with me, but as he shows his devotion to my body, they sink in. He loves me.

I release a purr as he unleashes a sweet torture on my breasts, still over their cotton covering. He cups my right one with his rough hand as he devours the left. The words he whispers against my mound are a game changer.

"I love you, baby. You're the only one with rights to my heart. I'm never letting you go." His voice is thick with truth.

I don't doubt him with any bone in my body. I can feel his words are meant to soothe my anxiety and any remnants of the nightmare I'm quickly forgetting. Somehow, I begin to believe his love can bring the closure I need to my past.

I don't have to fear the shadows of my memories. Gutter is here to scare them and my scars away. His touch alone sets a flame to the twisted memories I have of being with a man.

My mind spins as I recognize his touch as his gesture of making love to me. Tears spill from my eyes, I never thought I could have this. I never thought I'd know the touch of love or intimacy.

Gutter moves back up my body to hover over me. His breath fans my face as he locks his gaze with mine. I cradle his face in my hands, but before I can kiss him, he dips his head to kiss my tears away.

"No tears, remember," he murmurs.

"They're tears of joy." I smile up at him as our eyes catch again.

He searches my face, before he nods his response. I shiver beneath him as he rests his hand on the side of my face and caresses my lower lip with his thumb. He's taking more caution than usual with me. He kisses my chin.

I love the tenderness he's giving me, but this fire isn't going to extinguish itself. I push at his shoulders, causing him to turn onto his back. I follow his body, straddling his hips.

He sits up, palming my sides. His lips return to my chin, while he kisses and nips at me. He drags his hands up my sides, reaches for the hem of my shirt and yanks it off over my head.

With both his warm hands, he palms my breasts, kneading my flesh as he looks at them in awe. I watch him closely. It's as if he can't believe he's allowed to touch me or something.

"You're so beautiful. Your skin looks made for my hands. I always want to have my hands on you," he says, peeling his eyes from our connection long enough to see if I hear and understand his words.

I start to grind in his lap. I want him so much. His erection tries to push free of his boxer briefs. I look down between us, rocking against it.

"I always want your hands on me," I breathe back.

He groans from deep and moves his hands to my shorts to unbutton them. I'm losing my battle with patience. I reach down to wiggle out of my shorts and stand up to shimmy out of my ripped stockings.

Once they are at my feet, I kick my shorts, stockings, and panties free from my legs and return to his lap, locking my fingers in his hair. He latches his eyes onto mine, then slides his hands down my back, meeting my curves and squeezes. His length pulses beneath my pussy.

Yet, he's still taking his time. I reach between us and release him from his confines. He lifts his hips up into me when I go to push his boxers further down.

A loud moan escapes my lips, when his bare flesh slides through my wet lips, but doesn't enter me. I need to do more than grind against him. There's this deep need to feel him inside of me. It's as if I'm going to burst any moment now.

Gutter reaches between my legs and fingers my slit. I bite my lip and roll my eyes in my head. His touch is everything and more, but I still need more. I'm greedy for him.

"Mmm," he moans, causing me to focus my eyes to look at him.

I respond with a moan of my own, when he sucks me off his fingers. The lust in his eyes is enough to have my juices gushing forth. Men as gorgeous as Gutter are meant to be imagined, not experienced.

Fuck that, I'm here and I'm going to experience every inch of him.

With a smirk on my lips, I reach between us and start a slow descent down his offering of pleasure. No, scratch that. This is his offering of love.

True love because he's just as damaged as I am. I keep my eyes on his, knowing how important that is to ground us both right here in the moment. I start to ride him slowly. He rocks his hips up into me at the same controlled measure.

"Pierson," I gasp.

He reaches between us, placing his thumb on my button. I can't help crying out and circling my hips while he circles my clit. With the same hand, he glides his fingers up to my throat, massaging the column of my neck.

Then he glides his hand back down between my breasts, pushing me back as he continues to rock into me. I continue to ride him, leaning back until my head meets the mattress.

"Fuck," Gutter growls, shifting to swivel and thrust into me. I use my thighs to guide me up and down his length. He grasps my hips, taking advantage of my flexibility. With each of his upward thrusts, I come down to meet him. Not once have we lost the connection through our eyes.

I think that connection makes it more intense. My heart swells. His eyes are telling me more than words ever can.

I cry out, when he moves his hands to my ribs and tightens them. He draws me back up into a sitting position, bringing my mouth right to his. He takes my lips and devours me.

His soft lips taste of salt and copper from the mix of his own sweat and blood. Then there's something with a sweet note coloring the flavor of his mouth.

Breaking the kiss, he looks up into my eyes. When he places his forehead to mine, it's like our connection deepens. I part my lips and so does he. It's like we are breathing each other in. We pleasure each other just like this for longer than I think possible.

"I'm coming," I whimper.

"Together."

I nod, feeling him swell inside me. I know he's about to come. I dig my nails into his shoulders as I ride the seconds out. My climax is right within my reach.

When Gutter roars into the room, I can't hold back, even if I wanted to. It's like I burst into flames as my heart tries to come through my chest. I drop my face into the crook of his neck.

"I love you, baby girl," he says so softly, it makes my heart ache.

I would never expect to hear such gentleness from a gruff man like him. There's a heart of gold inside this man. Knowing that I own a piece of it, warms my heart in places I didn't know existed.

"I love you too, Pierson."

Covering Bases

Gutter

I didn't sleep last night after Sal's nightmare. We talked for a while before Sal drifted off to sleep and I spent the night thinking about her words. Not just her declaration of love.

Those were words I will cherish with every breath, until I have no more. However, what kept me up all night was her worry. It was the fact that in her dreams, I couldn't be there to protect her.

I plan to find and kill the motherfuckers who have stolen her peace for much too long. There's a beauty in Sal I will make sure is never touched. I see it. It remains in spite of.

If I'm real about it, baby girl is healing me. Watching her slay her demons is giving me the courage I didn't know I needed to fight my own. I itch to climb on the back of my bike and take her with me.

One ride, just one, where I can show her true safety. It would be a ride where we'd leave our past in the wind. I plan to give that to her when this is all over.

For now, we need to get our asses up and get on the road. The thing about being a Lost Soul, we have access to shit. Grim and Reap were able to fly in with their rides.

They're going to flank us back in the truck. Well, after Grim checks a little something out. They won't be far behind.

King might not like it, but Grim and I agreed last night we wanted to take care of something before he and Reap joined us. We also thought it best not to draw too much attention for the almost two and a half day drive.

My bike on the back of the truck and those two riding alongside me will draw a hell of a lot of attention. Like I said, they won't be too far behind. I'm more than capable of getting us down the road on my own.

"I can hear your brain frying eggs," Sal says softly.

There's a smile in her voice. It brings a rare smile to my face. I've smiled more with this woman at my side than I have in my entire life.

"Well, you've been making bacon for the last ten minutes yourself, darlin'." I chuckle.

She lifts her head from my chest to look up at me. She's just as gorgeous first thing in the morning as she was all dolled up last night. She blinks those beautiful eyes at me, and my heart skips a beat.

I don't know how she does it. Each day since the first time I laid eyes on her, she's blown my heart out of my chest, just to revive me again. However she does it, I don't want her to ever stop.

I run my fingertips down the side of her cheek. It feels so soft to the touch. I want to get lost in her, but that will need to wait.

"I see it in your eyes. We have to go, don't we?" She sighs.

"Yeah, we need to move. You can head into the shower. I want to check in with King and look into a few things before we go," I reply.

I start to get up, before her body tempts me into staying right here. I swing my legs over the side of the bed and palm my head. I have so much shit going on in there.

I feel her moving toward me before she wraps her arms around me. Her sweet scent soothes my mind in a way that feels like being enchanted. I'm sure as shit gone for this woman. My thoughts alone, scream I'm her slave in every way.

No words are exchanged. She holds onto me for a few moments. Although I know she's doing this to comfort me. I get the feeling she needs it for herself just as much as I do. I lift her forearm to my lips and kiss it.

My lip is still a little sore from last night, but I've had much worse. Sal has a nice right hook. My lips curl into a smile. She's a fighter, whether she knows it or not. I love that about her.

Just as my body relaxes under the feel of her warm breasts pressed to my back, the moment ends too soon. Sal kisses the back of my head, before pulling away and heading into the bathroom. It's for the best.

I was ready to turnaround and have just a taste for the road. Shaking my head clear, I reach for my phone and shoot King a text. I want to check in before he starts to wonder why I can never do so while I have his sister.

I know I have problems ahead of me. No use in making them worse.

Me: *Getting ready to hit the road.*
King: *Good. Eyes open.*
Me: *Always.*

I shoot Grim a text next to see if he's ready to head out. I snort to myself when he replies that he and Reap have already gone. I'm not surprised at all. You can take the soldier out of training, but never the training out of the soldier.

My next call is important. I need to talk to one of my brothers. There are few who I've made a bond with. Diggs is one of those few. It was one of the reasons I listened to King when he suggested Diggs and I go into business together.

I had the funds, and some know how. Diggs had the expertise and the support of the brothers behind him. We're a good fit.

"Hey, Gutter, you on your way in? I have some contracts I need you to look over. I'm finally getting some shit done with this lockdown," Diggs answers the phone.

"No, King has me on a little something special for him. I sent some shit over to Matrix last night. I was wondering if you could peek over his shoulder and make sure he figures it out. I need to know what the fuck I'm dealing with," I grunt.

I grit my teeth at the mention of the lockdown. King has been sharing on a need-to-know basis. To him, all I need to know at the moment is to get his baby sister home safe.

That doesn't stop my jaw from ticking. I also know how King is about sharing over the phone, so I take a breath and crack my neck. I'll have details when I get home.

"No problem, Brother. Is this business, business or Club business?"

"For now, it's *my* business. I'm trusting you, Brother. This stays with us, until I figure out some shit. Not disrespecting. I'm protecting. I'm going to need you to reel it in for a bit," I reply.

"Not sure I like the sound of that," Diggs says slowly. "A lot of shit going on around here."

"Shit I plan to get a handle on. Trust me. Grim is in on it. Prez will know as soon as we get a grip on it. No need to put more on his shoulders," I reply.

A long pause passes on the other end. "Got it. You need anything else?"

This is why we get along. Diggs is always ready to step up. Sometimes without being asked. I respect that.

"That's all for now," I say and end the call.

I check on a few other things, before my finger hovers over my phone. I think of my cousin. We haven't spoken in... I'm ashamed to say how long.

My mind has been heavy with thoughts of him all week. This is never a good time for me. It's a time when I try to tie up all that's twisted inside and keep it there.

I've been thinking even more about Terry, since letting Sal into my past. There's so much damage between us. I sigh and shake the thought off. I'll deal with him, when I have my girl safe. I don't need to add anymore to my plate now.

I get involved with him, I may just be throwing myself down a rabbit hole. I told myself I wouldn't go there for him again. I know he has grown, but I don't know if it's enough.

I stand and stretch my aching bones. I'm not looking forward to spending all this time in a cage. I'd much rather be on the back of my bike, but I have a gut feeling we should remain in the truck.

I move to shuffle through the bags Stormy left behind. I find the T-shirt and jeans she insisted I purchase for myself. Just as I straighten, Sal comes from the bathroom wrapped in a towel.

I lick my lips. *I wouldn't mind a taste of her this morning. I really wouldn't.* I shake my head at my own thoughts.

"There are more clothes for you in the bags. You don't have to put that stuff back on," I say, when she goes to collect the things she wore here.

"Oh, thanks." She smiles at me.

I shake my head again as that smile draws me in. Instead of walking over to her, I take my ass into the bathroom. This is going to be a long fucking ride.

I Want Names

Grim

There's nothing like crushing skulls first thing in the morning. Only a foolish man believes he's untouchable. I've never been foolish, but I've caught a few fools slipping a time or two.

This morning is no different. Gutter and I spotted the Devil's Masons' tat on the side of one of those fucker's necks in the video. I knew right away where my next trip would be.

It's this bastard's unlucky day. I've owed Blaze an ass whipping from a while ago. That's what brought his ass to Nevada in the first place.

I've known he was here. He got sloppy when I made it seem like I wasn't looking for his ass anymore. Silly mistake, I never give up.

I've been biding my time for such a time as this. He's going to remember this day and all the glory that comes with it. I told him never to touch my woman.

He made the mistake of grabbing Reap's arm while he tried to press her for information. Wrong fucking move. I'd piss on a Devil's Mason on a good day.

Touch my girl and imagine the wrath that would bring. He's only still breathing because I couldn't get to his ass that night. Reap nearly put him to ground, but King was there to pull her off him and get her the fuck out of there.

It was a sticky situation. One where the Prez and the club had to come first. Now, I need information.

I haven't decided yet, I might spare his sorry ass life. If he coughs the right shit up. Speaking of coughing, his bitch ass coughs up blood and turns his head to the side to spit it out. Reap snarls at him in disgust.

"This can all be over nice and quick. Just tell him who the fuck that is in the picture," she hisses next to his ear. Matrix was able to get me a still pic of the guy with the tat from the video. *That's my baby.*

We've been working him over for over an hour at this point. Getting an early start gives us more time to handle this. We won't be far behind Gutter. I promised that.

I wave my phone in Blaze's face once more. He's going to break soon. I can smell it.

"Listen man, I don't want any trouble. I told you I was sorry for what happened that night. I left to call a truce," Blaze grovels. "I don't want to be in the middle of this."

"In the middle of what?" I sneer.

He groans and shakes his head. I send a fist into his already broken ribs. I hit just the right spot. I don't want to go puncturing anything, before I get what I came for. This all takes a certain skill and finesse.

Blaze's lips vibrate when he blows out a pained breath. Snot and blood cover his face. *Pussy.*

Reap cocks her gun. "I'm tired of this. Start talking," she says, pressing the barrel to his forehead.

Blaze's eyes grow wide. He looks at me for help. I rock back on my heels and grin.

I fucking love this woman.

Seeing I won't be coming to his rescue, Blaze nods frantically. "All right, all right." He swallows. "This is what I know. That's Slim in the pic. Man, he's been running with some joker that's been making big promises.

"Shit's falling apart with the club, since Griff had his stroke. I was just about to head back home, until my brother told me how bad things were. The club is divided and whoever this dude is, he's taking advantage of that," Blaze rushes out.

I wrinkle my brows. Slim, I'm not coming up with any memory to go with the name. I know a lot of those pussies across town, but this one isn't ringing a bell.

Blaze seems to read my thoughts. "Slim just came up from prospect. He was a Hang Around not too long ago. Real piece of shit kid. No one special," he huffs.

"I need to know where I can find this Slim," I growl.

Blaze tries to shrug his shoulders but gets the sudden reminder that one is broken. That one is courtesy of Reap. I smirk at my girl.

"I don't know where he's been." Blaze licks his dry lips. "Word is, a few of the new recruits in the New York, Lost Souls chapter are Devil's Masons. Slim's a dumb ass. He would've forgotten to cover that tat or he's just being a cocky bastard."

I take a step back and narrow my eyes. Looks like I'll be going to New York when all of this is over. It's time to clean house. I look Reap in the eyes and I know she's thinking the same thing.

King isn't going to like this, but I'll handle it before he can stress about it. I tilt my head, eyeing Blaze. I nod my head at my decision.

"You heal up," I say to him. "Your ass needs to be back in South Carolina when you can move. You're going to help clean up your pig pin. I'll be in touch."

I have plans for Blaze and the Masons. I swear, he looks so relieved, I think he pisses his pants. He still needs someone to find him and get him help.

I pull my phone to call in a favor. I don't want this asshole dying just yet. Gutter's friends here in Nevada will handle this for me. We need to get on the road.

"We're done here, been here too long," I say, wrapping my arm around my girl. I kiss the pout from her lips. "We still have plenty of heads to roll. This one will prove valuable."

"Fine," Reap grumbles and tucks closer into my side.

CHAPTER TWENTY-TWO

Need a Break

Sal

I smirk to myself. I've seen the lust in Gutter's eyes since this morning. I wanted to explore what I saw there and almost followed him into his shower, but I knew we needed to leave.

I was surprised to find that Grim and Reap had already left when I stepped out of the bedroom. I thought we were all leaving together. Gutter explained they had some business to handle, but they would be right on our tails.

I was curious, but being King's sister, I know the deal. I didn't push for information. I knew Gutter would tell me what he needed me to know.

Although, there was something nagging at me once again. Gutter had figured out who the first intruder into my apartment was. Or at least, the persons behind it. I still wanted to know about the second party that took off with my bike.

They were looking for something. My blood runs cold and I shiver in the hot truck cabin, causing Gutter to pull his eyes from the road to look over at me. We've been on the road for about ten hours already. Though, it seems like so much longer.

I shift under his gaze and move closer to his side. He throws an arm over me and kisses the top of my head. I melt right into him.

"I plan to make a stop soon. We can get something to eat and stretch," he says as his attention returns to the road.

"Are you tired? I can take over after we stop," I offer.

"I'm fine. We'll cover a few more States before I stop for the night."

I nod and get lost in thought again. I absently play with his big fingers. The cab of the truck is silent except for our breathing. Neither of us have been in much of a talking mood. That suits me just fine.

I'm learning that we have a way of communicating without saying a word. I like that. I start to drift off to sleep, when his voice rumbles through my body.

"I have an apartment in South Carolina, but I spend most my time at the clubhouse," he says, out of the blue.

I lift my head to look at his face, knitting my brows. He glances down at me through the corner of his eye. I pull from his arm and slide back to the other side of the truck.

I kick off my flip-flops, pull my feet up onto the seat, and curl my upper body around my knees, before looking down into my lap. I'm wearing the white distressed jeans and white tank top Stormy left for me. I focus on the tears in the thigh. I'm so much cooler today, but the icy feeling in my heart is coming from the dread that tries to take me over.

"Is there something you're trying to tell me?" I finally say, not able to hide the tight edge in my words.

I look up through my lashes, holding my breath. Gutter turns his entire head toward me, a frown on his face. He glares at me after getting a good look at my scowl.

"I'm telling you I need to change somethings when this is all over. My apartment is a mess and it's not fit for a girl, my girl, to live there." He rolls his eyes at me, before turning back to the road. "Get your ass back over here."

I crack a smile, but I don't move. I slide my feet over to wiggle my toes underneath his thigh. He reaches for my calf, massaging it just before tugging at me to get me to move closer. This time I go willingly, when my butt starts to slide under his strength. Turning my back in the seat, I then lean up against his side again.

I stare out of the passenger side window. "Things are about to change," I say almost to myself.

He brings his arm around the center of my waist and kisses the back of my head, then the side of my neck. It's all the comfort I need.

"That, they are, but all for the better," he says, sending warmth spreading through me.

I reach for the stereo. "Do you ever listen to music?"

He shrugs. "Sometimes, most times, I spend time with my own thoughts. Dangerous, I know."

I smile at the teasing in his voice and crane my neck to look over my shoulder at him. He looks away from the road to peck my lips. I smile, registering the country music filling the truck.

Not what I imagined Gutter listening to. Rock, maybe, country ballads not really. I don't say anything.

I just bob my head to the music and watch the road fly by. We're five songs in when I get the shock of my life. Gutter starts to sing along with one of the songs and his voice is amazing.

I'm stunned at first. I can do nothing but sit and listen. His voice is like velvet kisses and chocolate covered sex. I sit up and turn to look at him in astonishment. I swear, I see a blush creep up his cheeks.

I throw a light punch at his arm. "Oh, my God, you can sing," I gush.

He shrugs. "Not really. I like this song," he replies.

"Not really, my ass. That was amazing. Your voice is beautiful. Come on, you have to know you can sing," I say, shaking my head in disbelief.

"My mama would sing to me when I was little. I started singing with her at some point." He lifts his shoulder again.

"Wow," I say with a goofy smile. "Tell me something else I don't know about you."

The face he makes is adorable. His lips purse and his brows wrinkle. He's truly thinking about what he's going to tell me.

A small smile curls the corner of his lips. "I don't eat pork and I'm allergic to shell fish," he says.

"Ooookkkay, that's the best you could come up with after that," I tease.

"It's the best I could come up with because I'm starving." He chuckles.

"I love your laugh." I sigh like an airhead. I have to roll my eyes at myself. "I promise, I'm not this mushy."

"You're not bothering me, darlin'," he says, turning to wink at me. "There's a burger joint I know of at the next exit. You up for a burger?"

"I could take down an entire cow, right now." I laugh.

"Burgers it is," he mutters.

Gutter

This place has great food. It will also give Grim and Reap a chance to catch up. It seems their visit this morning took longer than they thought it would.

From Grim's text, they're about three hours behind us. They need to stop for food and fuel soon too, but they should still be able to cover a little ground while Sal and I are here.

Sal hisses from behind her burger, while she chews and holds the massive sandwich before her face. I turn from my own burger to look at her. Her face is twisted, looking as if she smells something sour.

I drop my burger and wipe my mouth. "What's up, baby?" I ask, leaning to peck her full lips.

"I don't like the way that waitress keeps flirting and swaying her ass pass our table. I'm gonna drag that bitch, she walks this way one more time," Sal says heatedly.

I lift a brow at my girl, before turning to look around for the waitress she's talking about. The brunette comes into view, but I'm not impressed. She has long silky hair and both her arms are covered in tattoo sleeves. Her look suits this place, but she doesn't suit me.

I shrug my shoulders and look back at Sal. Her brown eyes are trained on me. I lock gazes with her and let her see my disinterest.

When my eyes roam over Sal's tight curvy body, that's when my cock twitches in my pants. She looks hot. The white tank top she has on is loose, but it shows the right amount of cleavage to make me stare.

Those white jeans are skintight, and the random patches of brown skin peeking through are sexy as fuck.

"She wants what she can't have. I'm not paying her any attention. Only one I want is sitting right next to me," I reassure her.

Sal makes another sour face. "It's rude and disrespectful," she mumbles. "It's clear that I'm your girlfriend."

I feel like teasing, so I lift a brow. "Is it really? You haven't shown me much affection since we arrived. I was wondering if you're ashamed of my dirty white ass."

Sal's mouth falls open. "Shut up," she gasps. "I'm not ashamed of you. You're not even dirty."

"But you admit that you haven't shown me any affection," I push.

She narrows her eyes. "I'll do better on my PDA," she says, with a little twist of her lips.

"I hope so. I'm developing a complex."

"He has a real sense of humor," she says to herself and grins wider. "Learning something new every second, babe."

"I can ride a bull too," I say with a straight face.

"Bullshit," she says, lifting a brow and popping a fry into her mouth.

I laugh. "Just wanted to see what you would say, but yeah it's actually true."

"You're twenty-five, right?"

This time, I lift a questioning brow and nod. Sal shrugs her small shoulders. She pops another fry in her mouth, before explaining.

"I had time while waiting for you at the station. I may have read up on your profile," she says and bites her lip.

"Interesting. How old are you?"

"Twenty," she says softly.

I almost spit out the drink I just sipped. I mean, she doesn't look old at all, but I thought she was at least twenty-three, maybe twenty-two. I groan and rub the back of my neck. King is going to have my ass.

"Sweet Jesus," I huff out.

"Is that a problem?"

"Not for me. Not sure how Prez is going to feel."

"It's none of his business," she mumbles, crossing her arms over her chest.

"Doesn't mean he's not going to make it his business."

"Are you telling me you're scared of the big bad King," she taunts.

"I respect your brother a hell of a lot. Don't confuse that for fear. Especially, when it comes to where I stand with you."

"So that means you're going to tell him as soon as we get back?"

I hear the need for reassurance in her voice. We have definitely moved fast in all of this. I should've thought a lot more through, but she's mine. I'm not backing down from that.

"Once you're safe. As soon as we get there," I say with confidence.

"I'm holding you to that, cowboy."

"You're welcome to," I say and return to my burger.

I intend to keep Sal. King and I may bump heads on it, but I have no doubt I'll be claiming my woman in front of the Prez. Suddenly, I'm not sure why we're rushing back to South Carolina. When we get there, everything is going to be turn on its head, but there's no going back.

Can't wait

Gutter

We've fallen into silence through the rest of our meal. I love that I can do that with Sal. I've seen how some of the brothers' old ladies can nag for attention. Sal is just laid back.

Halfway through the meal, she slides over and snuggles into my side. I don't mind that. It actually takes the edge off of some of my thoughts. My head is swimming with so much.

I need to get Sal home safe, handle both threats against her safety, deal with King, and get some girly shit for my apartment. Then there are the real issues in my life. Things have been quiet in my head the last few nights, but I'm not sure how Sal will take my night terrors.

Her nightmare and reaction last night were mild next to the shit I've done coming out of mine.

"So, this apartment. I'm not a picky girl, as long as I have a place for my shit, I'm good," she says with that gorgeous smile.

I stare at her eyes, feeling like she's reading my thoughts. I can't even begin to tell you how it makes my heart swell. Hearing her making my place her own already, feels like I'll be going home for the first time.

I know I mentioned her moving in but hearing her see herself in my place does all types of things to me. I've never wanted anyone in my space before. Hell, I lock myself in my room at the clubhouse every night.

As I think of my apartment and why I don't stay there much, my demons try to rise up and tell me this is all wrong. I can't possibly live with Sal, but I shut that shit down. I turn away from her trusting eyes and look down at the table.

"It's a three bedroom," I stare at my plate. "I… there was a point where I needed the space. I couldn't sleep in the same bed every night. I felt trapped. At the club, it's different. I've become accustom to the round the clock hustle of the place. The sounds and life are familiar now. I can't explain. I just feel safe with my brothers."

The revelation tumbles out of my mouth without my permission. I used to sit up at night in the clubhouse, when King would ask me to stay close. Eventually, it became more home than my own properties.

I furrow my brows. My tongue tastes like sandpaper. When Sal learns more about me and my crazy ass habits, she may just run from me. I think that would shred me more than anything.

She covers my hand. "Like I said, I'm not picky. We can move around from room to room if that's what you need."

I turn my hand over and lace our fingers together. God, I'm falling so hard for her. Honestly, I've slept the best I ever have since she's been in my bed at night.

I smile tightly, squeezing her smaller hand in mine. Her words and gesture mean more than she knows. I vow right there to work harder on my shit. Sal deserves a whole man.

I'll shelter her from my crazy shit as best I can. My phone rings, breaking the moment. I pull it from my pocket and frown. I don't know the number.

With all the shit going down, it could be anyone. I take the call and lift the phone to my ear.

"Hello."

"Hey there." When I hear the voice, I frown harder.

"Hold on," I say into the line. I look at Sal and mouth, *"I'll be right back."*

She nods and gives me a sly smirk. I want to know what she's thinking, but this call has my attention for now. I don't go too far away, wanting to keep an eye on her while taking this.

"Speak," I grunt into the phone.

"Hey, young fella. This is Old Henry, from the Woodlong B & B," the man says.

I narrow my eyes as if he can see me. "Why are you calling me?"

"I have your number from that time you stayed with me and helped me out with those thugs. I'll never forget that, I won't," he rambles on. "I get those types of low lives around here from time to time. I was glad you were here.

"Jody didn't get that lucky. The poor girl. She said you were here the other night. She thinks the fellas who roughed her up were after you and your little friend you had with you."

"How do you know about my friend?" I hiss.

"Jody said you had a pretty little thing with you. She said the guys wanted to know if a black girl and big guy passed through here. I'm calling to warn you, son. I do appreciate what you'd done for me. I don't want trouble finding you, I don't."

"Jody, who's Jody?" I ask.

"My desk clerk. Well, her daddy ain't too keen on her coming back. I think the poor little thing has been sweet on you. That's why she took that beating." Henry sighs.

"Fuck," I growl. "Listen, I'm sending some friends to check on you and watch over the place for a bit. I'm sorry."

"Oh, boy, I don't hold this to ya. I know bad seeds when I see them. I think I scared them off when I arrived. I was just in time. You be safe now, you hear. If you're still in the area, you be safe," he says and ends the call.

My body trembles with fury. I need to know who's looking for us and how they found out we were at the B&B. I remember the feeling I had the morning we left.

I knew something was off then. It seems we left in time, but I still need more answers.

Just as I get ready to call my team, all hell breaks loose. I snap my head up and my eyes grow wide. I can't believe what I'm seeing.

It only takes a minute for me to snap into action. My only thought is to get to my woman. I don't give a fuck about anything else.

Sal

I smile when Gutter mouths, '*I'll be right back.*' I was hoping I would get a chance to be on my own for a few minutes. I have something that I need to address.

I watch as he walks off to take his call. When I see his focus turn to his phone, away from me, I make my move. I flag down the waitress who has been working on my last damn nerves.

Yeah, Gutter said he's not paying her any attention and he was right. Maybe she wasn't clear on who I was to him when we first arrived, but I made sure to make that shit clear. Yet, she has been passing our table for no reason and trying to pull his attention since we sat down.

She's not even our waitress. That's the shit that's pissing me off. She's just being straight disrespectful.

If Rose Kennedy ever made anything clear, it was always clear you don't fuck with her man. I got it honest from my mama. I hate that shit and I'm not about to let it happen to me right in front of my face.

Enough is enough.

This heifer tries to pretend she doesn't see me waving her over. That's fine with me. I get the attention of the waitress who served us and call her over.

I don't want to make this too noticeable in front of Gutter. I take a quick glance in his direction to see he's engrossed in his conversation.

Great.

"You guys need anything else? Y'all want some dessert?" our waitress asks, with a bright smile on her lips.

She has been great the entire time. She'll get her tip for the night. It's her co-worker I have a problem with.

"I just wanted to talk to your friend." I nod my head at the other waitress. Then, sweet as sugar, I place my request. "Would you mind calling her over?"

I watch the waitress follow my nod and frown as her eyes land on the other woman. Obviously, she's not a fan favorite. I'm not the only one with a problem with her from the looks of it.

She turns back to me and looks me in my eyes. I turn up my sugary sweet smile that reads, *"yeah, I'm petty."* Our waitress gives me a smile of her own. Her blue eyes sparkle, saying, *'hell, yeah, I got you.'*

"Sure, hun, no problem." She winks. Then she turns and waves the other girl over. "Hey, Crystal."

Crystal frowns and rolls her eyes, but she comes over. My lips turn into a sneer when I watch her eyes search the room for Gutter. I see the moment she finds him. Her chest rises and her gaze roll over him. I follow her glance.

Gutter is totally absorbed in his call. I turn back to Crystal as the other waitress called her. She's now a foot away, but her eyes are still on my man. She's so focused on Gutter, she nearly trips over some guy's foot.

My waitress snorts, drawing my attention to her. She has her hand on her hip, while she shakes her head. The distaste for her co-worker is apparent in the twist of her lips.

"Hey, Autumn. What's up?" Crystal says with a forced sense of cheer.

"Actually, I wanted to talk to you," I interrupt before my waitress can answer. I got this from here.

"Oh, how can I—" I cut her off again.

"You can do nothing for me or my man. You need to learn some respect, you trifling cow. I'm going to tell you once and once only. Stop eye fucking my man," I snarl.

She whips her head back, a sour look crosses over her face before anger takes its place. She's about to make a very bad mistake. Cage didn't just teach me to shoot. I will not be disrespected.

"Oh, I didn't realize he was attached," she snaps at me.

"You can save that bullshit. I made it more than clear, since you couldn't catch a clue and continued to stroll your ass pass our table," I say through tight lips and narrowed eyes.

"Well, from the way he was staring at me. I figured he was fair game," she clips back. "And another thing, you're not going to come in here talking shit to me."

When she says Gutter was staring at her, I draw my head back. I barely hear the rest of her words. Gutter didn't so much as glance in her direction, until I pointed out her behavior.

As all of her words hit me, my vision turns red. I jump from my seat and grab her by her throat. Crystal is shorter than me, causing her feet to dangle from the floor, when I snatch her up, bringing her face to face with me.

I growl in her face like I've lost my mind and jerk her body with my words. "You disrespectful skank. I'll drag your ass through this restaurant. Let's see how fair you find that game," I hiss.

"Oh, shit." Autumn chuckles, not making a move to help her co-worker.

I draw my hand back to punch Crystal in her face. The first punch connects with her eye, causing it to swell instantly. I reach back to deliver another punch, but my arm is caught mid-air.

I turn my head to see a pissed Gutter, staring pass me. At first, I think he's angry with me, but the look on his face reads something more. I turn back toward Crystal, who I still have in a chokehold.

Her one good eye is wide with shock as tears running down her cheek. She shrinks away from me, all that mouth dried up now. Gutter releases my arm, wrapping his around my waist.

The movement brings my attention to what has Gutter looking like he's ready to murder. Three other guys have gotten up from the other side of the restaurant where Crystal was supposed to be working. They've made their way over in our direction.

From the looks on their faces, they have every intention of stepping in. It's obvious they're not going to be on my side at all. I hate to judge a book by its cover, but these guys look like the type of rednecks who would have no problem hanging my ass or dragging me behind one of their trucks.

Gutter pulls my body behind his, causing me to release the waitress in my grasp. He pulls a hand full of bills from his pocket and tosses them onto the table we were sitting at. His words are directed to our waitress.

"That should cover what we owe, what I'm about to fuck up, and your tip," he says darkly. He then calls over his shoulder to me. "I move, you move."

I nod, even though he can't see me. I'm coiled for a fight. I didn't start this for my man to have to finish it and get hurt. I've always admired Erica and my mama for being willing to fight at their man's side if they had to. I plan to do the same.

"You need to get your little—" one of the men starts.

"You don't want to finish that sentence. Not if you want me to leave here without knocking your teeth down your throat," Gutter snarls low and rough.

"I think you're out numbered, boy," one of the others says.

Gutter snorts, tilting his head to the side. "I look like a boy to you?" He scoffs. "I've seen worse odds and survived. I'm not as concerned as you should be."

The third guy looks Gutter over, his gaze stopping on Gutter's Lost Souls patch. I witness the recognition in his eyes. He takes a step back, reaching for the arm of the guy closest to him. He quickly becomes the voice of reason.

"Let these kids be on their way. Us men don't need to get in these girls' business," he says, with a slight tremble to his voice.

"Shut your trap, Earl," the dark haired, greasy looking one says.

"I think you should listen to your friend," Gutter warns.

"See, I don't think I should. I think you and your little ni—" He doesn't get to finish his words.

Gutter sends a hand flying right into his fat greasy face. The meathead falls to the floor like a sack of potatoes. In the next moment, Gutter has the other one in a throat hold, much like I had Crystal. He head butts him, sending a crunching sound into the air.

I wince as the guy's face seems to explode. He screams and covers his face with his hands. I stand in shock.

Gutter moved so quickly to take the two down. Neither of them were small men to begin with. That didn't seem to matter to Gutter at all.

He tosses the bloody guy back, causing him to stumble, before falling on his ass, crashing into a table and knocking over a few chairs. The other guy with all the mouth is snoring on the floor. Gutter rocked his ass to sleep. That may even be a pee stain in the front of his pants.

"Let's go," Gutter says, grabbing me by my arm.

Earl, the guy who had a lick of good sense, backs away with his hands in the air. Gutter doesn't even glance in his direction, guiding me outside. Silent rage swirls around him.

Opening the passenger side door, he helps me inside the truck. The door closes hard once I'm in. Gutter rounds the truck and climbs into the driver's seat, slamming his door shut as well.

I feel like a small child that's in big trouble. Now that my temper is somewhat in check, I know I could have handled all that differently. I look at the side of his face to find it's a mask of stone.

"Gutter, I—"

"Not now," he says firmly.

I'm affectively silenced. I turn to look out the passenger window, not saying another word, no matter how badly they're burning in my mouth. Honestly, if it happened all over again, I would probably do the same.

CHAPTER TWENTY-FOUR

Unleashed Passion

Gutter

I'm so pissed I can barely think straight, forget talking, but I can't afford this type of distraction. Someone has been following our trail. This should be damn near impossible to do. That just tells me one thing.

We have someone we can't trust in the ranks. No true Lost Soul would take kindly to that, but a Squad member sees it as ten times the offence. We have a code we live by. You don't lie to your brothers and you don't betray their trust.

The Lost Soul's way of life and the rules they live by was one of the things that made me stay around. King, Brick, Grim, and Diggs showed me they had my back, and it was safe to have theirs. Slowly, the trust I'd lost in people returned when I became a Lost Soul.

To know there's one among us who has disrespected that balance so many of us need, gets stuck all the way in my craw. My true brothers would never do something like this. We've all found a small slice of hope in one and other. Our souls would truly be lost without each other.

However, none of that has me as livid as the fact that those fuckers back there had planned to lay hands on my woman. I'm sure Sal thinks I'm angry with her. I'm not.

I think it's sexy that baby girl feels she needs to stake her claim on me. I knew that waitress was getting to her. I just didn't think she was going to go upside her head over me. That shit turned me on.

Salalia takes action, it's something I'm starting to pick up on. I like that about her, but she'll have to reel that shit in from now on. We have enough on our plates as it is. Starting fights in dives isn't helping me keep her safe. It sure as hell isn't helping to keep the attention off of her.

I look behind us for the millionth time to make sure we're not being followed. I still need to make that call to my boys, but not until I put some distance between us and that bullshit back there. I relax a bit as I see a clear road behind me.

It's been at least an hour now. Salalia hasn't turned my way the entire time. I turn to look at her, while she stares out of the passenger window.

I have an unbelievable urge to have my hands on her. Reaching out, I place my hand on the back of her neck. She flinches a little, which stabs me through the heart. My chest loosens as I start to rub her smooth skin and she relaxes under my touch.

I take in her sweet scent and warmth. It's a balm to my soul like no other. Giving a gentle tug, I pull her toward me. The tension leaves my own body, when she comes willingly. She curls into my side.

I rest my hand on her taunt belly and exhale, knowing it's time for me to speak. My anger is still boiling on the surface, but her feelings matter to me as well. I don't like this tension between us. I need Sal to understand the way I operate.

"You shocked me back there, baby girl," I mutter.

She turns her face up to look at me. I turn my eyes from the road to look down at her. Her big brown eyes have a sadness in them I never want to see. I look at the road quickly, before turning my eyes back to her and dipping my head for a quick kiss.

"I know I fucked up. She just pissed me off," she says softly.

"Salalia, I'm not pissed because you felt you needed to set that girl straight. I'm pissed at a few things, but that's not actually one of them," I reply.

"Then what are you pissed about?"

"One, those low life bigots thought they were going to put their hands on you. It will always be my first job to keep you safe, baby. Just the thought of someone thinking they can harm you sends me off the rails," I explain, feeling my pressure rising as I do.

I take a calming breath and continue. "You had nothing to worry about with that waitress, darlin'."

"I didn't like that shit. It was disrespectful," she grumbles.

"Yeah, I get that, but you're going to have to learn sometimes you're just going to have to trust me. If I say I got it, I got it. Just like I'll keep you safe, I won't let no one disrespect you." I look down at her face from the road once again.

Without a thought, I reach to caress the side of her face as she pouts. While I let my words sink in with her, I turn my attention back to the road. I figure she's not going to reply when she rests her head on my chest and a hand on my thigh.

"My mom was the Prez's old lady. When I was home from school, I watched a lot of shit go down at the club. Mom never played games when it came to Cage. She loved him.

"Cage only had eyes for Mom. He loved her so much. He could give a shit about the Lost Bunnies that threw themselves at him, but Mom wanted them to show her respect. She demanded it.

"It's what I know, Pierson. Mom and Dad are the only example I know of a truly loving couple. So, you're going to have to bear with me and some of the things I can't help. I will never be okay with some skank throwing herself at you, without me letting her know she's out of line." She looks up at me again with her final words.

I think her words over. I understand them. I don't like it, it'll put her in danger every time she feels she needs to demand respect for our relationship. I'll never be okay with that. For now, I don't want to argue, so I nod and let it go.

I shift in my seat. Yeah, I might be angry, and I don't want Sal placing herself in dangerous situations to stake her claim, but that shit has me wanting to take her, hard. Having her so close isn't helping. The warmth of her full breasts pressed into me floods my entire being with a feeling I can't describe.

I squash those thoughts, finding an off road to turn down. I travel down the road a bit before I drive out into a clearing. This is just what I need. A place to stop for a moment.

I say a silent prayer I'll be able to get a signal out here. Checking my phone, it's a weak one, but enough for me to get out a few texts. Maybe if I get out of the truck, I can get a better signal. I cut the engine and run my hand down Sal's side, just because I need the contact.

"Stay here," I say, before detaching myself and climbing out of the truck.

I text Grim for an update on his location. I don't wait for a response, knowing most likely he's still riding. My nostrils flare, when I can't get a stronger signal to make the call I need to make.

Frustrated, I look back at the truck and find Sal's eyes on me through the windshield. I need to make this call. I pace hoping for just another bar. Finally, my call connects.

"Hey handsome, you miss us already?" the voice on the other end comes back to me.

"I need to call in that favor."

"Name it," Stormy replies, her tone changes to all business. "Is your brother around?"

"I hear you," Ramon's voice comes through the line.

I should've known Stormy would be with her brother. Hearing the tension in my voice, I'm sure she put the phone on speaker without a thought.

"Someone is riding in my dust. I want to know who and how? I stopped at a B & B two days ago. Someone roughed up the clerk, asking questions about me and mine," I explain.

I don't want to mention Sal over the line. I look over to her, she's the most important cargo I've ever had to protect. I don't know what I did right in this life to end up being the one King trusted with his sister, but I will forever be grateful for it.

I continue, while keeping my eyes on her. "I'll text the address. Send someone over and find out what happened. Have a few of your guys hang around there for a while as well."

"We're on it," Ramon replies.

"Gutter?"

"Yeah."

"I'm getting the feeling you need to watch your back out there," Stormy says, her words laced with worry.

"She's right," Ramon adds. "I've put out feelers for what's going on. You need to get home. Shit is brewing in your backyard."

"I figured that." I blow out a breath.

"Remember we're here for whatever," Stormy interjects.

I grunt and end the call, having said all I need to say. I shoot off a text with the address of the B&B. I trust Ramon to get guys he trusts there as soon as possible.

Now that I know we have a problem in house, I think it's best to outsource this. Shoving my phone into my pocket, I run my other hand through my hair. There's so much sitting uneasy with me.

My muscles bunching with the tension running through me. Once again, I lock eyes with Sal through the windshield. My chest squeezes with the silent conversation passing between us. Her gaze questions what I need.

I know my eyes tell her, it's her. She has become my compass, my anchor, and my refuge, all in one. My feet are moving before I register, I have commanded them to.

It's as if she's controlling the movement of my body with her come hither look. I move to the passenger side of the truck, where Sal opens the door to me. She backs across the bench seat on her palms, while I climb inside.

I reach back, tugging the door close, placing us in tight quarters. Slowly, I reach for her waist, wrapping my arm around it and tug her against my chest. I press my forehead to hers as our eyes stay connected. Turning, I sit in the seat she vacated, bringing her body with me. Sal straddles my lap and cups my face.

The look in her eyes says a thousand words. The last few hours have heightened my need for her, and I believe hers for me. The gravity of the danger surrounding her hits me hard.

When it does, I grasp her face and run my thumb over her plump bottom lip. Everyone I've ever loved has been taken from me. The thought of losing Sal as well is unbearable. My eyes go to my trembling fingers.

My fear is taking on a physical form. Sal covers my hand with hers, bringing my palm to her lips. The kiss she places there is like air to my lungs. I feel it in my veins igniting my blood with a renewed fire.

Her brows draw together as she looks at me. "Tell me what you need. What can I do to make it better? I need to do something," she whispers softly.

Her voice is a sweet blanket of love, something I haven't known in so long my chest aches. She wants to do for me, when it's my job to be there for her. I'm the one with her safety in my hands. Safety, I have a deep feeling will be tested.

I cup the other side of her face without answering her words. I need to steal this moment for my memory. A fucked up bastard like me shouldn't even be allowed next to an angel like her. It's only a matter of time before I find a way to fuck it up.

"Pierson, stop," she commands gently. She leans in to brush her lips against mine. "I see your thoughts. I've been waiting for you for so long without even knowing I have been. I'm not going to lose you now that I have you."

"Baby girl." Her words are exactly what I'm saying to myself in the back of my mind. I just don't have the words to explain how I'm feeling now.

"Gutter, I will always fight for us. Even if I have to fight one of us," she says fiercely, again breathing my thoughts.

I move my hand to grasp her jaw, dragging her face to mine, needing more contact. I know we need to be moving, but I need this moment or else I won't be able to focus. I take my time, slanting my lips across hers.

My soul savors my lips upon hers. I surprise myself with the tenderness of the kiss. So much so, I nip her lip softly and pull back to watch the connection of our flesh and bone. Her lip, my teeth, the softness of her full lip slowly slipping from my teeth, it's all mesmerizing. I chase her mouth to soothe the slight sting I know I've created.

The moan that fills the truck from her sweet lips echoes in my core. It takes another piece of me. In this moment, I know I want to gift Salalia. She has given me a gift I can never repay. This is the least I can do.

"You don't always have to be a force to be felt, baby," I say low. "You can set a fire without burning everything in your path. They'll still feel you."

The puzzled look on her face brings a smile to my lips. She'll understand soon enough. I learned early in life how to consume with just my presence. It's something I never thought I'd want to do ever again.

However, for Sal, I'll do anything. I plan to be felt in ways she's never known. In ways, a skilled man understands.

With my eyes, I unleash an intensity I've held back from her. The cage we're in fills with my energy, wrapping around us both. She parts her lips and her breathing becomes audible. I ghost a hand over her cheek, causing her breath to hitch.

"I can make love to you without penetration. It's the most powerful feeling in the world. Do you trust me?" I ask.

Her eyes fill with so much lust and desire, my own blood revs in my veins. She bites her lip, nodding slowly. I lift a brow wanting her words of confirmation.

"Yes," she nearly pants out.

My lips curl into the largest smile I've had in years. I even show teeth. When her eyes focus on my lips and go wide, I can imagine I look like the big bad wolf to her.

"Good girl," I murmur.

Sal

My eyes widen further as his words rasp through his sexy lips. This is a side of Gutter I've yet to see before. I surprise myself, when I take in the fact that I like it.

The confidence and charisma rolling off of him has my stomach and pussy churning and clenching with want. With us seated like this, the space in the truck is already tight. However, Gutter's current presence is making the space stifling. The air crackles with a current his demeanor has created.

I try to remember to breathe. His gorgeous face and intense eyes aren't helping in the least. I've been drawn to Gutter since the moment I laid eyes on him, but this... I just can't even explain.

His presence is all consuming. The look in his eyes says he sees right through me and my every thought. Not a single one of my desires are hidden from him.

His words play lazily in my head. *I can make love to you without penetration. It is the most powerful feeling in the world.* I want to know this feeling.

I want to know it with him. My skin is already vibrating with anticipation. I have no doubt he will deliver. I'm already soaked between my legs and he has barely touched me.

I can sense there's so much he isn't telling me. Things that he feels I don't need to know, things he intends to handle. On some level, I'm fine with that.

I just need to do my part somehow. If I can ease his mind a bit, I want to. At least, that was my plan before he entered the truck. Now, with my chest heaving, and my own breathing in my ears, I don't think I'm the one in control here anymore.

I don't even think this is about him at this point. Gutter has again turned the table to make this about me. I'm gradually learning this to be a pattern. Gutter always turns things around, making them all about me.

"Stop thinking, baby girl," he commands.

It's sharp, but the twinkle in his eyes softens the blow. I blink away my thoughts in time to register his gentle assault. He leans in, nipping my chin lovingly.

He doesn't stop there. He darts his tongue out to flick over the spot he just nipped. I shiver in his lap and close my eyes. I try not to burst into flames in his lap.

Gutter turns my head to the side, blazing a path with his lips to my ear. The hairs on his face heighten my sensitivity as they whisper across my skin. The burn is sweet and welcomed.

I squirm, feeling my core flood with liquid desire. I'd be embarrassed if I had my wits about me. However, my brain refuses to fire off any rational thoughts.

I've become all sensation. He follows the path of his kisses with a long, slow lick of his tongue, stopping at my ear to bite down on my lobe. My whole body jerks in reaction as if I've been shocked.

"A man isn't worthy of your body if he can't make you come without being inside of you," he breathes into my ear.

I moan, dragging my fingers into his hair. Shit, my body is already coiled tight. I just need him inside me, and I'll come harder than I've ever come before. I rock my hips into him, but he has other ideas.

He grips my waist with his free hand. "Oh, baby girl, the things I'll teach you," he groans. His breath fans across my face as he talks. When his nose ghost along my jaw, my skin heats and prickles. "Keep your eyes closed. Just feel me."

"Gutter," I gasp, feeling my core clench as if begging to be filled.

"That's it, feel me in that pussy, baby. I'm the only one that will ever turn you on like this," he whispers.

His every word pierces me on such a deep level but offers safety as well. It's overwhelming, yet I can't get enough.

"You make me so hard for you. Just thinking about it, I can taste you on my tongue. That sweet pussy is all I want to eat for an entire day. When I get you home, I'm going to feast on you for hours. Make you scream my name until your voice is raw and disappears."

"Oh, shit," I breathe and gush inside my panties.

He runs his fingertips down my arms as I come apart from just his words. His touch throws me into overdrive. This is unreal.

"That's it." He chuckles sexily. "Feel me, baby. Come for me. Don't fight it. That's what I want, that's what I need. I need you to come for your man."

"Pierson," I cry out in awe, my body shaking harder than ever before.

He growls, gripping my waist tighter. He captures my lips, pulling my cries from me. When he breaks the kiss to place a chaise one on my forehead, I try to catch my breath. Silly me for thinking it's all over.

"Turn around," he commands and gently starts to turn me in his lap.

I maneuver as much as I can in the tight space, placing my bottom in his crotch. He hisses in my ear. He's throbbing against my butt cheeks through his jeans. I reach beneath me to squeeze him, but he captures my hand before I can.

"This is about you," he says huskily into my ear.

Placing my hand in my lap, he splays his other on my belly. I lean my head back against his shoulder, turning my head to look up into his eyes. Those blue-gray eyes are blazing back at me.

I can almost taste his essence in my mouth. I want to taste him and offer this amazing force he's creating back to him. His scent is clouding my head as much as his words and his trust.

He traps my thighs together between his. Not taking his eyes from mine as he flicks out his tongue against my lips. I part them on a sharp gasp, I can't help it. The gesture sends sparks through me. My response to him is so strong.

I lift my arms behind my head tentatively, watching for his approval. He gives a slow nod of assent. I knot my fingers in the top of his hair.

He palms my breasts in his large hands, causing me to arch into him. He takes his time circling his thumbs over my nipples through the fabric of my shirt. I bite my lip so hard; I'm surprised I don't draw blood.

Electricity swirls through my body. His touch has awakened so much within me. If Gutter's touch could burn away my past, he'd be well on his way to incinerating the darkness of old.

My body is building again. His aura takes on a life of its own, curling around me, caressing me, penetrating my mind and my soul. His next words only serve to slice right through me.

"I can't wait to throb inside you. You're going to drip all that honey all over me," he groans, before licking the shell of my ear. "I'm going to drown in your love, darlin'."

"Shit, Gutter, please," I beg.

I need him. I want to slide down onto him so badly. The need to welcome him into the place he has claimed for his own is so overpowering, I don't know if I can stay sane without it. He slips one hand underneath my shirt and bra, connecting his palm with bare flesh, then slides his other hand down between my legs.

"Squeeze your thighs together," he demands as he cups my heat. I do as he orders, squeezing my thighs tightly.

The heat of his hand burns right through my jeans. I start to roll my entire body, grinding to find my release. The tight coil of his body tells me he's restraining himself from rocking into me. The feel of the tension within him is a turn on to my own body.

"Take what you need, baby girl. You're in control. You give me as much or as little as you want," he whispers.

His words hit me in my core. His understanding of my needs is so profound in this moment. I may seem wanton in his arms, but there's a part of me that screams for me to remain safe. I battle her every time I allow Gutter to touch me.

He's safe, I whisper to her in my head. Her whimper of joy and trust echoes in my mind. *We can feel, we can allow this. We are safe every time this man touches us.*

My breath hitches and my emotions crest on overload. I'm overwhelmed. I take this offering for what it is. The tears spill over, but my body has a mind of its own. I lift one foot, planting it onto the dashboard, rocking against his heavy hand between my legs.

"That's it, you can give it all to me, baby. Never be ashamed to feel with me. You're safe in my arms. Always," he pants the words that my mind and heart have come to take for truth.

I explode, screaming his name out. He put his arms around me, rocking me slowly from side to side. I don't even realize I'm sobbing loudly as I come down from a Gutter created heaven.

He kisses the top of my head repeatedly. "With each piece of me you give back. I promise to return one back to you," he says gruffly.

No words are needed from me, even if I could find the right ones to say. I know something just changed within the man who's wrapped around me. His touch and command of my body was different this time.

The assurance in his touch was heightened on so many levels. Our love making has been intense from the start, but what just happened was something mind numbing. I'm emotionally wrecked.

"I love you, Salalia. Whatever we face, remember that," he says with so much emotion, I sob a little harder.

Lurking Past

Gutter

I can't help watching her sleep. It's been a long day. Sal has been passed out, since her sobs subsided in the truck. I'd held her, while she allowed her emotions to drain.

When she was all cried out, I slipped from beneath her, placed her in the seat, and fastened the belt. I wanted to leave as much road as I could in the rearview mirror.

I can't deny feeling the change between us in that cage. I'm not just talking about in our relationship. Something shifted on the inside of me, and I know something has on the inside of my girl as well.

For once, Salalia was able to stop and feel. She was able to give over control and not have to take action, if she didn't want to. I would've gotten her there either way.

From what I'm learning about her, Sal's always ready to go. Always ready to take action. People don't understand the energy it takes to run for your life, to make sure that you survive.

Watching her sleep, seeing her at peace, causes my mind to run through all she's been through. It pains me to think of how much of it all she's had to endure on her own. There was a time when I wasn't so alone.

In all the shit I had handed to me, I had Terry. In the beginning, we had each other's backs. I took on more of the responsibility, but Terry being as smart as he was, took some of the burden off my shoulders by handling shit while I made us money.

Listening to Sal tell it, she doesn't ask King for much. When she needs something, she relies on herself. I want to change that. I plan to change that.

I look down at my phone. Grim and Reap are about an hour out from us. I told him to stop, eat, and get some rest the last time he sent me a text. He wanted to ride through, but I think Reap must have started to show signs of fatigue, which forced him to text me just now that they're stopping.

I'm confident they will eat up that distance in the morning. I rub my forehead, knowing I need to get some sleep myself. My thoughts won't let me.

My demons are clawing at my collar. I don't know if it's from unleashing a part of who I really am with Sal in that clearing or if it's a result of the build up from the last few weeks. My own shit hasn't miraculously gone away.

This time of year always brings back the darkest times of my life. I've had a lid on it all since having Sal with me, but tonight the devil is knocking. I just refuse to answer. I'd rather lie awake than allow my demons to surface in my sleep.

Sal stirs in the bed beside me. I look down at her as I sit with my back to the headboard. She still looks peaceful. I allow my eyes to roam over her curves beneath the thin sheet.

I haven't removed her clothes, just her shoes. There was a time where Terry slept fully clothed. It took months before I got him to at least take off his shoes.

Given my many triggers and remembering Terry's, I don't want to set any of Sal's off unintentionally. Not wanting to disturb her sleep, I swing my legs over the edge of the bed and run a hand through my hair. Then, I draw the same hand down my face, grunting to myself as I feel the hair lining my jaw. It's been a few days since I've shaved.

I stand and make my way to my bag, might as well shave while I'm up. I make my way into the bathroom, shutting the door behind me. I'm lost in thought and the act of shaving, when my phone vibrates on the countertop.

When I see the name that comes up on the screen, I freeze. Not sure why, but it's the last name I'm expecting to see tonight. The silence of the last few days gave me a false sense of comfort.

I'm thrown back in time. It happens so fast I can't stop it. I can only reach for the countertop and hold on.

"You're really going to just walk away?" Terry said in a small voice.

"Yeah, there's nothing here for me. I don't want any parts of this house. I can barely stand here as it is." I shook my head and turned away.

I don't want him to see the fear and anger on my face. This place is filled with nothing but fear and anger. So much fear.

We feared what would happen to us when my mother died, and my father lost himself, becoming the living dead. We feared what would happen to us when my dad died too. We feared Melody and what she would allow her friends to do to us.

It all made us so angry. I wanted nothing to do with this place. I don't want the money either, but it's better than living on the street, trying to strip for money or being an escort just so I can eat and have a place to rest my head.

"Pier, I'm sorry about all that shit," Terry starts from behind me.

"Don't," I say, unconsciously lifting my hand to my scar.

"Are we ever going to talk about it?" he whispers.

"No, I don't want to talk about shit. We're toxic for each other, Ter. I can see it in your eyes. You're still on that shit. I can't watch you self-destruct."

"I thought we would make this work together. I... I need—"
I cut him off.

"Don't, don't say it. Don't do it. Don't trap me here with you. Do what you want with the place. I have more bad memories here than good. I don't want any parts of this place," I replied, heading for the door.

It was the last time I saw Terry in person. It was also the night he tried to commit suicide. It's the night that has haunted me for years. I wasn't there to save him from himself. Again, I failed him.

I was in the habit of failing him, but I knew I would be destroyed right along with him if I tried to pull him from the darkness. Alba, our only childhood friend found him in the bathroom with slashed wrists and an empty bottle of pills.

Terry had called her sobbing that he didn't want to die. She got there in time to get him help, but not before a bloody, fucked up Terry texted me photos of his situation. That text will never wash away from my mind.

I didn't even see it until the next morning. I was wasted out of my mind when Alba's call woke me the next day. Terry was stable, but Alba was a mess over it. She'd known bits and pieces of what we'd gone through.

Terry had told her and made her swear never to tell her parents. She had sobbed for me to come to the hospital. What she didn't know was that I had tried to drink myself to death that very same night. My head was too fucked up. I couldn't face Terry. I had failed him over and over.

I was barely holding my own shit together. We were better off without each other. We would only remind each other of the fucked up life we shared and I would forever be reminded of how I failed him.

I'm brought back from the past by the ping of my phone. Terry's name flashes as a missed call and a voicemail. My hand shakes as I reach for the phone.

I don't know if I'm ready to open that door. We're only two weeks away from the anniversary of the night we both tried to take our lives. I can still remember waking in a pool of my own vomit.

I squeeze my eyes shut, but that's a mistake. The images of Terry in a bath of his own blood, his lids heavy as he gave me the finger is so vivid. I feel like he has been giving me the finger ever since.

I open my eyes and grunt at the phone. Looking up into the mirror, my scar screams at me. Nothing good comes from getting involved with Terry.

From what I know, he's gotten his life together. At least, that's what the reports say. I'm just not ready to open that door. Not with Sal's life still in danger. My own shit will wait.

We Got Company

Sal

Something is different with Gutter this morning. It's more than his clean-shaven jaw. I was surprised to wake to the sight of his smooth skin.

I was also surprised I slept through him bringing me into the hotel room as well as all through the night. Better yet, I slept peacefully. I can't remember the last time that happened. I never sleep soundly through the night.

Gutter has seemed distant and distracted since I woke. Something is definitely going on with him. He's even a little more gruff than usual.

I thought we connected on a deeper level yesterday. This change has me on edge. I can't help but wonder if I've done something wrong. Maybe my sobbing in his arms was too much. Perhaps he realizes how damaged I am and doesn't want to deal with so much baggage.

I chew on my lip, trying to figure out where things went wrong. I'm frustrated and the silence is enough to kill. I brush imaginary lent from my skirt, frowning down at the fabric.

Stormy could've traded this one out along with the leather one. The flirty yellow skirt is totally not my thing. I smirk at my black riding boots, now those are all me.

"It has nothing to do with you," Gutter mutters into the silence.

I look up to find him watching me out the corner of his eyes. I blink a few times to make sure he's talking to me. He reaches to place a warm hand on my thigh.

I feel like one of these silly girls, I went to boarding school with. The ones who teased me for being a bookworm. The ones who fell all over themselves when boys gave them attention.

I melt under his touch before I can think better of it. I slide across the seat to be closer to his warmth. He moves his hand from my thigh and wraps his arm around me, pulling me into his side.

"Then what is it?" I ask.

He kisses the top of my head. A long silence stretches out between us. So long, I don't think he's going to answer me.

"You have enough of my burdens in your head. Leave this one be."

I purse my lips to keep from opening my mouth to pry. This change in him is huge. Not like when his dominate side came out yesterday. This is something different.

His eyes seem to carry darker shadows. His energy is off. He's more guarded, all while anger, frustration, sadness, and—dear I say—fear ooze off of him.

I want to reach for the thin thread that's hanging between us and pull, but I fear what it will do to the trust we've given each other and started to build our relationship on. It takes just as much trust to know when to let things be as it does to be willing to share. I think this is a time I need to let things be.

As if reading my thoughts as he seems to do so often, he gives a gentle squeeze to my side and kisses the top of my head. "One thing at a time, darlin'. We have a ton of shit flying at us. When we clear our plate, I'll open up as best I can." He heaves a heavy breath.

"Okay." I nod. "I can give you that."

I reach for the radio to turn it on for a distraction from the silence. I frown at the somber country song that's playing. The mood in the truck is already quite depressing, but the song comes to an end and the song Gutter had sung yesterday comes on.

I smile, turning my head up to look at him. His lips draw into a frown. I know he can sense I'm about to ask him to sing for me.

I run the backs of my fingers over his lightly stubbled face. God, the man is beautiful. Reaching up higher, I run my fingers through his dark waves. His hair is a sexy mess today. He looks like he hasn't slept.

"Please." I pout.

He shifts his gaze to mine. I give him my version of puppy eyes. The light crinkles in the corners of his eyes when he smiles back at me takes my breath away. His lips turn up into a crooked half smile that makes his full mouth so sensual and alluring.

I can't resist leaning up to peck them. That seems to do the trick. Gutter starts to croon to me while returning his attention to the road. His voice is simply amazing, like a velvety smooth, sweetest chocolate ever.

I don't know the song, but I know he's doing a damn amazing job singing it. I could totally see him with a guitar in his hands, singing while training those intense eyes on me.

I feel safe and warm in his arms, but I need to see this. I want to watch him sing for me. I'm still in awe that this voice is coming from this gruff man. I'm learning that there are so many layers to Gutter. The more I peel, the more I learn.

I scoot back over to my side of the truck and just watch. I think I fall in love with him a bit more when he turns toward me and winks as he belts out the lyrics. It's in this very moment it dawns on me that I'm happy. Despite all the shit coming my way and going on all around us, I've never been this happy.

In the blink of an eye that all changes. I don't even have time to relish in the joy I feel before it's taken right from my hands. It all happens so fast.

Gutter

I love that pretty smile on her face. If me singing a song puts that smile on her sweet face, I'll sing to her for the rest of our lives. Salalia has crawled deep into my darkness and turned on the lights.

The song pours from the speakers as I croon it out for her. I turn to wink at her and get a glimpse of that beautiful smile. My heart does that thing it's been doing since I first saw her at that bus station.

My chest aches as my mind tries to tell me I'll fail her. At some point, I won't be enough. I'll fail her, just like I did Terry.

Again, those images of Terry soaking in his own blood fill my head. I begin to blink them away as panic tries to seize me. I clench my jaw.

This is why I didn't want to open Pandora's box. My level of fucked up will send Sal running before she can get to truly love me. I can't have that. I shut all that shit down, singing through the madness in my head.

I'm mid-song, when I go to turn back to the road. Something catches my eye in the rearview mirror, sending my hackles up. It's been too quiet. I've been watching my mirrors for Grim and Reap. They should be flanking us soon. We are closer to home, but we still have a ways to go.

I pause and narrow my eyes on the mirror. Two bikes and a cage are on our tails. The bikes keep weaving around the cage. I get that feeling something's off.

"Baby, I'mma need you to reach under that seat," I grunt to Sal.

Before I can finish my instructions, the back window blows out. I duck and shift my eyes to see if Sal is okay. I tighten my jaw when I see her turning in her seat, placing her back to the dash. Sal uses her booted foot to kick out the remaining glass.

"What the hell are you doing?" I bite out.

She doesn't answer me with words. Instead, she reaches under the seat, pulling my shotgun. Sal pumps the shotgun and fires. More fire is returned, flaring my ire. I turn back to focus on the road to get us out of here. Cars in the other two lanes swerve out of the way and speed up.

I'm in the center lane, taking advantage of that fact. I swerve right and then left. Sal fires again, causing her to tilt over from the movement of the truck and the kickback of the gun.

"You okay?" I growl, reaching to hold her down. I'm on the verge of losing my mind. I hadn't meant for her to use the shotgun. I wanted her to hand it over. "Stay down. I need you safe."

She's already reloading. I grab the shotgun, using it to hammer out the driver's side window. With all the force I have, I hit it once, twice, the third time's the charm.

I pump the shotgun, then reach out of the window. I look through the side view mirror and fire. I get the front tire of the rider on the left.

I grin, when the bike turns flat on its side before sliding off the road onto the shoulder. This shotgun isn't what I wanted. I need something a little faster. I reach under the seat for another special something I have hidden.

When my hand touches the cold steel of the semiauto burner, that dark part of my soul awakens with joy. The bloodlust is real. I can taste it on my tongue.

My shoulders lighten as if my wings have unfurled, just as a Lost Soul's Grim Reaper would. The Squad member in me lives for this shit.

More fire bounces off the truck. I grit my teeth and aim at one of the three riders behind us. Shit is getting thick, but I know one thing. I'm getting me and my girl the fuck out of here alive.

I drop two more bikes, but two more seem to appear. "Fuck," I roar, but continue to fire. It's the sound of movement, within the truck that grabs my attention.

"Sal! What the fuck are you doing?" I hiss, when I turn to find her body half hanging out of the window. Her brown legs are still halfway in the truck, while her little yellow skirt reveals her panties as it flaps in the wind.

"Your bike," she yells back. "They're going to ruin it. I can help, just cover me."

I honestly don't know if I want to kiss her or strangle her right now. It's hot as fuck to see her snap into action like a ride or die chick. My very own badass. However, I have no control over her safety if she jumps into this fight.

I don't have time to snatch her back into the truck. I hear the gunfire rather than see it. She must have taken one of my pistols from the glove compartment. I shake my head and cover her. It's the only option I have. A glance in the rearview, shows me Sal unhooking my bike as she ducks and fires.

I snap out of it and get to seriously covering her ass. Panic rises as more bikes appear. *Fuck this.* I need Sal safe. I smash the radio off so she can hear me as I yell out.

"Baby," I bellow. "Get on the bike and ride. Get the fuck out of here. I'll catch up."

"No," she yells back. "I'm not leaving you."

"Don't fucking argue with me. Get the fuck out of here, now."

I throw the truck in reverse and spin to face the fuckers shooting at us. I shoot out the windshield, before fisting it out of my way. The moment Sal starts my bike, I breathe a sigh of relief.

I know that bike like my own body. I listen closely for any sounds that she might be damaged. She purrs perfectly. I'm confident she'll get Sal far from here.

I bang my fist on the roof. "*Go!*" It's an order.

I look in the mirror at Sal's scrunch up face of indecision. It would be adorable if shit wasn't so real at the moment. Suddenly, her features clear.

She nods her head and in a move that makes my heart stop, she rides my bike right off the back of the truck bed. She bounces onto the pavement, turns and takes off in the direction I need her to go. I focus back on the road and see what placed that look on her face.

My motherfucking Squad. Grim and Reap have arrived right on time. Grim rides right by one biker, blowing his head wide open.

Reap has her machine guns, one in each hand, arms stretched out, blazing. I throw the truck into drive, moving into head on traffic and fucking light shit up. I gun the truck, headed for the cage that's been riding in the middle of it all.

I laugh when I home in on the face of the motherfucker driving. His eyes widen and he looks like he's seen the devil himself. Fucking right.

I put a bullet in the head of the passenger sitting beside him. From the looks of it, the driver only remains in this game of chicken because he's in shock. I roar as I floor the gas.

I prepare for impact only to bare my teeth, when Reap rides up and blows the driver's head off. She shoots right through the passenger window. I shift my eyes to hers and her little ass shrugs.

The car swerves out of my path. I slam the brakes and growl. Grim rolls to a stop, beside my truck and bangs on the smoking hood. The look in his eyes sends alarms off. Reap pulls to a stop, jumping off her bike and climbs on the back of Grim's.

"Let's go. A few slipped by. They're on Sal's ass," Grim roars.

I don't even think. I throw the door open and head for Reap's bike. I reload and take off right behind Grim and Reap. My heart is racing out of my chest. How did this happen? I fucked up, just like I knew I would.

Sal

I didn't want to leave. I saw the fear in Gutter's eyes for me, but I wasn't going to leave my man behind to fight by himself. I'm not built that way. I had planned to get the bike down and help.

Once I saw Grim and Reap, it was the only reason I decided to go. With Gutter's gun in my hand, I took off as fast as his ride would take me. I wish I had time to relish in the way he's beast opened up and purred beneath me.

For a moment, I felt a pang of loss for my own stolen bike. Gutter's custom ride is much sweeter, but my girl was getting there. Just a few more tweaks.

Shoving those thoughts aside, I open the bike and ride the fuck out of it, weaving in and out of traffic. I think I'm in the clear, until the first bullet flies by my head. My heart almost tears out of my chest.

I lean in and crank the bike, pushing forward, but they're on my ass. I ride hard, trying to dip them. I'm not dying today. Not like this. I refuse.

I'm no one's victim. Never again. *Never!*

It dawns on me I'm not going to out ride them. I have to fight for my life. Fine, I'm willing this time. I have shit to live for.

I release the bar I'm holding, gun still in hand. Crossing my right arm over my body, reaching under my left, I tuck my arm against my chest and fire. I thank God for my daddy.

Cage taught me more than a kid should know about guns. Hell, I plan to kiss King for teaching me to ride the fuck out of a bike. Yup, I'm getting my ass home.

I lean to the side, just as another bullet whizzes by my face. My confidence weans a little, but a glance in the rearview and my heart soars. Lost Souls always find their own.

I hear King's voice in my head. *We get elbows deep for ours.* Relief floods me. Grim is riding hard toward me and Reap is blasting.

You've survived. You did it again. Breathe.

Gutter

It is a known fact that Reap can build the hell out of a bike. She built the shit out of her ride, too bad I'm about to run it into the ground to get to my woman. I push this pink and black bike to its limits.

I can taste the bile rising. Sal dips and dodges on the back of my bike. Damn, my girl can ride, but I'm not sure it's enough. They're still firing at her.

Grim's riding as hard as I am. Reap aims around him and starts blazing. My eyes widen and a smile comes to my face, when I see Sal firing back behind her. She's still keeping that bike upright and riding like a fucking pro.

That's my girl. I'm coming, baby. I chant the words in my head, more for myself.

Grim's bike is a little more souped up than Reap's so I'm not surprised when he pulls away. This is why these two and I click. They get shit done.

I watch with pride as Reap flips her little body around so that she's facing me, her back to Grim's. Grim rides pass the fuckers shooting at Sal. Reap, with both arms stretched out before her, does what she does best. I watch two of the bikers as their bodies are blown clear off their bikes.

I dodge the fallen bikes, headed for my girl. There's one more bastard on her tail. Not for long. This bike is either going to give the performance of its life or its going to die beneath me, but I'm getting to my girl.

I move out to the side. I need to clear Sal of my shot. Finally, I have the angle I need. I lift my gun and take the life that owes me. You don't fuck with what's mine. My soul roars when I see the fucker fall. It takes Sal a moment to register she's not being chased anymore. At least, I think it does. She doesn't slow for a few.

I ride up beside her and lock eyes with her. Tears are swimming in those beautiful brown eyes, causing me to only want to pull her into my arms, but I just nod.

She did good. She did real good.

Squad

Brick aka Owen

I'm pissed as fuck. First, Grim sends me a text to say he and the team bringing Sal in had a full out gun fight in the middle of the fucking highway. Then, I find Mags lurking outside of Eva's room and King finds us in a heated conversation.

This day has started out as shit. I just want to get to my Squad and get them back safe. Someone has lost their fucking mind going after mine. It's going to get handled. All this shit is going to get handled.

I look to my side and nod to Diggs. I have him, Beau, Axle, and Vault with me. That's a whole lot of Lost Souls muscle. There's nothing pretty about this escort back to the clubhouse. You'd be a fool to come at us in this formation.

Diggs signals that we're in the right place. He and Gutter have a place out here they use for business. Grim, Reap, and Gutter were able to get Sal to safety while the rest of us rode to bring them in.

As we ride around to the back of the structure, it hits me that someone tried to kill the sister of my woman. My blood is already simmering. Knowing someone tried to hurt someone who means so much to Eva has my veins on fire.

I shut down the engine of my bike, bringing a silence to the roar. All the other bikes around me do the same. I roll my neck, still feeling the fatigue of the last four days. I'm getting too old for this shit.

"They're inside," Diggs says beside me.

Just then, the large doors of the warehouse looking building slide open. Grim and Reap are the first to come into view. I move my gaze and I swear my head almost explodes.

I blink a few times to make sure I'm looking at what I think I'm looking at. Gutter is sitting against his bike and Sal is in between his legs with her head resting on his shoulder. Gutter's hands are resting comfortably—too comfortably on her ass.

I groan and pull a hand down my face. I've never seen Gutter even so much as look at a woman. *Damn.* King is going to kill one of my best Squad members. *Shit.*

"Ah, fuck," I say, pointing at the two. "You knew about this?" I direct my question at Grim.

Reap throws her head back and laughs. I look at her with impatience. She stifles her laughter. Grim frowns and shrugs his shoulders.

"The man rode and killed for her like she's his property. I ain't got shit to say. Brother is the happiest I've ever seen him. I'll vouch for him with the Prez," Grim rumbles.

"Shit." I'll be losing two of my best. I point to Grim. "You mind your fucking business. I got this one. I'm already on death row," I mutter the last sentence for my ears only.

This shit just keeps getting better and better. King is going to go postal when he finds all this out. His baby sisters are not babies anymore. Two of the craziest brothers in the club have claimed each of his girls for their own.

I rub the back of my neck. I have to minimize some of the blowback from this shit. I know King. He's going to feel betrayed by the both of us. We'll be no better than the fuckers out to get our club.

"Gutter, you let me handle this shit, kid," I huff.

The crazy bastard turns his head toward me and glares me down. I didn't expect anything less. He's been this way since he showed up at the club with King.

I was one of the first King introduced him to. Neither of us were sure we were going to like the other. After spending time with him and learning he's loyal and just wanted to be left alone, we gained a mutual respect for each other. I don't fuck with him; he doesn't piss me off.

This here though, it's going to get him killed if he doesn't listen. I narrow my eyes at him. I'm still his Squad captain.

I'll put his ass to ground if he fucks with me. I actually like the kid, so I don't lose my shit on him.

"You feel me, Brother?" I lift a questioning brow.

"I ain't feeling shit," he grunts. "I made my girl a promise. I'm keeping it."

The fuck he just say to me?

I should let King kick is mean ass. Old ornery son of a bitch. I snort.

Well, fuck.

Gutter

I like Brick, but I made a promise to my woman. I don't make promises I don't keep. I promised Terry I would never let him pull me under again and I haven't. Even if it meant walking away from the only person I had.

Brick snorts and looks me in the eyes. He's not amused. I'm sure he's trying to help me, but I'm going to handle the prez my way. I won't disappoint Sal.

Shit, I almost lost her. I've failed her enough for a lifetime. When I thought, I wouldn't get to her in time, I was sure my life was going to end right there with hers. I would never have recovered from losing her.

"I'm going to tell you this once, kid. Let me handle this. King isn't going to like this shit. He has enough on his plate. Don't make this worse," Brick says, holding my gaze.

I grunt my reply, not committing to a damn thing. If he wants to think I have, I'll let him. He's my squad captain. I won't disrespect him, especially not in front of all these other Squad members. It's not my style.

Brick runs a hand through his hair and blows out a breath. "Let's get the fuck out of here," he rumbles.

I climb on the back of my bike, before holding out my hand for Sal to climb on after me. My heart smolders when she settles behind me and wraps her arms securely around my waist. Knowing that she's safe on the back of my bike and that I'm taking her home to safety, calms every nerve in my body.

Yup, I'm letting the prez know. I'm not giving this up and I know I can't go a day without touching her. He needs to know she belongs to me. I'll take whatever the repercussions are. Sal belongs with me.

CHAPTER TWENTY-EIGHT

Killer Prez

Sal

I'm so nervous, when we pull into the gates at the Lost Souls clubhouse. This compound is my second home away from home. Everywhere I look there's a memory.

I never thought I would dread coming through these gates so much. I never thought I would fear being here. Seeing Brick's reaction sort of put things into perspective. I know I talked a lot of shit, but the truth is, King is going to lose his mind.

I could be minus a boyfriend or minus a brother. King could kill Gutter, or I could end up not talking to King because he's too bullheaded to understand I belong to Gutter, there is no other way.

I curl my fingers into Gutter's shirt. My palms have become so sweaty. I inhale the scent of his cut. It's familiar and allows me to relax just a bit.

It doesn't last long. King comes rushing out of the clubhouse with that swag only King can pull off. My older brother is a force within himself. His blond dreads hang down around his shoulders, which is a sign of one of two things.

King is either highly stressed or he has been partying hard all night. It doesn't look much like a party has been going on around here. Everyone looks tense. Which tells me King isn't in a very good mood.

I unconsciously give Gutter's waist a gentle squeeze. He pulls his bike to a stop with all the others. My brother heads straight for me. He's about a few yards away.

I go to climb off the back of Gutter's bike on my own, but he snakes his arm around my waist to steady me. I turn from watching King approach to look back at Gutter.

He lifts from the bike and stands beside me. When I see what he's about to do—here in front of everyone—I part my lips on a gasp.

Gutter tilts my head back with his free hand under my chin. He dips his head and nips my bottom lip. I can't help sagging into him.

It has been a long and emotional day. When I open for him, he seizes my mouth in a passionate kiss that has my toes curling in my boots.

He moves his arm around my waist so he can palm my ass over my skirt. Everything around us goes deadly silent. That's until Brick's loud huff and a growl fills the air.

"Ah, fuck, kid," Brick huffs in frustration. "*King!*"

"You little motherfucker," King roars.

I break away from the kiss to find my brother charging at us. Well, at Gutter. I've never seen my brother's face so red with anger. I jump in front of Gutter and throw my hands out.

"No, King, no," I try to shout.

Brick has already jumped into action. He runs to block King's way as he tries to calm him with words. I can't hear what Brick is saying to King, but it doesn't seem to be working.

Gutter reaches for my waist and pulls me to his side, stepping forward. This isn't what I meant when I asked him to be up front with King. *Note to self, Gutter is very literal.*

"Your ass is squaring up on me?" King hisses, his eyes narrowed on Gutter.

"Naw, Prez, but if you want to beat my ass for falling for my girl, then I'm ready," Gutter states matter of factly.

"There will be no one kicking anyone's ass," I groan.

"His girl? *His girl.* Motherfucker, you don't even like pussy," King seethes. "That's the reason I sent your big ass to get her in the first fucking place. I thought I could trust you."

"You can trust me," Gutter says without question.

"You sneaky, pretty motherfucker. I'm going to cut the rest of your fucking face up. You will never touch my sister again."

Brick has had a firm hold on King, but in a sudden move, King spins and dips under Brick's arms. It's amazing to watch with King being such a large guy. He does it so quick and fluidly.

I yelp and go to run forward, but Gutter catches my waist, restraining me. Brick throws his arms around King's waist and plucks him right off his feet. Again, I'm surprised and in awe. I also know that shit isn't something anyone, but Brick can try.

"Get the fuck off me. That's my baby sister," King bellows.

"And I love her," Gutter yells back.

Brick and King freeze. Brick releases my brother and they both turn to glare at Gutter. King places his hands on his hips and gives Gutter the look of death.

"Motherfucker, you haven't known her but a second. How the hell are you in love with her?" King frowns and looks Gutter up and down.

"I didn't know you at all, but I knew there was something about you I was willing to risk my life for," Gutter says pointedly.

I note the pause in King. He looks to be thinking over the words Gutter just said. He nods and looks like he may accept them.

Then he looks at me. A myriad of emotions crosses his face, before he scrunches it up in anger all over again.

"No, I know the way you left here. Something was off. This motherfucker took advantage of that," King spits.

"No, he didn't," I find my voice and speak up. "I love him too, King. Don't do this, please," I plead.

King closes his eyes as he vibrates with anger. "Come here." He holds his arms out for me.

I run into my brother's arms, closing the gap between us quickly. I want to sob, when I reach him, and he envelops me in his embrace. It's been too long since I've been comforted by my brother. I've avoided him a lot in the past few years.

"Are you okay?" King breathes into my hair.

"I am now."

"You don't belong with one of us," he whispers. "Especially not him."

"The hell I don't. Tell that shit to Eva while you have a chance. I'm already gone, King. I belong to him. Especially, him."

"Well, fuck," King says, releasing a long breath. "I'm gonna kill him."

King releases me and moves like lightning to get around me to head for Gutter. This time Grim and Brick restrain him and head to the clubhouse. The small crowd parts to get out of their way.

Most are looking at Gutter as if they want to step in for King. Reap steps up beside Gutter and eyes them all down. I'm grateful to her when her words fill the air.

"This shit is between Prez and Gutter. Don't none of you get any ideas. I'll put you to ground before he has a chance to. Don't fuck with what you don't understand."

Reap looks around. "Prez is processing, but when he calms the fuck down, he'll have your head for fucking with his Squad and breaking his baby sister's heart. Don't try it."

Her warning is heard loud and clear. Those who looked like they were going to leap, back down and turn away. I notice Gutter's hard glare, taking in those who looked like they were going to try to take a stab at him. I'm sure he's banking that information for another time.

Suddenly, I'm exhausted. All I want is to get inside and find somewhere to relax. My nerves are shot. I don't know how much more I can handle.

Never Letting Go

Gutter

"Fuck," I mutter to myself.

This has been the longest fucking day ever. As I watch the prez claim his pregnant woman, I shake my head. I'd seen them ride off together once before, but that shit was none of my business.

Just like it's none of my business now. Sal looks exhausted. I'd planned to get her fed and take her to my room to get some rest as soon as we arrived.

I managed to get her belly full, but the moment she saw her sister and Misty, I knew the rest of my plan wasn't going to happen. As tired as she looked, there was determination in her eyes to spend time with the girls, which to my surprise, included Reap.

Now that the prez has lost his shit for the second time today, I think it's time for us to at least try to get some sleep. I'm sure King is going to want to go another round with both Brick and myself when the girls aren't around. I'm ready to give my pound of flesh.

It is what it is. Nothing is going to change between Sal and me. I walk up behind her, wrap my arm around her waist. Then I lean into whisper. "Let me tuck you in, baby girl. You're home now."

That pretty smile is on her face when she turns to me. I don't know how I've survived this long without that smile in my life, but I don't plan to find out what life is like without it.

Without words, she tucks into my side, allowing me to walk her back to my room. I can't believe I'm a little nervous. I was ready to stand up to the prez without flinching, but knowing I'm taking my girl into my space has me breaking out in sweat.

I never have people in my space. Seeming to feel me about to lose my shit, Sal squeezes my waist and snuggles deeper into my side. I calm right as we reach my door.

I pull out my key, licking my suddenly dry lips. It's as if I'm opening the door in slow motion. When I finally get it unlocked, I push it open for Sal to walk through the door first.

I watch her as she walks pass me into the mid-sized space. The Lost Souls take care of their own. I know for a fact we have nicer quarters than most clubs.

While the room isn't as big as the one the prez is in, it's a decent size, big enough to place a king-sized bed in. There's a bathroom attached on the right side. I haven't done much with the place.

It still has the same bare beige walls that were here when I moved in. I don't have pictures from my past and there's nothing to really say the place is mine. My apartment is sort of the same.

I never got around to making either mine. Sal walks right over to my bed and sits on the right side, facing the bathroom. I step inside and close the door behind me.

Watching her move about as if the space belongs to her as well, causes me to I relax a little more.

"I'm going to shower," she says tiredly, while unzipping her boots.

"You need anything?"

She looks up at me, a soft smile on her lips. "Just you," she replies.

I nod, shrugging out of my cut and tossing it over the chair in the corner. My boots are the next thing I get rid of before I tug off my T-shirt. When I get my shirt over my head, I find Sal standing by the bed naked.

I'm distracted by that sexy brown skin of hers. I allow my eyes to travel up her curvy body. I take my time to savor it.

The fact that I have the luxury hits me. We're here, home in the safety of the club. When my gaze reaches her face, I have to close my eyes and say a silent prayer.

She's so fucking gorgeous. I open my eyes to find her watching me cautiously through those long as fuck lashes. Her lower lip is caught between her teeth. I lift a questioning brow.

"You're staring." She giggles nervously.

"You're gorgeous." I shrug.

I remove the rest of my clothes, not taking my eyes off of her. I grin when she shifts from foot to foot. A shy Sal is a sexy Sal. I walk toward her, lacing my fingers in hers when I reach her.

She reaches for my chest with her free hand, running her fingers up to my shoulder and back down again. I flex my pecs, while her fingers travel over my skin. My eyes remain on hers.

"You're real," she says, with a slight catch of her breath.

"As real as it gets," I reply, placing a hand on her waist. I gently tug her closer.

"I…" The tears I saw in her eyes earlier on the road, begin to spill over. "You saved my life. For a minute, I didn't think I would get to touch you again."

"That wasn't an option," I say between tight lips.

I reach to wipe her tears away with my thumb. Her plump lips purse and she nods her head. Her breasts press against my bare chest and she lifts onto her toes. Our lips don't touch, we just breathe each other in.

I cup the side her of face and touch my forehead to hers. No words are needed. I'm not even sure how long we stand like this, but I can feel the electricity flowing between us the entire time. A fire burns in my soul for this girl.

Despite throbbing against her stomach, I choose to ignore that need. My need to be close to her and close to her only, overrides all else. Her words hit home. There was a moment when I feared I wouldn't make it in time.

I don't know what makes me, but I start to sway our bodies together. Before I think better of it, I'm finishing the song I sung to her in the truck before all hell broke loose. It's a song by Kevin Urban, *Blue Ain't Your Color.*

I think it's fitting. Sal wasn't happy when we met. I could see it in her eyes. It was more than running from danger. I saw her, the real her, deep within those big brown pools.

Sal wraps her arms around my neck and holds me tight. I sing the song all the way through. When I release the last note, she lifts her head that has been on my shoulder to look me in my eyes. Her face is soaked with tears.

I use my palms to wipe them away, then lift her in my arms and carry her into the bathroom. Once I step into the shower, I place her on her feet. Then I reach for the leaver to turn it on, but Sal reaches for my hand.

"When you turn that water on, we wash it all away. This is our fresh start. Everything will be okay from here. This is real, we can breathe again."

I nod, swallowing the lump in my throat. If I didn't love her before, I know I love her now. I turn on the water and let the washing begin.

Sal

I wake to a dark room and the warmth of a big body beneath me. I'm still naked from our shower earlier. I have to pee, and my stomach speaks up, telling me I didn't eat enough.

I slide from Gutter's chest, appreciating the warmth once it's gone. There's a little chill in the room. I look around. I've never seen one of the brother's keep such a clean room.

Another thing I notice, there isn't a single thing in here that didn't come with the room. I would know. My mom redid the entire clubhouse when Cage made her his old lady. Cage always took care of his boys.

Mom made every room here feel like home. Some of the brothers tried to pretend they could care less, but I remember the looks on their faces when mom was done. Everyone loved her.

I feel the weight of thinking of Mom and Dad press down on me. I shake it off and move to the dresser to find a T-shirt. I smile at the second drawer that I find full of tees.

Gutter's scent drifts into my nostrils. I grab one and slip it over my head. It's a little oversize on my curves, riding high on my mid-thigh.

I pull the neckline to my nose and inhale as I walk to the bathroom. My stomach growls again, causing me to roll my eyes. After I relieve myself, I move to the sink to wash my hands.

A look in the mirror brings a sigh from my lips, once I see the mess that is my hair. I comb my fingers through the wave on top, combing it into some semblance of a style.

It may be time for a cut or maybe something new. I shrug at the mirror, when my stomach protests for the third time. Pushing my thoughts aside, I move back into the bedroom and find my underwear. I pull them on and tiptoe to the door.

I slip out of the room, it's late. Some of the brothers are probably milling around in the main area of the clubhouse, but

I can get to the kitchen from here without being seen. I turn the corner and smile when I see Misty standing in King's doorway talking to Eva.

My smile falls when I see they're in an intense conversation. I move closer to hear what they're saying. My brows wrinkle as their words reach my ears.

"You are in no condition to come with me," Eva protests. "I've got to go."

"Go where?" I ask, concerned and curious. King said were on lockdown. No one should be going anywhere. "I thought we were on lockdown. What's the matter?"

"Oh, God, Sal. I just got the weirdest call. Some lady says she's Mom's nurse and that Mom just woke up from a coma," Eva says.

I feel the blood drain from my face. I stumble back as if her words have pushed me. I feel his heat at my back before I see him.

It's like he knows I need him. My brain is reeling. I'm having a hard time processing my sister's words.

"What?" I push pass my lips, when I finally find my breath.

"You can't go alone," Misty calls out as she moves back inside the room.

The sound of her moving around inside greets my ears, while my brain tries to catch up. I can only imagine she getting dressed, ready to be there because she knows Eva needs her.

"You're not going anywhere. You three are under my watch until King and Brick get back," Gutter says from behind me.

"Oh, the hell I am. I need to go find out what the hell is going on," Eva demands.

"Calm down, Eva. How do you know you can trust this woman? I mean, this just sounds crazy. You can't go running off. Think about the baby," I say, worry setting in while my mind still whirls. I think I'm in shock.

"What if she's telling the truth?" Eva stomps her foot like a little child. "I can't not go. It's Mom."

I nod, feeling the tears gather in my eyes. My brain snaps into action. What if this is real? What if Eva is right? We have to find out.

I turn and look up into Pierson's eyes. He has to understand how important this is to me. How much it means. He looks down at me and his gaze softens.

I know then and there he understands without me saying a word. I still choose my words wisely. I know how these bikers stick to their instructions. Gutter is already in the shit house with King.

"Pierson, please, babe. She's right, what if it's real? What if my mom is alive somewhere?" I say softly.

He closes his eyes and nods. "We all go." He sighs. "I'm not letting the three of you out of my sight."

"Thank you," I say and hug him around the waist, before releasing him and turning to Eva. "I just need to throw on something to wear. Don't run off, we're doing this together."

Eva bobs her head. It's written all over her face she's been crying. More tears surface and spill over.

My own heart squeezes. This could be real. That means my mother is somewhere out there, still alive. If it isn't real, I know Eva will be just as destroyed as I will.

I don't want to get my hopes up, but it's already too late. After all I've been through, I could really use my mom. Whatever happens tonight, I know it will change my life forever. I have a feeling nothing will be the same after this.

Lost

Sal

I can't explain the mood around here lately. It's like being hit by a Mac truck, but you keep moving because you have somewhere to be. So many people have been affected by Mom and Dad's return.

"Mom and Dad are alive," I say to myself as I walk through the clubhouse.

It's like I'm going mad. I repeat those words to myself a few times a day to insure I'm not. It's only been a few days, but it's still such a shock.

With the attack on Eva, I think it's taking everyone longer to process what's happened around here.

Secrets, so many secrets have come out. In a way, I'm sort of glad mom doesn't remember much. On the other hand, I feel for Cage, but I don't know how to feel or how mom would feel about the Jacky thing if she could remember.

They weren't together, but... I think Mom would have wanted to know. I guess.

"Hey, you," I say cautiously as I walk out to the backyard of the clubhouse.

Jacky turns and looks back at me. He's out here all by himself. Finding out Mom and Dad are still alive has been a hard blow. I can't imagine how Jacky feels in all of this.

To find out the man he thought was his real dad—the same man he watched kill his mom—isn't his father at all. Not to mention finding out his real father, Cage—the one he knew nothing about—is actually still alive... as I said, I don't have words for this.

I totally get the brooding. He's hurting. Jacky seems to always be on the shit end of life. I feel for him.

"What are you doing out here?" he says as he looks at me with a sour expression on his face.

"You do know I'll still kick your ass," I tease.

"I'm a grown man now. Besides, you know I don't beat up on woman, Brat or not." His words are sharp, but the humor in his eyes tell a different story. "You know, I used to tease you because I thought you were pretty. Now that shit is sickening. You're my fucking sister for Christ's sake."

"Technically, I'm your stepsister, but, ew, I totally get it." I burst into laughter.

"So much shit has changed in a matter of days. I feel like I don't know who I am."

My shoulders sag with the weight of his words. I move around the bench to take a seat beside him. I know exactly what he means. There are moments when I don't know if I'm coming or going.

"Yeah, I hear you. The hardest part is having my mother back, but her not having any idea who I am," I say.

Jacky turns his green eyes on me. It hits me like a ton of bricks, I have another brother. Just one more thing I've been trying to process, over the last couple ofdays.

I don't know how none of us saw it before. Jacky looks so much like Cage and King, just with green eyes and a little darker skin. His hair is also honey brown and not blond like Cage and King's. It's crazy, but now that I know, I can see it so clearly.

"Sorry, I probably shouldn't be whining about this shit with all you and Eva are going through."

I lean in to bump his shoulder. "Are you kidding? You aren't whining. We're all going through a lot."

"Yeah," he says and pulls a face.

"You know, Eva and I are here for you. You've been like a little brother to us forever anyway."

"Thanks. I'm fine."

"Sure, tough guy." I grin. "So… I hear you're thinking about going up north."

"Maybe, Grim has something he needs handled that way andI could use a break from all of this. Why not?"

I shake my head. "I so did not see that coming," I scoff.

"What?"

"Come on, Jacky. Squad. You've always been so sweet. You couldn't even bully me properly. You always brought me treats after you got on my nerves," I say through light laughter.

"I told you. I liked you." He cracks his first real smile, but it fades as quickly as it comes. "I've seen a lot of shit in my life, Sal. I've done some shit too. I belong as much as any of the rest. Youngest member and all."

Sadness takes over me. That's the part that bothered me when I learned he was a member. He's so young. Squad members are a different bred. They're built different, from a broken place.

"Don't feel sorry for me. What doesn't break you makes you stronger. Everyone thinks I was too young to remember what happened to my mom. I remember all that shit."

He lifts his shoulders. "I need to be stronger. Someone has to call in that debt."

Without, saying another word, his gets up and walks away. He doesn't have to explain. Jacky has been an angry boy for years. I know exactly what he means.

Pop may be after Cage, but he has a target on his back as well. My heart aches as I watch jacky's back as he walks across the yard headed for the parking lot. I stare after him long after I hear his bike rev and pull off. I'm so lost staring after him, my phone startles me when it rings.

I look at the screen and smile. It's Mom. Cage got her a phone and programmed all of our numbers into it.

Hope blooms. Maybe she's remembered me or something about us. I take a deep breath before I answer.

"Hey, Mom, what's up?"

"Mom. I'm still trying to get used to that. You two are so grown up and beautiful," she says. "Um, I was wondering if you would like to come have dinner with me? This house… it's… big."

I chuckle despite the disappointment. She still doesn't remember me, my own mom. The one who gave birth to me.

"Cage has always spoiled you with the best."

It's true. The house he bought for her is gorgeous. We never thought to sell it. Eva and I couldn't.

"Um. He's here. Cage. I… uh… he eats with me. If you don't want to come, I understand."

Yeah, this has been one of the biggest adjustments for everyone. Awkward to say the least. Mom is a bit skittish around Cage.

We're all used to the two of them being so in love and wrapped up in each other. It's hard to see Cage look so longingly at his wife as she darts away from him every time, she sees him. Despite the lockdown Cage insisted on moving Mom home.

He's giving her space, although he did move into the house to watch over her. If you ask me, I think he moved in with hopes she'd remember him sooner. He could've had any number of brothers watch the house for him.

King would have made sure she had the best. Heck, Jacky loves my mom. He would have done it in a heartbeat.

"I would love to have dinner with you. I can be there in fifteen. Is it okay if my boyfriend comes along?"

"Oh, okay, yes, that's fine. I'd like that. Maybe you can tell me more about you or more about... *him*."

I smile, knowing which him she's talking about. I get the feeling she wants to know more about Cage than me. "Sure, I'll tell you anything you want to know."

"Thank you, Sal."

I close my eyes as tears spill. My mom used to call me Salalia, not Sal like everyone else. I sweep at my tears.

Give her time.

"No problem, Mom. See you in a bit."

Gutter

I feel like shit as we step into the bedroom Rose offered to us after dinner. I've been so damn distracted, but I can tell Sal really wants to stay.

Terry has been calling more and my demons are barely hinged. I won't sleep tonight for fear they will slip out with Sal's mom and Cage only a few doors away.

"Do you want to talk about it?" Sal says in a quiet tone.

I've known this was coming. She's been burning a hole in the side of my face all night. I hate that I'm adding to her already full plate.

"Not really."

My phone rings, giving me an escape. However, when I see who the caller is, I contemplate taking my chances with Sal. I'm not taking this call, but I still excuse myself as if I am.

"Give me a minute," I murmur.

Stepping out onto the balcony of the bedroom, I take a deep breath and run my hand through my hair. My phone starts to ring again in my other hand, and I swear, I get ready to chuck it.

It's King's name that stops me from tossing the thing. There's still a lot of tension around the club. After all, we still have so many unanswered questions and shit in the shadows.

"Prez," I answer the call.

"Need you back at the clubhouse."

The line goes dead. I groan. Sal isn't going to like this.

I don't like it. I don't want to leave her here alone. Yeah, Cage is here, but I've seen how distracted his is with Rose. Besides, I don't know him well enough.

I want to know Sal is covered while I'm away. No offense, it's just the way it is. I make a quick call to check on something.

"What's up?" Reap answers.

"Have you guys been called in?"

"Grim has. I was going to ride in with him."

Figures. "You mind coming my way to sit with Sal? We're at Cage and Rose's place."

There's a pause for a brief second. When she replies, there's a smile in her voice. "Sure, I can do that."

"Thanks."

Ending the call, I turn and head back inside. "Babe," I call out as I look around, not catching sight of Sal.

She comes from the en suite in her panties and a T-shirt. She looks sad, but I'm failing at knowing how to make that go away. I drag a hand down my face.

"I need to head back to the clubhouse. Reap is coming to hang for a bit."

"I don't need a babysitter, Gutter. Dad and Mom are here."

I close the distance between us and press my lips to her forehead. "Humor me."

"Yeah, okay. You clearly don't know my father."

I don't. Which is why I'm not taking any chances. I have enough at war in my head.

"Darlin', I…" I can't find the right words to tell her all the fucked up shit going on in my head. My phone vibrates and I close my mouth.

I pinch her chin and bring her lips to mine. The kiss starts soft, but I devour her mouth to let her know I'm still in this. I'm shit on figuring out what to do next, but I'm here.

"I'll see you when I get back," I breathe against her lips.

"I love you," she says just above a whisper.

My heart does that thing she always causes. However, the caution in her tone causes my heart to sink at the same time. I need to figure things out soon. My girl is slipping away.

"I love you too, baby girl," I say with all I am. I kiss her forehead again. "Don't wait up."

"You all right, son. You're looking a bit green," Mix says as he walks over to the group of recliners, where I'm sitting and hands me a beer.

The meeting with King was over an hour ago and yet, I'm still here. I haven't been able to force myself back to Sal's parents' house. A glance across the clubhouse tells me I'm not the only one avoiding the place.

I'm glad I followed my first mind and had Reap head over to watch things. Cage has been sitting at the bar nursing a beer since I step out here to the main area.

"Yeah, I'm fine," I say then take a long pull from the offered drink.

"Since Cage says Sal is at his place, I'm assuming there's trouble in paradise. Want to talk about it?"

I grunt. No, I don't. Do I get the feeling he's going to do the talking anyway? Yes, I'm pretty sure he intends to.

When I don't reply, he nods his head toward Cage. "I remember when he first saw Rose. He was a goner." Mix chuckles.

I sit back and make myself comfortable. I don't know why everyone thinks I've become more social now that I'm dating Sal. I want her, not all of this bullshit.

Mix continues to plow right into his story, not picking up on my need to be alone. "You see, Cage knew even then, love requires work and patience. Rose was younger, scared, and had a hell of a lot on her shoulders."

"Can you get to the point?" I huff.

He laughs and levels me with his eyes. "What I'm saying to you, son. Sal is a lot like her mama. It's going to take patience and finesse to keep her. Every relationship has its challenges. Don't look so defeated. Only a few days ago you two looked the happiest I've seen either of you."

I stay silent as I think his words over. Things weren't perfect but they were a hell of a lot better than where they've been headed. It's not Sal's fault, it's mine.

"Son," Mix says breaking into my thoughts. "If you need to talk, I'm here."

I nod as he stands and heads for the bar where Cage is. It's time I take a ride and clear my head. Then, I'll face Salalia.

Unanswered

Gutter

I walk into the office in a suit and tie, with Sal at my side. I asked her to look at our systems and see if there's anything she can do to improve them. It was my way of having her around so I can keep an eye on her.

I have a few meetings I couldn't get out of. I've taken off more than enough time for my personal shit. Work maybe the distraction I need to clear my mind.

"I need to talk to you, Brother," Diggs says the moment he sees me walk in.

From the sound of his voice, I know this isn't going to be a good start to my morning. Brick has us looking into New York's Lost Souls chapter upon Grim's suggestion. King wants to know who in our South Carolina and Georgia chapters needs to be exterminated.

Not to mention, I'm looking for those motherfuckers lurking in the shadows and keeping Sal up at night. A full plate is an understatement.

"Matrix," I call out. "Show Sal to my office. Get her set up. Then head my way."

"Got it, boss."

My phone rings as I go to tell Sal to follow Matrix. I grimace at the call and send it to voicemail. When I turn my attention back to Sal her gaze is on my phone.

"That's the third call you've ignored. Is everything okay?" she asks as she searches my face.

"It's fine. I'll deal with that later." I peck her lips. "Matrix will get you going. I'll check in before my first meeting."

She goes to reply but closes her mouth and nods. Sal turns and follows Matrix to my office. From the greeting they give one and other, I get the feeling they're already acquainted.

My chest loosens a bit. I trust Matrix, but that's me, not Sal. I wouldn't leave her with anyone she's not comfortable with. I'm learning everyday which brothers she tends to stay away from.

There aren't many, but I've noticed her caution with a few. None of those guys are around here. I roll my shoulders and allow more of the tension to release.

I'm lost in thought as I saunter to the meeting room Diggs ducked into. When I step inside, my attention is drawn by the small stack of files lying on the table in front of Diggs. I stop at the table across from him.

"This one has all you need to know about the New York issue. You're not going to like that one. I was ready to roll out, but Brick thinks it's premature," Diggs says as he slides the first file over to me.

I grunt as I pick it up and begin to look through. My brows shut into my hairline. I lift my gaze to Diggs and give him an, *are you shitting me look.*

"Wish that was all a joke, Brother. It seems shits been out of control up there for a while."

"I have some connections up that way. We can have them sit on the club and report back if it becomes a risk to us all," I reply.

"Sounds good. Brick took care of the authorities around the chase. However, we may owe a visit to some noisy motherfucker."

"What's the problem?"

"Some dude has been sniffing around asking questions about that day."

"Get me anything you can on them. I want one of ours to pay the visit, you feel me?"

"You're speaking my language." Diggs words come out so harsh I have to take a deeper look at him.

He looks exhausted and angry. Sugar comes to mind. I don't know if I could function if Sal were in the hospital recovering from someone almost poisoning her to death.

I know it's not that same, they're not a couple, but anyone with eyes sees Diggs is crazy about Sugar as is Axel. Tough shit falling for the same person as your best friend.

"You sure this is where you want to be?" I ask.

"I have the guys covering the Georgia office. I want to get answers."

"That's not what I'm talking about. I can handle all this. Shouldn't you be at the hospital?"

"I'm where I'm needed. I'll talk to you later about needing to assign someone to run the other office. I'll be staying here from now on."

I figured that. A part of me considered asking Sal if she wanted to move to Georgia. I would take over the office there, but all her family is here.

I won't burden her with my consist need for change. As far as Diggs goes, he has been a great business partner. I'm here for whatever.

"We'll do whatever we need." I nod at my own thoughts.

"Same, which brings me to these fuckers. They were able to slip off the grid," he says with a bitter expression as he hands me the next file.

I clench my teeth so hard they nearly break. Hoover and Spencer. I wanted to put them both to ground before the week's ends, but I'm not going to get that lucky.

The more I flip through the file, the more pissed off I get. These two are pure scum. I slap the file closed and toss it down.

"I want to know the second they resurface. Call in all my favors if you need to," I say.

"Don't worry, Brother. I'm on it." He eyes me as he slides the last file in my direction. "This is your personal shit. I'll leave you to do what you want with it."

I look down at the file as if it's burning a hole through the table. I won't look through it. Not now.

"Is he breathing?"

"Yeah, he's alive," Diggs replies.

"That's all I want to know."

I turn and leave the room. Diggs will put that file with all the others. I might look at it, I might not. What I know for sure, it won't be anytime soon.

I have enough shit to handle.

Sal

Something is going on with Gutter. I mean, everyone has been on edge with all the drama going on around the club, but this is something else. Since his two meetings, we've been in his office and he's been so distant.

I think the only reason we have lunch sitting before us is because Matrix asked around for who wanted to order out. Gutter pops a fry into his mouth and chews. Just as he swallows and reaches for another, his phone rings.

That's the fifth call I've watched him ignore. The grimace on his face says so much. I've wanted to push, but I keep telling myself, he'll talk when he's ready.

He pushes his fries away and wipes his mouth with his napkin. He's face is covered in shadows. Almost like he's seen a ghost from the past or a bad memory has surfaced.

I hold back the sigh on the tip of my lips. He has barely touched his food. His thoughts have been occupying him.

"Do you want your tzatziki sauce?" I ask as he stare off into space.

"Huh?" He turns his gaze on me and it's evident he didn't hear my question.

"Do you want your sauce?" I repeat and point to the little container.

He shakes his head and hands it over. "We should head back to the clubhouse. I need to change and it's safer to be there."

"Will you eat when we get there?"

He frowns and looks down at his mostly untouched food as if confused. "Maybe."

This is what I mean. I know there's more on his mind than he's letting on.

I've been feeling like he's shutting me out. One moment he's as attentive as can be, the next... I don't know what to think.

Suddenly, he stands and start to toss the food he hasn't eaten. I lose my own appetite watching him. I toss my food along with his and start to pack my things.

I have my back to him when he comes up behind me and wraps his arms around me. I bit my lip and close my eyes. I need to have patience.

"I love you," he murmurs into the top of my hair.

This new roller coaster has my head spinning

My Mom, Dad?

Sal

It's been two weeks since we found out my mom and dad are both still alive. Two weeks, since Eva was kidnapped, and I've never felt more helpless in my life.

"Shut up, shut up, shut up," I mutter to myself as I flip through a magazine while I sit with Sugar. My thoughts are louder than any have a right to be.

Ugh! To top it all off, Gutter is becoming more and more detached. I don't think it has anything to do with me. The haunted look in his eyes most nights tells me it's something more. I'm just frustrated that he won't let me in.

Add to it all, the fact that I'm trapped here in this clubhouse with all my problems glaring at me. I think I'm going to go crazy. That one trip to Gutter's security firm wasn't enough.

I need out of here. I can only dream. Since Eva was kidnapped, King has been a beast about our safety and knowing where his girls are at all times. It's driving us all nuts.

Not that Eva or Misty want to do much these days. I'm guaranteed to find the two of them doing one of three things, sleeping, eating, or puking. Trust me, I don't want to be around for any of those.

I've spent a lot of time here in Sugar's room. Or should I say, her makeshift hospital room here in the club. She still hasn't woken. Diggs and Axle rose hell in the hospital until they released Sugar into our care, thanks to Thor.

"You going to sit in here all day?" Reap asks from the door. "It's a nice day out. You could use some fresh air for yourself."

I look at Sugar. "Thought I'd spent a little time with her before heading out there."

Reap moves into the room. "I think they would've busted her out of that hospital if they didn't release her," she says as she sits in the other chair in the room.

The infirmary wasn't good enough for Sugar. Axle insisted she have her own room. Diggs has spared no expense to bring in a doc to see to her around the clock care. The good doctor, Pike Fisher aka Thor, is an interesting character. Then again, Lost Souls come in all shapes, sizes, and professions.

"You and me both. At least Thor seems hopeful. He says he expects Sugar to wake and have a full recovery with time. Her body is resting and taking its time," I reply.

"What's going on with you and Gutter?"

I blow out a breath. "I have no idea, Erica. One minute everything is fine, the next he seems so angry or distant. Or… I can't put my finger on it."

"You know the brother had a lot of shit going on in his head before you guys hooked up."

"Yeah, I got that, but that's also what we started our relationship on. Honesty and transparency. Something's tearing him up. I feel like this is something I can help with if he'll—"

I cutoff before I can expose anymore of my thoughts. Erica narrows her eyes at me and nods to herself. Turning, she leans in to kiss Sugar's cheek before turning back to me.

She bounces up to stand. "Listen, you're coming with me. Sug will be fine. I saw Thor and Axel headed this way. King stopped them for a sec but I'm sure they'll be here any minute," she says.

I purse my lips but toss the magazine down and follow her. The aura around here is so somber. I need to get away to breathe.

It doesn't help that my past is always haunting my brain. That crazy bastard and his friend are still out there, and I have no idea what they want. I don't even know where they are.

"Fix your face," Reap commands and pitches my side as we walk outside. "Look at that. Sunshine. Enjoy it."

"Yo, Reap. Come here," Grim calls across the yard.

She rolls her eyes but takes off in his direction. I smile at my friend she seems so happy those days. Grim really is her other half.

"Perfection takes time, right?" I mutter to myself.

My mind turns back to the two out there lurking. I get this eerie feeling as if I'm being watched even now. I wish I knew more.

Gutter won't talk about it. He keeps telling me not to worry. That's total bullshit. How can I not worry?

They broke into my place, went through my things, trashed my stuff. The worst part is, I don't know if that was the real Marvin Hoover in my place or the bastard who raped me, Philip Spencer.

I'm creeped out either way but knowing it could be Philip turns my blood cold. I rub my temples and take a seat on the back step of the deck, staring out into the large backyard area. Eva and my mom are walking side by side.

Two weeks and it still hurts like hell that she doesn't remember us. I've tried repeatedly to get her to remember me, somehow. I've told her stories; I've shown her pictures. None of that has seemed to work.

My heart breaks every time she looks at me with those sad eyes. As if she's disappointing me by not being able to remember. I can see how much she tries. I'm disappointed, sure, but I hurt more for the last six years of her life that she's lost.

I hurt for Dad. Cage looks like a wounded puppy every time Mom looks up at him in fear. Dad's a large man. Mom is short like Eva. She flinches every time Cage towers over her. Yet, you can see she's curious about him. That magnetic pull is still lurking between them, I saw it the night I spent with them.

I think she's just scared. I know the scars don't help. Cage will always be a handsome man. However, his right side is a mess.

It looks like someone dragged his face across the pavement, which is basically what they said happened. It's painful to look at if you knew him before, but his true good looks and big heart shine through it all.

I watch my parents and wonder if they will make it through this. If there's no hope for Mom and Dad, then I don't know how Gutter and I can hope to make it through all of this. I release a heavy sigh and look away from two of the most important women in my life.

"This shit ain't easy," the a rough gravelly voice comes from behind me.

I look over my shoulder to find the only man I've ever called Dad. At first glance, Cage stands there looking like the pillar of strength I remember. Upon further inspection, I see the slight trimmer in his right arm. It still doesn't change the fact that he's the greatest Dad in the world.

He nods at Mom and Eva. "You've been out here for about an hour now, staring and lost in your thoughts. Dangerous, darling," Cage says, turning to lock eyes with me. "I know how that mind works. You'll drive yourself crazy trying to fix everything. Some things you're gonna to have to learn to let go. This is one of 'em."

I shake my head, feeling the tears burn the backs of my eyes. "There's so much going on. If I could just do something," I say, feeling like the little girl I used to be when Cage would fix my little world.

He moves to sit next to me on the step. He rests his big arms on his thighs, letting his hands hang. Leaning over, he bumps me with his shoulder, bringing a small smile to my lips.

"What's going on with your mama is something we all have to be patient with. You think I don't want to hold my woman in my arms and hear her laughter ring out around me. I'd die for that sweet sound. Just to know I brought it to her lips would make me a happy man," he snorts and gives a small grin.

He rubs his jaw and continues. "That boy, Gutter. Don't know him well enough yet, but your brother says he's loyal." Cage chuckles. "King wants to kick his ass for touching you, but he still believes he deserves to be here.

"I trust King's judgement. I think I would've made the same decision when it comes to Gutter. It's in his eyes. He's a Lost Soul, all right. I don't doubt his role in the Squad either."

He takes a pause and looks me in my eyes. He's probing. I don't have it in my to shut him out.

He continues. "I know you're not telling us something, little one. It's written all over both of your faces. That boy is determined to make whatever it is right. He asked King to trust him. Said we don't want to know and if we find out the truth, it should be from you.

"Turned around and told us, don't fucking ask you either." Cage gives a full belly laugh. "The boy has a lot of balls, I tell you that much. You're my baby girl. I raised you as my own. I know you better than most."

He gives another pause, reaching to cup my face. There's hurt in his eyes. In this moment, I want to tell him everything. I just can't find the words.

He clenches his jaw as he reads something in the depths of my eyes. It's his way.

"I'm so sorry I wasn't here for you. Whoever the bastard is that touched you. He's a dead man," he says, without me telling him a word.

I throw myself in his arms and start to sob. I've needed this for so long, my daddy. Between Gutter and my daddy, I know all will be right in my world.

"I love you so much," I sob through my tears.

"You have no idea how much I love you. That boy loves you too, but he's one of the truly lost, Sal. You don't give up on him. Women like you and your mama are what keep us from going over the edge.

"I see him struggling. He'll find his way to you," he says with so much reassurance I truly believe him.

Gutter

I push off the wall just inside the back door. I'd been looking for Sal. It's been a hard week and I just wanted to try to talk to her.

I know I'm fucking things up. I just haven't figured out how to stop. My demons are riding my ass and I don't want to drag her into that.

Seeing her with her dad twists a knife in my chest. Cage has been nothing but welcoming to me. I'm learning to understand him, and I've already developed a deep respect for him.

I've watched him with Sal, Eva, Reap, and Misty. I've also watched him with his wife. He tries not to get too close, to give Rose space, but he's always there, watching over her. It's how I've become with Sal over the last few weeks.

She sees too much when she looks at me. I fear what she'll really see if I let her look too deeply. My past has come back with a vengeance. I can't say the last time I've slept.

I usually lie in bed until Salalia falls asleep. Then I sit there staring at the ceiling, doubting myself, my future, my happiness. Terry has called every day since we arrived in South Carolina. He has left a message each time, but like a coward I won't listen to them.

I can't handle all of that now. I may have gotten Sal home safely, but there's still a threat out there I need to handle. That Spencer fucker is a slippery bastard, but I'll find him. He's bound to fuck up.

"You got that for me?" King grumble beside me.

I turn to face him, nod, and reach into my cut. I pull out the drive with everything Ramon and Stormy sent me. They found a few guys still lurking around the B&B.

"It's essentially the same shit Grim and Reap got from Blaze. Devil's Masons are getting behind some motherfucker," I say.

"Pop, that motherfucker is Pop. I know it is," he growls.

I shrug. "Still not getting a name from any of them. It does sound like he's bringing in some muscle to help with this. Not talking about your friend from Brazil, either."

King's jaw tightens, he rolls his neck. Ignoring my statemnt, he looks into my eyes. "Fix whatever you fucked up with Sal. I hate seeing her like this," King demands, before walking off.

I huff and turn back to look outside. Sal is now standing with Eva, Cage, and Rose. Rose looks like a frightened bird as she tries not to look up at Cage.

I release another huff and rub my forehead. I couldn't handle if Sal were ever to look at me with that type of fear. I never want to hurt her and have her look at me that way but letting go isn't an option. I have to figure this out before I cause the most important person in my life pain.

"*Fuck*," I grunt under my breath.

CHAPTER THIRTY-THREE

Our Family

Sal

Big strong arms go around my waist, bringing a smile to my face. I tilt my head back to rest on his shoulder and Gutter places a kiss on my forehead. It's been two days since my talk with daddy.

I've given Gutter his space. Every time I think he's about to open up to me, he shuts down again. I'm trying to be patient.

"I thought we could go shopping for somethings for the apartment tomorrow," he murmurs.

"I thought you wanted to wait until King called this lockdown off." I wrinkle my brows.

Gutter gives an unusual smile that takes my breath away. "What do you think all the partying is about?" he asks.

I palm my forehead. "I wasn't thinking. I was lost in my own thoughts. I just wandered out here, really. I needed some fresh air."

He turns me in his arms, lifting my face to his. "I know I haven't been what you need. I have a lot going on in my head. It's grating on my fucking nerves that we…" He stops, his nostrils flaring. "Just know I want to make you happy," he says while holding my gaze.

"I told you before I'm not hard to please. Just stop shutting me out," I plead.

He closes his eyes. After releasing a long deep breath, he opens them again. "Take a walk with me."

I nod, lacing my fingers with his. Everyone's buzzing about, getting the grills started, lighting a few bonfires, and setting chairs around in little groups and cliques.

I smile to myself when I see the Squad forming their own group. I now know who all the members are. I have to say some surprised me, others not so much.

"You're lucky to have so many people who care about you," Gutter speaks, drawing my attention back to him.

"Yeah, I guess I am. It's been a while since I've had this feeling. Having Mom and Dad back has changed a lot," I muse.

"I bet. How are you holding up?" he asks with sincerity in his eyes.

"Honestly, some days are better than others. I swear, Mom remembered something today. Then just like that." I snap my fingers. "It was gone."

"Yeah, that has to be hard on her. I know she wants to remember you guys."

"I just wish there was more we could do."

"Just keep at it. You don't want to have regrets later," he says, the emotions in his voice catching me off guard.

We stop a ways from everyone else. I turn to look up at him. For once, his face isn't totally guarded. I'm hopeful he will let me in.

"Do you have regrets?" I ask cautiously.

He closes his eyes and nods. "I have a lot of regrets. They're eating me alive," he responds. When he opens his eyes, I see a sea of emotions running through them. "I tried to commit suicide once. It was the same night my cousin, Terry tried. He was a little more successful at it than I was."

I gasp and move closer to wrap my arms around his waist. "Is he okay? I'm confused."

"The only friend we had as kids found him in a tub of his own blood. When Terry is fucked up, he has this mean streak. If he's hurting, he wants you to hurt too. It's one of the reasons I needed a clean break from him.

"He chose to take his life and he wanted to leave me a reminder of it. I was supposed to have taken off out of town. I guess he thought it would haunt me that I left and couldn't get to him on time.

"He texted me pictures of the fucked up mess he pulled. I didn't get them until the next morning, when I woke in a hotel from my own attempt." He blows out a long breath and rubs his forehead. "That shit haunts me, already. Now, Terry has been calling me.

"I don't know what he wants, and I don't know if I want to be pulled into all that shit again. People change, but when you're as fucked up as we were." He shakes his head. "I just don't know. I can't go through any of that shit again. It all still fucks with my head."

"Wow, I… I can't imagine going through that." I purse my lips and look away. I know he's not going to want to hear what I'm about to say. "Pierson, what if he has changed? What if he's reaching out to you because he's changed?"

"What if he hasn't?" he says with so much bite in his voice, I turn to look up at him again.

I lift my hand. "Wait, just hear me out. You said yourself you two were like brothers. You were all each other had. Yeah, things got bad, but you're all he has and he's the only family you have… other than me.

"What if we have a baby, like Eva and King? Don't you want your only blood to be a part of that? If you can fix it, you should fix it."

I shiver as his face turns cold. I'm shut out again. I can't read any of his thoughts. I bite my lip, thinking I just may have said too much.

He shakes his head. "I would never have children," he says.

I whip my head back like I've been slapped. I don't even realize I've taken a step back until a breeze seems to pass through us. I know his childhood wasn't the greatest, but it never occurred to me he wouldn't want children.

I kick myself inwardly for not taking more time to get to know the man I've falling so deeply for. I don't even think he takes in the fact that I'm drawing into myself. He's too far gone in his own head. I can now see the wheels turning.

"You haven't even begun to see how fucked up I am. I would fuck a kid up, trying to play Daddy. You just said it, if something happened to me, I have no one. My kid would be fucked." He shakes his head adamantly.

"No, I won't do that. As for Terry, I… fuck, I just don't know." He passes his hand through his hair.

"You don't have to decide tonight," I reply. "Listen, we can go shopping tomorrow. I'm going to head over and sit with Sugar. You have fun with the guys."

His eyes grow wide. It must finally hit him that I'm upset. I've lost my appetite and I'm not in the mood for fun. I just want to be alone with my thoughts.

"Sal," he starts, but I hold up my hand.

"We'll talk later. I'm not feeling so well," I say over my shoulder, already in motion.

Gutter

Fuck, fuck, fuck.

That was not the way I expected this to go. I don't even know what just happened. I wanted to open up and tell Salalia what's been going on with me. I didn't think she would take Terry's side.

I puff out my lips in exasperation. I don't know how to do this relationship shit. I feel like it's over before it has gotten started. Nothing I do seems to be right, and we have too much shit going on.

Prez handled some of the shit headed our way, but there's more just lurking. I haven't felt this out of control of my surroundings and life in so long. Fuck, I have no idea how Sal is going to handle living with me.

"So, you thought love was easy." I turn my head to find Cage watching me closely.

"No, but I sure as fuck didn't think it would be this hard."

He throws his head back and laughs. When his laughter dies down, he hands over one of the beers in his hands. I take it and welcome a long pull. It's been a long fucking day.

"I hear my little girl is moving in with you," he states more than asks.

I nod. "Yeah, that's the plan if I stop fucking it up."

He chuckles and pats me on the back. I turn to look him in the eyes. Cage is a big and tall man like me.

"Sal is the easiest to please out of my girls. She has a need to understand everything around her so she can fix it. She'll take anything she can apart to piece it back together," he says the words as if they have so much more meaning, so I stop to think them over.

"Does that mean she feels the need to fix me?"

"Eventually, she'll pick at all that shit you're hiding away. Then she'll figure out how to set you right," Cage says, then furrows his brows. The way he stares into my eyes makes me feel like he can see through me.

"You sure you can handle that? I see those demons swimming. She's going to strip you bare. It's what those women do. It's how her mama made a real man out of me."

"I'm not worried about me. I'm worried about dumping all that shit on her," I say gruffly.

"Now see, that would be your problem, son," he grunts and shakes his head. "I know something happened to my baby girl while I was gone, but she's still a survivor. Sal does what she needs to survive. Even when she's motionless, she's in motion."

"Yeah, I get that." I sigh heavily.

"I say we get over there and get some of that barbeque before the rest of 'em polish it all off." He nods at the lines forming by the grills.

"All right." I bob my head and take another pull of my beer.

"Oh, and Son," Cage calls. I look at him again. "I'm not King. I won't be asking Sal shit. I'm telling you. Before the night is over, you're going to tell me what the fuck happened to her."

"Figured that was coming," I snort, humorlessly.

"Damn right."

My Baby Girl

King

I saw my father when he stormed out of the club like a bat out of hell. I'd gone to follow him until Mix stopped me told me to let it go. I almost didn't until I saw Rose staring after Dad with worry on her face.

"Do you know what happened?" Rose says from the seat beside me in my truck.

"Not sure," I reply, but it's a lie. Mix told me Dad had a conversation with Gutter.

"He looked so angry. Do you think he went to the house?"

I can't help the smile that comes to my face. Rose is worried about Dad. That's a good thing.

I'm hopeful for my dad. He loves this woman. I take my eyes off the road to glance at her.

"He just might be. I'll stay around until he shows up if not," I say.

"You don't have to but thank you."

"It's not a problem. We used to hang out a lot. You would bake and cook and shit. You also kept me from being a knucklehead."

"What about the girls? Did they spend that time with us?"

"Not Sal so much as Eva. Sal was away at school most of the time."

I catch her nod as I look away from the road. The confusion in her expression makes my chest tight. She's trying so hard to remember. It's written all over her face.

"Why would I send my child away? That doesn't feel like me."

"Oh, you were against it. Dad had the hardest time showing you it was the best thing for Sal. I think you guys took more trips to visit Sal at school than anything.

"In the end, you agreed it was right for her. She's so damn smart and the schools around here weren't doing much to keep her interested," I explain.

"That would make sense, but Eva seems to be very smart too. Why not send them both? They would've protected each other."

I shake my head. "Eva is different. Sal was fine..." I trail off as it hits me how much of a lie that is. She wasn't fine, at least not in college. That's when things changed.

"Eva is always in her own bubble. Sal has this thing. She's recording everything around her even when she and everyone else thinks she's not. It's a hell of a survival skill.

"I think Dad saw that as a protection mechanism. Something to help Sal adapt and handle herself," I share.

"She's not adapting now," Rose says matter of factly. "I don't remember her well, but I sense something is wrong or... off, maybe."

"A mother always knows." I give are a sad smile.

"All of you guys are close to Cage? I mean, he seems like a good father. He has been good to my girls?" I hear the real question in her voice and the defensiveness of a mother.

"Rose, when my daddy was chasing you, I wasn't that much younger than you. I thought he was crazy. I was even angry for a bit.

"I got over it and we became real friends. Now, when it comes to my daddy and your girls. He has always been the father they needed and would put a motherfucker to ground for thinking of hurting one of them.

"I may know where a few bodies are. Trust, there were a few who wanted to test the theory and Daddy made good on his word every time. Eva and Sal think Cage hangs the moon, because for them he would. They are always safe with him," I say.

She blows out a breath. "I feel safer with him at the house than not. I hope he's there."

The smile returns to my lips. Yeah, there's hope for my pops. I think the old Rose is somewhere in there.

It's not possible to forget a love like theirs. She'll come around. We all need to give it time.

I pull up into the massive driveway and Cage's bike comes into view. Lights are on throughout the house. One of the garage doors is open.

"You want me to come in with you?"

She stares out the windshield. "Um, no. You go home to that pretty girl of yours."

"You need me, call. I'm always here for you and Dad. No matter what the problem is."

"Thank you, King. I hope we can be friends again."

"We are that and more. You never tried to replace my mama or disrespect her memory. I have a deep respect for you because of that."

"When we respect what was before us. It makes us care for what we have," she says the words so easily, I would swear she remembers saying them to me a million timres.

However, the way she turns so nonchalantly to get out of my truck, I know she's only saying them as a reflex. Again, I'm hopeful. It will all come back.

Cage

I crouch in front of the bike I'm trying to work on in the garage of my home, shredded to pieces. I've walked every each of this home remembering when I kept my girls safe. When I had no doubts about every detail of their lives.

I played this all wrong. In hindsight I see everything I could've done differently. My baby girl was raped.

"Son of a bitch. Why?" I growl brokenly as I tug at my hair.

I knew it from the look in her eyes. However, hearing Gutter rundown what happened, I feel like I failed my baby girl. I failed Rose.

I haven't felt like this since I thought I would lose Rose to that accident, but this is a different kind of hurt. I promised Rose I would protect her and our girls.

I never should have hid away. Six years was too long. King had so much on his shoulders. Sending Salalia to school was my idea. I kept an eye on her studies and boarding every school year.

I would have done the same when she went off to College. I've always been so protective of my girls. Sal is tough, but she's always been so innocent and trusting too.

"Cage?" Rose's soft voice breaks though my thoughts.

I pull my shit together and stand to my full height. She takes a step back out of the garage door. I release a long breath.

I wish she would stop flinching away from me. I would never hurt her. The thought of it makes me sick to my stomach.

"Are… are you all right?" she asks cautiously.

I nod my head and swipe at the moisture in the corners of my eyes. "I'll be fine."

Rage fills me as I think of all the ways I plan to make those motherfuckers suffer. Especially the one who put his hands on Sal. When I notice Rose shrinking back, I reel it in.

I look around. "We have a bunch of photo albums in here. The ones I was telling you about. Would you like to sit with me to look through them?" I pause and redirect. "Or I can get them out and you can have a look at them."

She makes her way further into the garage. "No, no. We can look together. I probably would be lost looking at them by myself."

I nod and wave her over. "Come on over, we'll take a few books inside." I lift my chin toward the house.

She comes over as I move to the cabinets holding the albums and pull a few out. I hand her two and take out a another four to carry in myself.

Rose settles on the couch, once we get into the living room area. I sit beside her and place my stack of albums on the coffee table. Cautiously, I reach for the one on top of the two in her lap and flip it open. Rose looks up at me for a long moment.

I hold my breath, hoping she remembers something about me. After a few beats she shakes her head and looks down at the photos. She reaches to run a finger over one photo.

It's of the girls. My heart breaks as I look at Sal's bright open smile. She looks so innocent and happy.

She moves her hand to a picture of all the girls dressed in Lost Souls softball uniforms. Eva, Sal, Misty, Erica and Sugar are all filthy with smiles on their faces. I remember that game. People are always underestimating those girls.

They are fierce in their own right, but together they are an unexpected force. They made me proud that day. Rose releases a breath, pulling me from my musing.

"I wish I could remember them like this. They played softball?"

"Sure did. We coached them. You swing a mean bat yourself." I wink at her. "If you check the front closest in the foyer, you'll find your slugger."

"I'll have to check that out." She gives a soft smile and looks back at the photos. I watch as she chews on her lip, waiting for her to ask the question I see swimming in her eyes. "I... um. You're not their father, are you?"

"No, not biologically, but in every other way, I've been their Daddy for years."

She nods and looks up at me. "Do you know what happened to their father?"

"Yes. I'll tell you, but can we hold off on that? It's been a long night."

She reaches to cups the smooth side of my face. I hold stock still. I don't want to send her running for the hills.

Rose searches my face with her pretty brown ones. It takes the strength of God, his angels and all the disciplines to keep my ass from taking her lips. I miss my wife so fucking much.

"Whatever's hurting you, it has to get better," she says. "You seem like such a strong man."

I grasp her hand and turn my face slowly. That startled look comes to her eyes and I think better of kissing her palm. I smile and turn my attention back to the photos as I release her hand.

While we look through our past, I vow to right everything that has happened in the gape in between all of those good memories and the painful ones I wasn't around to prevent.

Our Place

Gutter

"It's not much," I mutter.

I thought I was nervous the first time I took Sal to my room at the clubhouse. I'm ready to shit a brick as I open the front door to my apartment. Don't get me wrong. It's a nice place.

It's clean and the layout is nice. However, it's still the box I signed the lease for. other than some professional enhancements no one knows about. I can't help feeling this place is going to reveal my secrets.

Sal tugs at her T-shirt and twirls her fingers in it as we stand in the foyer. I shove my keys into my pocket and reach for her waist with the other hand. She stiffens a little and my heart sinks.

She hasn't said much to me since our fight yesterday. Fight, I think that's what happened. I hadn't notice how bad it was until the end of the night.

Sal slept damn near on the edge of the bed away from me. Normally, she falls asleep across my chest. I played our fight over and over in my head while I sat awake.

Definitely a fight and I'm totally in the doghouse. I keep fucking up. Hopefully, being here in the apartment—without a ton of people around—we can figure some things out.

I follow as she moves forward into the place and stops in the open kitchen and living area.

"Wow," Sal says as she looks around. "Pierson. I... wow. You weren't lying."

"We can get whatever you want. You know, make the place feel like home for you. The couch and TV can go too, if you want to replace them."

She turns and looks up at me with a weak smile. "We'll build around them. Sometimes all you need is a little change."

Her words hit their mark. I'm going to have to change to make this work. I know this, doesn't make it any easier.

I take a breath and try to push forward. "We need some place to eat. I should probably get some pots and things for the kitchen." I place my hands on her hips.

She ducks her head away and the sting of her words runs deeper. "I'll make a list and we can head to the stores. It's way better than the clubhouse. It will be good to finally get out of there."

It runs across my mind to sit her down and talk about what could happen with us living here together. It's right on the tip of my tongue, but she spins out of my hold and starts to move through the apartment, popping her head into rooms and closet.

"For tonight, we need bedding and towels and things. Hey, no radio?"

I frown. "No."

She takes a pause in the doorway of the third bedroom. Spinning to face me, she gives me a quizzical look. At first, I think she's going to drop it like she's been doing everything else.

Something I've been grateful for, but she presses forward with her thoughts this time.

"What's that about? Why'd you say it like that?"

I blow out a breath. I don't want to add to the tension so I give her an answer. Staring down at my feet, I begin to speak.

"My stepmother used us as show pieces. We were the entertainment. Terry and I can both sing and play instruments.

"Listening to music in the truck with you, singing for you. Those are things I'm doing solely for you. I'm not big on listening to music for pleasure. It jogs memories sometimes. Especially if I'm listening to some random station or something," I say.

"Oh, I didn't know. Music calms me. I'll make do with headphone from now on."

"You don't have to. We'll get a system for the place."

Sal closes the gap between us. "You don't have to do that. I'll be fine."

"It's our place. If music calms you, we'll have a system. You can have this room, by the way. It can be your office," I say, pointing to the room at her back.

"Add office furniture to list."

I hold her gaze. "I'll replace it all, you just say the word, but if you want anything from your place in New York, I'll arrange that too," I offer.

Watching her place be invaded couldn't have been easy. I've been thinking about this for the last two weeks. I don't want her to have any triggers here. This is a safe space.

"Mix already sent someone for the things I need. I'll need to get some clothes to replace my wardrobe, but my tech stuff is already on the way. Thanks for being so thoughtful."

I place my forehead to hers. The surge of energy between us starts to fill the space, but she turns away breaking the connection. I throw my head back and stare up at the ceiling.

"Gutter," she whispers.

I turn to look at her sad face. "Yeah, baby girl?"

"I don't think—"

Her phone chimes cutting her off. She pulls the phone from her pocket with a grimace on her lips. However, her lips turn up and she looks at me with bright eyes when she looks up from the device.

"Sugar's showing signs of responsiveness," she says as she types back quickly. Her shoulders slump. "Eva says they're not letting anyone in her room for now. Thor is running tests."

"We can go shopping and head over after we get everything back here. That should give them some time to sort things out and then you can check in on her if you like, if they'll allow."

"Yes, please." She throws herself into my arms and hugs me around the neck.

I'm a Lost Soul, of course, I'm going to take advantage of this moment. This is the most she's said to me all day. I take her lips and force back all my doubts and demons.

She whimpers into my mouth and reaches to link her fingers into my hair. I groan and push her back against the nearest wall, lifting her onto my waist. I'm so fucking hard.

Sal starts to grind against me, causing my need to shoot through the roof. I palm her ass and claw at her tight jeans as I grind back into her. When I break the kiss, she whimpers and bites her lip as she gives me a lust filled look. As soon as I go to tug her lip loose, my phone rings.

"You have to be fucking kidding me," I growl.

I roll my eyes when Sal unwraps her legs from around my waist and her heavy boot hit the floor. The sound is like a door closing. The moment is gone. I loathe this person, no matter who the call is from and I have this sinking feeling in my gut telling me just who it is.

Sure enough my past strikes again. I bare my teeth at the phone as I send the call to voicemail. What doesn't he get?

"Baby, I—"

"I'm going to make that list. We should head out. We have a lot to get."

She turns and heads toward the front of the apartment. Frustration runs through me. And as if the world knows my mood has turned to shit, text messages start to file in left and right.

Sal

This day is ending on a sour note. We've done all of our shopping and put a lot in place, but it's all been done with me silently brooding. I have to say, I'm glad we were interrupted. We're not going to solve our problems with sex.

I'm still pissed from our fight. Earlier was a small moment of weakness. I was vulnerable after getting the news about Sugar. My mistake.

I chew on the last bites of my burrito like I'm chewing on cardboard. Nothing has any favor to me, or it might be that I'm too busy in my thoughts to taste a thing I've eaten. I'm startled out of my musing as the lights flash.

It's been raining since we got the last of our things in the building. Thankfully, we didn't get caught in the downpour. However, we decided against heading out to the clubhouse in the storm. Word is, Sugar hasn't woken yet anyway. The lights flash again, and I groan, I didn't think to get candles.

"There's a backup generator," Gutter says. "Come on, I'll show you where the flashlights are in case it ever doesn't kick in."

I get up and follow him. He stops at the closet in the hall and opens the door. Running a hand through his hair, he looks at me as if he's thinking something over.

He reaches for the top shelf and pulls down a flashlight before turning it on. "This isn't just a closet. Step inside," he says.

I stare at him for a beat before cautiously stepping in. He shines the light ahead of me, while reaching around me after entering behind me. A lever comes into view as he grasps and turns it. I take in a sharp breath when a door opens to some sort of control room.

This is the last thing I was expecting. I quickly realize there are screens revealing every room in the apartment. Gutter's eyes are on me as I move around and take it all in.

"It's a safe room. It has its own generator if all else fails. If something were ever to happen and I'm not home, you bring your ass in here and lock the door. You feel me?"

"Yeah, but…" I shake my head. "Never mind."

"What?"

"Nothing."

He closes the space between us. "I'll always come for you. You just sit tight and wait for me."

"And if you don't come?"

He shakes his head. "Never gonna happen."

"But if you don't?"

He frowns and laces his fingers with mine, tugging me across the room. "We'll get you printed. The lockbox only opens by fingerprint. Not that you will ever need to unlock it, but I keep the guns in here."

He turns and pinches my chin between his fingertips. "I'll be there when you need me."

He kisses my forehead. I can't help wondering if that includes emotionally and physically, because we're falling out of sync. Whatever, he's been keeping to himself has changed us and his fears are only widening that gape.

Don't give up, Sal.

CHAPTER THIRTY-FIVE

Settling In

Sal

Gutter enters the office he gave me and taps the doorjamb. I look up to find a shy boyish smile on his lips and it hits me how much I miss him. We've been in the same apartment together for three days and yet it feels like we've been a part for five years.

"Hey, come take a break."

I narrow my eyes. He's up to something. I glance at the clock on my computer screen. I've done it again. Gotten loss in my work and forgotten to eat.

"Okay," I murmur and stand. It's when I walk pass him out of the room, I notice he looks nervous or something.

I shrug it off as him being cautious around me because I haven't been talking to him much. When we're at the club we don't even speak. Gutter seems to be spending a lot of time with King, Mix, Brick, and my dad lately. Not sure what that's about.

When I step out of the hallway into the open living, dining area, I stumble to a stop. Tears well in my eyes and I feel like a total bitch. There's a reason I fell in love with this man.

I'm completely blown away. Before me is a candlelit table with dinner set for two. It's the same dining table that arrived yesterday, the one he let me pick out for his place.

When we arrive three days ago, I couldn't believe how bare the place was. I think his room at the clubhouse has more character. When I say he had the bare necessities, that was all he had. A couch, TV, and in each bedroom a bed. That's all.

I'd heard him banging around in the kitchen, but I was so engulfed in my work. I hadn't let the scent of food or what he could be doing sink in. As I said, I tend to get lost sometimes when in front of a computer.

All of this says he's trying. He pulls my chair for me and I can't help the tremble in my lips. I suck it up and take a seat before he sees my reaction.

"It smells great."

"Thanks," he replies.

We both dig in. My mouth waters as I open for the first bite and it doesn't disappoint. I moan around the fork and nod my head. It's delicious.

"This is so good."

He smiles, I mean, a real smile and I'm stunned for a moment. It's so gorgeous. He should smile like this all the time. My God.

I reach for my glass of water and take a sip. I'm forced to look around at the romantic display before me to keep from melting into my seat as I look at him. I don't think he has come to play with me tonight.

That smile alone is the perfect weapon. I gaze at him again and long to kiss him. What was I so mad about again?

Oh, right... babies. I want them and he doesn't. My frustration returns. More so with myself.

I promised myself to him without knowing him. Now, I'm in love with someone that doesn't want the things I want.

I push those feelings down and continue to eat. This silence thickens and not in a good why. After about twenty minutes of quiet, I try to think of something to say to lighten the mood.

Here goes nothing, I think before I speak.

Gutter

Things have been strained between Salalia and me. Ever since the barbeque, she's closed me out. We've been living together in the apartment for three days. It's suffocating enough in this place without this tension.

I thought making her dinner would help break the ice so we could finally get to the bottom of this. I think I would rather her pick me apart than have to deal with this. This isn't the comfortable silence we had in the beginning of our relationship. This is my girl closing me out. I need to fix us.

"It's so romantic."

Sal smiles as she looks over the dinner table for the millionth time. I've noted her surprise from the time she saw the table. I think this was the last thing she was expecting when I asked her to take a break.

"You say that as if you're surprised," I murmur, after swallowing a fork full of lasagna.

"Hell, yeah, I'm surprised." She giggles and it's so sweet.

I reach to brush my fingers across her cheek. Her cheeks warm with color. It's gorgeous on her chocolate skin.

"I promised I would do my best at this." I wave my fork between us. "I'm trying."

Salalia's eyes soften, and her smile grows. "Thank you."

"I was hoping we could figure things out. You know, fix what went wrong," I try, feeling completely out of my element.

When she looks away, my heart sinks. We're back to square one. Yes, her body reacts to my touch. That chemistry is still burning between us, but something is on her mind. Something she won't spit out and tell me.

"Can we just... Pierson, this night has been perfect so far. Can we just enjoy it and see where things go from there?" she says softly.

I nod my head, frustrated, but willing to do as she asks. We live together, we have to figure this out eventually. I'm not much of a patient man, but for her I'll be just about anything.

So, for now, we eat in silence. Cage, King, Brick, and Mix, spent hours prepping me for this. I'll just try another route.

Sal

We finish dinner in silence, and I feel terrible for it. I have so many questions in my head. I just don't know how to deal with them.

I don't know where we should go from here, but I don't think I can bare going separate ways. It's the reason I don't want to ruin tonight.

"Help me with the dishes." Gutter breaks through my thoughts. I get ready to offer to do them, but the grin on his face says he just wants me to tag along.

As I enter the kitchen, he lifts me onto the countertop. He brushes my bare thighs with his hands as he pulls away. After my request to just enjoy dinner, something changed. He's been placing subltle touches to every bare surface that's exposed by my short sundress.

I've been in a constant blaze of fire from the inside out. Every place he has touched, aches for a repeat. I know I'll breakdown soon.

He licks his lips and it's as if he has licked my pussy lips as well. I cross my legs and squeeze. I can't bare being this close to him.

I can't breathe. I just feel. I feel him everywhere.

I have to have him before I lose my mind, but I bite my lip. I'll wait, waiting will make this so much better.

We haven't touched since we moved into this apartment. I see the hungry stares he gives me. I've been processing it all. Gutter hit me with a heavy blow the other night.

Yet, my body doesn't care about any of that. It wants the man standing before me with those hungry, piercing blue-gray eyes. Yes, this wait will be worth it, and my brain is sure to short circuit.

As if reading my mind, he says, "When I finally take you, you will lose your sanity. Don't worry. I promise." His rough voice washes over me.

I'm stunned as I watch him move away from me to the sink. I blink rapidly, trying to get my brain to restart. He's giving off that vibe from that day in the clearing. That side of him that exudes sex and power.

I'm no match for that side of him. The smart side of my brain tells me to run, get to safety. The side of my brain that craves this man in ways I never thought I'd be able to, keeps screaming for me to strip down and make his job easy.

My gaze travels over him as I take in his profile. He moves to the other side of the room and I drop my eyes to his tight ass in his low hanging jeans. When he turns back for the sink, he catches me drooling over him.

Instead of heading for the sink, he walks straight to me. Placing one hand on either side of me, he leans in until we are face to face. Heat rolls off of him.

"We can fuck and talk this out or we can talk this out and then fuck. Those are your two options," he breathes against my lips.

I want to kick myself for panting. I miss his touch so much. I miss the bond we've built together, but if he doesn't want children, we shouldn't be fucking anyway. I'm overdue for my birth control shot.

I've been busy trying to get somethings done for King and the Club's books. I think King is about to do a major turnover. The details and changes he's asked me for are all red flags he's up to something. He just hasn't told me what, just that he needs it all done as soon as possible.

That was the reason I've been working round the clock. All of this drama has been a little bit of a setback. I need to get through—

"Shut that pretty brain of yours down, baby girl," Gutter growls into my neck, then places a kiss on my sensitive spot.

I giggle and heat everywhere, unable to stop either. My arms go around his neck of their own accord. Gutter pulls my legs around his waist, slowly, carefully as he connects our eyes, seeming to connect our souls.

"Gutter," I start, but he shakes his head.

"Pick one, talk and fuck or fuck and talk," he commands.

I lick my lips and scoot my butt forward. The words feel dirty leaving my mouth, but they feel safe with him. It's then I decide everything will work itself out. Gutter always makes sure I'm safe.

I know I can trust him to make safe decisions when it comes to me. We can figure the rest out. I know we can. I let go of the restraint I've been creating on my propensity to do.

If he wants to fix this, if he wants to talk, we can talk. However, there's something I need to handle first. I glide my hands up into his hair, tugging his head down toward me.

"Fuck, then talk," I moan against his full lips, just before he captures mine like a man starved for far too long.

A low rumble comes from his chest as he devours and savors me. I tighten my legs around his waist, clawing at his back. He begins to drag kisses down my neck to my collarbone.

"I've never wanted anything as much as I want you." He flicks his tongue out and mutters.

"Please," I plea. He's awakening the fire he's been setting all night.

In a single motion, he plucks me from the countertop and moves into the living room area. He's long legs eat up the distance swiftly. Still holding me tight, he snatches one of the pillows from the couch and tossed it onto the floor in front of it, followed by another.

Gently, I'm lowered to the couch. I look into his heat filled eyes and feel like I'm about to go up in flames. Gutter pulls his shirt over his head as he stands before me. My gaze follows the ripple of his ripped chest and abs. I move forward, unable to stop myself from needing to lick my way over his tattoos.

He groans, while cupping the back of my head in his big hands. I revel in the fact that this man will only ever want and receive my touch. No other woman has ever turned him on.

This I know and this I can use to fortify my resolve in sticking to our relationship. When I look up at him through my lashes, the desire I see there in his eyes nearly makes me weep. I continue my trail over his well-honed canvas.

I reach for his belt and release it. Unfastening his pants, I push them down his hips, until what I want springs free. I look down to see the precum dripping from the tip and lick my lips.

Just his scent alone makes me want a taste. It's a mix of his natural musk, citrus, and a freshness all of his own. I reach for him, wrapping my fingers around him in awe.

He's so silky smooth to the touch, but hard as a rock. I give a gentle squeeze and more precum leaks forward. I can't deny myself another minute.

I dip my head and flick my tongue right through it. I hum as his sweet, salty taste hits my tongue. It's like having my favorite caramel invade my senses.

"That good?" He chuckles.

The sound warms my chest. It's been too long since he has sound so carefree. That sexy bravado is oozing from him.

"Mmm, hmm," I hum around him, starting to swallow as much of him as I can.

"Fuck," he groans. I look up to find his head thrown back. It is such a stunning sight.

I did that, I'm doing that. Most of all, I want to do this as much for me as I do for him. I have the power here.

I smile around him and go into overdrive to bring him to his knees. Not because I can, but because he's allowing me to. For us, there's that difference. That's what makes this special, makes us special.

I make sure he's soaked and wet, not caring about the excess drool dripping down my chin. His groans and grunts are my fuel to keep going. I dig my fingers into his thighs for support as I twist my head to the side, shifting the angle in which he's entering my mouth.

"Aargh," he moans, pulling from my mouth. His lips are tight when he commands. "Turn for me."

I want to finish, but I obey his command. I turn on my knees, facing the back of the couch. Gutter reaches for the hem of my dress to pull it over my head.

My breasts bounce free, having no other restraints on them. I gasp when he rips right through my panties. He's right at my ear, keeping me in our safe place as he does this.

"You with me, baby?"

"Yes," I pant.

"Good, I'm going to eat this pussy. I've wanted to taste you every night you've been in my bed. You tap out on me; you make sure you mean it. If I can't have my mouth on you, I'm going to be in you."

My pussy clenches with his words. He waits for no reply. I hear more than see him drop to his knees, on the leather cushions he dropped on the floor.

It feels so good, I reach back with both hands and open for him. I press my face into the back of the couch. Gutter growls in response and shoves his face deeper. He covers my hands with his big ones, holding me open to his assault, not that I had plans to let go.

My eyes cross. I'm close to going over, but it's so strong I want to tap out. I just refuse to. I choose to go up in flames.

I accept it in all its glory, cresting and crashing hard. I'm drunk as Gutter gently lifts my body, bringing me down to the floor with him. The heat coming off of him is surprisingly welcomed to my own heated flesh.

"Put your hands and head on the pillows," he orders.

Dazed, I mindlessly do as he says, placing both hands on either side of the pillow and planting my head onto the cushions. The smell of leather and my essence fills my nostrils. It's like being welcomed home.

Gutter lifts my hips to meet his, bringing me into a standing position. He lines up with my entrance and starts to push forward slowly. He rocks into me gently a few times. Going deeper with each pass.

It's the most amazing feeling of my life. A long moan escapes my lips, followed by me crying out, while he slams home into me. I feel breathless, I can almost taste his desire as it comes off of him.

The punishing pace he sets proves he's not here to play. He meant it when he said we were fucking. This isn't the love making I know from him. This is something more raw and downright nasty. I like it and I don't feel ashamed that I like it, surprising myself and bringing tears to my eyes.

"Don't." He slaps my ass. "Don't you dare overthink this. You have a right to be fucked by your man and like it."

I have no words. It makes me wonder how he doesn't get that what he said the other night is a problem. I push that thought aside with the others to just enjoy this feeling. It takes no time to get lost.

"Fuck," he hisses. "You're going to tell me what I'm doing wrong and I'm going to deal with it."

His words aren't a command, but more of a demanding plea. I don't respond. Instead, I begin to give as good as I'm getting. I root my hands into the cushion and push my ass back as best I can.

His grip tightens on my waist. "You're mine. You promised. I won't lose you," he says huskily. "Fuck, yeah, keep coming on me."

I do just that. One orgasm, turning into another, then another. It happens so fast I lose my stride and my legs start to buckle. He doesn't stop pounding, not until his warm seed spills inside me.

He collapses against the couch, keeping his weight off of me. His strong arms go around me, guiding me down into his lap as he twists to sit. His warm lips meet my temple.

"Give me a minute, I'll carry us in the room. Then we talk."

Heavy Heart

Sal

The bed dips as he crawls his big body onto the bed. He'd gone to the bathroom after carrying me into the room and placing me under the covers. I shift in bed to face him.

He searches my face with his eyes as I look up at him. Gutter runs his fingertips across my temple, his brows furrowing. He releases a heavy breath.

"My past is a hard thing for me to deal with. I've spent so much time running from it. I didn't mean to scare you with my shit," he huffs.

I wrinkle my own brows. "You didn't scare me with your shit." I shake my head. "Listen, I totally understand you not wanting to deal with your past. Although, I do think you should see what's going on with your cousin. That's who keeps calling you, right? You should see what he wants."

"No," he cuts me off, before I can finish.

"Pierson, I—"

"I don't want to talk about him," he commands.

I whip my head back and pause. Suddenly, it all clicks into place. The vacant look in his eyes, the closed off expression on his face.

Gutter doesn't get what I'm upset about because he blacks out every time we talk about Terry. He's totally unaware of my reactions or his own words. I pause to look at this another way.

Clearly, we have a problem. A problem he's so unaware of because he guards himself from the topic. I sigh and rub my forehead. This seems to bring him back to the present.

"Sal—" This time I cut him off, holding up my hand.

"You don't have to explain. I get it. You're not ready to deal with him, but honey, at some point you have to. Otherwise, those demons win. You haven't been yourself since you started receiving those calls.

"It took a minute, but I figured out it's him. I confirmed it when your phone rung the other night while you were in the bathroom. You have to handle it sometime," I say cautiously.

His jaw tightens, but this time I watch my words penetrate their mark. His silence offers a lot of information as his emotions play in his eyes. He grunts and nods.

He closes his eyes. "I told you I'd fix the problem." He opens his eyes, cups my face, and places a kiss on my forehead. "So, I'm doing this for you."

I beam up at him. I want nothing more than to see him free of the prison he has allowed himself to be trapped in. Either way, it's time for him to find his own peace.

"I love you," I whisper in his ear, my heart still heavy with the topic I should address.

Gutter

I lie in bed, staring at the ceiling like most nights. Salalia has fallen asleep across my chest after we made love twice more. I crave her so much. These last few days have been torture. However, I know its torture of my own doing.

I need to deal with my cousin and make the right decisions to move on. I won't allow my past to rob me of another thing. It really has been long enough. My phone buzzes on the nightstand, drawing my attention.

I close my eyes. I know it's him. My first reaction is to ignore it, but I think of the woman snoring softly on my chest and I can't.

I reach for the phone and sure enough, it's Terry. I grunt and slip from under Sal, doing my damnedest not to wake her. Throwing my legs over the side of the bed, I then lift to my feet.

Quickly, I answer the call before it can go to voicemail. "Hello," I say low as I head for the living room.

There's no answer at first, but I hear breathing. My anger rises. I go to pull the phone from my ear and stab the end button, but a voice calls out.

"Pier, don't hang up," Terry's voice greets me.

I sigh and place the phone back to my ear. Those damn demons start their clawing, pushing at the hinges of Pandora's box. For Salalia and the relationship I want to keep, I push it all back.

"I... I was just surprised you answered. I've been trying for going on a month now," he says. "I miss you. I know I fucked up, but I really miss you."

I close my eyes. I can't blame him for what was done to us, but what he did to me. The shit I had to go through because of him. He blew a hole in the little security I created for myself, for us.

We were finally able to take care of ourselves, without selling some part of us. That bullshit he pulled snatched that all from me, from us. The anger, resentment, and torment consume me. I have to let it out.

"We promised to take care of each other. You turned your back on me… for what, Ter? Some sadistic lunatic who was beating your ass.

"I could've died fighting for you, but you didn't even give a fuck. You showed up at that hospital, high out of your fucking mind. Calling my mother, the whore that ruined everything.

"She was like a mother to you. She was your family too. She died in a fucking car accident, she didn't leave us or dad on purpose," I choke the words out because they cut as deep as they did the day, he spewed them.

"I… my God, Pier, I don't even remember saying those things. I was so fucked up." He's sobbing on the other end.

"Do you remember sending me pics of you trying to kill yourself?" I snarl.

"Yeah, that I do remember. I was so angry. The money didn't make up for what happened to us. It couldn't fix the shit I did to lose you in my life. I thought you would see how fucked up I was and come back," he whispers into the line.

"I couldn't, Ter. You want to know why?"

"I… you gave up on me," he says weakly.

"No, I couldn't be there for you, because while you were texting me, I was lying in my own filth, trying to drink myself to death," I seethe.

Silence, I'm greeted by nothing but silence. I want to crush my phone in my bare hand. His words from that night so long ago in that hospital, ring so loudly in my ears.

"You're a whore just like me, Pier. So, what you work for that fancy club and that overpriced escort service. If they want service, you're down on your fucking knees just like me," he threw at me.

"I suck cock, but your mouth is no stranger to giving head. If you look at me like I'm shit, your shit too," he taunted.

I hadn't looked at him like he was shit because of what we had to do. I looked at him like he was shit because of the bile that seeped from his lips. His words cut deep, they hit me like an arrow to the heart.

I already loathed myself. He didn't have to make it worse. Sure, by that time, I was no longer dancing, but I did work the escort service from time to time. Whenever, Terry fucked things up and I needed a little more cash, which was becoming more often.

His words stuck to me like cheap cologne. I couldn't get them off. The night I tried to kill myself, it was as if he were screaming them at me all over again, but louder.

"I didn't know," he finally says.

"Yeah, you wouldn't."

"I've changed, Pier. I got some help. I'm doing better," he whispers.

"I know. At least, that's what it looks like."

"What, what do you mean?"

"I run a security firm. I have my boys look in on you from time to time."

There's another pause. I just wait. I want to be done with this conversation. When Terry says nothing for a few beats, I open my mouth to find out what he wants.

"They mustn't have checked on me lately," he says, and for the first time, I pick up on something out of place.

He sounds scared, nervous. Something tells me it has nothing to do with this conversation. I never did look at the latest report on his life.

I stuck it in the bottom of my desk drawer after Diggs handed it over. I close my eyes because I know I'm about to butt in. I promised I wouldn't, but I'm going to break that promise right now.

"Yeah, they've been busy the last few weeks," I half lie. Ter, what the fuck is going on?"

"I'm in trouble, Pier. It's not drugs or any of that bullshit I used to get into. Well, it's one of the things I used to get into.

I've always been bad at picking partners," he snorts
humorlessly.

"Fuck, no, Ter. I'm not putting my life on the line for
some bullshit again, just for you to walk right back into it," I
growl. "I have my woman to think about."

"You found someone," the joy in his voice sounds genuine.

"Yeah."

"Good, good," Terry says. "But Pier, it's not like that. I
want out and I want out for good. He's trying to take my
business from me. I built everything I have.

"That money from Dad and the house. It's all in an
offshore account. I don't touch it. I'm sure he would kill me to
get his hands on that if he knew. Pier, you're all I have. I don't
know what else to do," his voice trembles.

I close my eyes, vibrating with anger. I only calm when she
wraps her arms around me. Salalia places a kiss on the back of
my neck and then my back.

"Pier, are you there? Please, he left town for a few weeks.
That's why I've been trying to reach you. He has me watched.
You're the only person I know who can get my ass out of here.
Please," he pleads.

I'm thrown back in time, again. This time to one of the
nights Ter was balled up, pleading with me to figure out how
we could get help. He had begged me then, before things had
gone too far.

I was too young to do anything at the time. Now, I have
the resources and the muscle. For once, I know I could save
him if I tried.

"You bring this shit to my door, to my woman, we're done,
Ter. I save you, it doesn't blowback on my woman's doorstep.
Otherwise, I'll be the one you need saving from," I snarl.

"I'm happy for you," he says. "I don't want to take that
from you. I just need your help."

"Who's this fucker?"

Terry takes a minute to respond. "Sergio Rossi, I met him in Milan, when I did my first showing."

"Christ," I hiss. Terry really does know how to pick them. "Do you just sniff shit out?"

"I had no idea," Terry sobs. "He was so nice to me in the beginning. I thought my love life was turning around like everything else."

"How long?" I grunt. "How long do we have before he returns?"

I need time to get a team together. I've been stretching my men thin, looking for Spencer and Hoover. I'll need a little time.

"Three days. I only have three more days," he replies.

"I'll be in touch," I grumble and end the call.

Box Opened

Gutter

The room was so dark. I could hear the moans and groans of both women and men. I moved forward and in the corner two guys sucked each other off.

"You're worthless. You couldn't even stay beautiful like my other pet," she hisses at me.

My skin crawled. I hated the sound of her voice. It grated my nerves. I spun around looking for Terry. When I found him, he was across the room being held down.

"No," I yelled and take off to help him.

The more I ran the further across the room he was. I pushed my legs harder, but I couldn't get there. Suddenly, I could see him, but no one was holding him down.

He was in a bathtub full of blood. She's there beside him, stroking his hair. "My pretty one. Come fellas, you can all have a taste," Melody purred.

"No, get away from him. I'll kill you all," I bellowed.

Someone grabbed me by the shoulders, restraining me. I go into survival mode. This wasn't going to happen again.

Sal

I blink my eyes open, groggy and disoriented at first. Whimpers fill the room, and the bed is rocking. I turn my head to see Gutter tossing and turning in his sleep. He's soaked, sweat is dripping from his face and covers his chest.

He was so agitated after the call I found him on. It had taken him a while to fall asleep. I followed shortly after. He'd looked so peaceful then. Now, he looks like he is literally being tormented.

I reach for him and shake his shoulder. "Pierson, babe—"

I'm pinned flat on my back, he straddles my body with his big one with his hands around my throat. I can't breathe as he chokes me, crushing my windpipe. His eyes are unfocused, and a snarl is on his face.

"Gutter," I spatter, trying to get through to him. Tears leak out the corners of my eyes. "Gutter."

I see the moment his eyes clear. Panic replaces rage. He releases my neck and shoves his hands into his hair. He pulls at his damp strands.

I sit up, rubbing my neck. He jumps up from the bed and backs away from me. He shakes his head as if to clear it. Pulling his hands from his hair, he looks down at them as if they belong to another.

"Fuck, *fuck*," he roars. "I'm so sorry. I knew this shit would happen. I'm so sorry, baby."

"I'm fine," I say in a raspy voice.

His eyes widen. He starts to move closer to the bed but stops. He closes his eyes and beats a hand across his chest as if doing so to punish himself. When he does it twice more, I jump from the bed to run to him.

I grab his hand in mine, needing both hands to match his strength. "Please, Pierson. Stop it, I'm fine." My voice still comes out raw.

A sob rips from his chest and he buries his face in my hair. "I'm sorry, baby. I'm so sorry," he sobs.

He wraps his arms around my waist, pulling me in tightly to him. His entire body shakes against me as he breaks down. I try to wrap my arms around him, but he slides down to his knees, burying his face in my belly.

"I'm so sorry," he says again, sounding like a wounded animal.

It breaks my heart to see my big strong man falling apart at my feet. It's like I'm getting a glimpse of the frightened boy he once was. The anguish in his voice tears at my soul.

"You had a bad dream. You didn't mean it," I say softly, hoping to soothe his ache.

"I could've hurt you. I could've killed you," he groans.

"I'd say we're even," I try to joke.

He looks up at me, tears swimming in his beautiful eyes. My humor is lost in the moment. He grabs the backs of my thighs squeezing tightly.

"You mean everything to me. I can't ever put you at risk like that again," he says in all seriousness.

"What?" I snort. "So, we're sleeping in separate beds for the rest of our lives?"

He turns his head away from me. I gasp. He's seriously considering this. I drop to my own knees and cup his face. He won't turn to me at first. I duck my head to search for his eyes.

"Pierson," I say gently.

He turns and locks gazes with me. "You and I are so fucked up. We're going to have times like this. Maybe we can go see someone together, but what we're not going to do, is let this come between us. We have enough shit going on as it is," I say with determination.

"Don't worry about it." He kisses my forehead. "I won't make it back to sleep tonight. Go to bed. I'm going for a ride."

I get ready to protest, but he silences me with a kiss on the lips. When he breaks the kiss, he pecks my forehead. Lifting to his feet, he reaches out his hand to help me up.

I stand and stare at him for a few moments. When I don't move toward the bed, he leads me to it. I reluctantly climb in, watching in silence as he gets dressed and heads out.

Boy, we're a fucked up pair. Even my thoughts sigh at that truth.

Gutter

I feel like less than a man. My job is to keep Salalia safe and I'm now the one I need to keep her safe from. I can't get her face out of my head. The fear, the panic, the pleading in her eyes for me to let go.

I would never put my hands on a woman. To wake up and comprehend that I had my hands around Sal's neck tore a hole through me. Even riding on the back of my bike isn't able to keep my demons at bay tonight. They're nipping on my heels.

I stomp my way into my office and stop in surprise to find Diggs in the waiting area. There's a gallon of Jack sitting on the coffee table before him. He looks up through his lashes and I can see the damaged soul staring back at me.

"I told them I wanted to be left alone," he says through a clenched jaw.

"Don't know what you're talking about. Got my own shit I'm standing in," I grunt back.

He closes his eyes and nods. I can't help but wonder if Sugar has taken a turn for the worse. Last I heard, she hadn't woken yet. I'm not about to pry. It ain't my business.

"I don't know if I want to drown myself in this bottle or ride so far away from here it all becomes a distant memory," he says almost to himself.

I feel him on that one. Only, I wouldn't get far. My heart and soul are tethered to that woman sleeping in my bed. I know I wouldn't make it to my next breath if I tried to leave her.

"You ain't ran from shit since I've met you." I amble over and flop down on the other side of the couch.

Diggs blows out a breath and looks up at the ceiling. "I need to get my mind off this shit. I need to get out of here," he says, scrubbing his hands down his face.

I rub my own jaw, contemplating my next move. I had planned to come here and get some work done. Diggs has been after me about signing some papers.

I figured if I'm here first thing in the morning, I could pull together a small crew to ride with me to get Terry the fuck out of the mess he's in. I talked to King about it, after I hung up and calmed the fuck down earlier.

He offered Terry the Lost Souls' protection without even asking for more information. When I said it was my cousin, there was nothing more to be said. I could just wake some of the guys now and take off.

"Hey, you want to ride out with me. I have that shit to deal with." I'd sent him a brief text earlier too.

His face brightens at the prospect of a distraction. "You said it's a family thing, right? Why wait, when we can do?" He shrugs.

"I put in some calls," I huff. "Rossi isn't going to make this easy."

"What's your plans for him? You know you're going to have to put him to ground." Diggs lifts a brow.

"So be it." I shrug. "Elbows deep, Terry and I have some bad history, but he's all the family I have left."

My thoughts turn to Sal. I need to do this, but I don't want to leave her unguarded. If I'm honest, she's my family. I just need to put distance between my fucked up head and her, for now.

"Vault can stay behind at your place. King doesn't need him. That way we can take our guys," Diggs offers up as if I'd spoken my thoughts aloud.

I nod. That's a good plan. If I have to leave Sal with anyone not in my crew, it would be a Squad member. Vault is smart and lethal. He thinks fast on his feet.

From what I've learned, Vault is also fond of the younger girls around the club. They're all like little sisters to him. The girls feel the same about him. I think Sal will be comfortable with him.

"Sounds, like a plan." I nod and start to set things in motion.

Distant Cousin

Terry

"He'll come for you, Ter. He promised," I say to myself as I stare in the mirror.

Crystal clear blue-gold eyes stare back at me. My long dark hair is pulled up into a top knot, showing off my long neck. I swallow and watch my Adam's apple bob. I get it.

I see what all the woman and men see when they look at me. I know why Pier and I were able to survive off our looks. What I don't get is what causes them all to abuse me.

I look away from the mirror not able to look at myself much longer. I ruin everything in my life with this face. Pier, he's different. His beauty brings him a respect I've never felt. Although we look so much alike.

I sink to the floor and turn to press my back to the vanity. I'm a prisoner in my own home. I start to sob.

"I don't blame him if he doesn't come for me," I say into my palms as I cover my face.

I can't believe the shit I said to Pierson all those years ago. I was so fucked up. I've been clean for a year and a half and doing all I can to change my life for the better.

Yet here I am in a screwed-up relationship all over again. Rossi has been married to his wife since he started with me. It's the reason he wanted us to be a secret. I didn't see all the red flags.

My phone rings causing me to jump. It's Pierson. I didn't think he would call back so soon.

I rush to pick up the call. "Hello," I say in almost a whisper in case one of Rossi's men are outside my bathroom door.

"I'm on my way. Get whatever you need together and be ready to move."

"Okay," I sniffle. "I'll be ready."

"Don't hang up. One of my guys is trying to get a trace on your phone so I can come straight to you. This is going to be hard and fast, Ter. You need to be alert."

"I'm alert. I'm ready. Please, just get me out of here."

"Calm down, I've got you. We'll get you out."

I nod my head as if he can see me and bite down on my lip, realizing I do sound a bit frantic. I can't take any more of this possessive torture. I'm a trophy in our circle, Rossi loves to show me off, but behind closed doors and out in the real world, he's a different man.

"I'll have to start over, again," I murmur the thought out loud.

"And lose what you've built? Nah, let me handle this shit. We get you out and make sure you're safe to live your life. You'll be fine." He pauses and it sounds like he's talking to someone else in the background. "We're ready. I'm coming."

The line cuts off and I suck in a breath. I stand and rush to the walk-in closet in my en suite. I grab a duffle back and shove a few things in.

I don't even care about the expensive clothes and makeup. I'm not getting my ass beat and being forced to suck cock in front of Rossi's friends ever again. I'd die first.

I rush back through the bathroom and that's when I hear it. An explosion that rocks the entire house. I spent a lot to make this place perfect, but today this entire bitch could burn down and I wouldn't give a fuck.

Gutter

Getting ahold of Terry isn't going to be easy, but we'll manage to. Quick and with a whole lot of force. That's the Squad way.

Diggs doesn't seem to mind being able to get his hands dirty. In fact, I think it's therapeutic for him. He gives me a grin and the signal.

"Move, move, move," I say to my guys and wave them in as the explosion goes off.

Gunfire rings out from my crew. After Diggs scoped the place out, we knew we had to come in blazing. Terry is being guarded more heavily than the golden child.

This was the only way we were getting in and out. I don't like any of this. I'm falling into an old habit of sticking my nose in where it's doesn't belong. I swear, I'll kill Terry myself if this threatens my life I have now.

"On me, on me," I call out as we move through the front doors of the house.

"Watch your six," Whispers says into the comm.

I brought my best with me. King promised he'd handle Rossi if necessary. The fucker already owes us some flesh for a bad deal a few months back. I bet that's why his ass isn't around now.

He begged for more time. He probably needed more time to get money out of Terry and whoever else he could find. None of that matters now.

I look at the app on my phone to follow the tracker to Terry's phone. The gun fight is still in heavy play. I rush up one side of the winding double staircase.

This place reminds me too much of the home we grew up in. I force the memories back. This isn't the time for me to spaz out.

When I get to the top of the stairs, I head for the double doors up the hall. I pop one of the guys guarding the door and Wolf gets the other.

"Thanks, Brother," I say before planting my boot into the doors and busting them open.

Terry comes into view, looking as if he's about to shit his pants until we lock gazes. Relief covers his face and fills his eyes, it's almost palpable. He rushes forward with his duffle slung across his back. I sidestep him, and his face falls.

I'm not about to hug his ass and shit. We still have a whole lot of shit between us. I don't have time process any of it.

We didn't have time for reunions. I grabbed him by the arm. We need to get out of here. Rossi has other men not that far away. We need to move before they are in motion and find us escaping.

"Let's go," I say tightly and turn back for the door.

I got what I came for. We can deal with the rest later. It's been hours since I left Sal and I'm feeling uneasy.

We head back through the way me and the boys came through. We have to scale a hill back up to where we left the my cage and a few bikes. Terry trips a little to my frustration on the way up.

"I'm fine," he mutters when I grab the back of his shirt to help him up.

I look down at the pointed toe boots on his feet and roll my eyes. They suit the tight jeans and button down he's wearing. Classic Terry, I'm sure his jeans cost more than my entire outfit. Heck, probably as much as one of my tailor-made suits.

We arrive at the bikes and my mustang. I nod for Terry to toss his bag in the back and climb in. He rushes to the passenger side and does as instructed.

The bikes behind us come to life and all take off. The ride home should take a few hours, depending on traffic. This is going to be a long tense ride.

We're silence for a good thirty minutes. I've been checking the mirrors for company, but it seems this extraction has gone as planned. I breathe a sigh of relief and settle in my seat.

Something is still nagging at my gut, but I think we're in the clear for now. Forward, I need to keep moving forward.

"Thank you," Terry murmurs toward his hands in his lap.

I grunt, not in the mood to talk. The faster I get Terry to my room at the clubhouse the better. Then I can go home and face what happened between me and Sal last night.

"How have you been?" he asks we come to stop at a light.

"Living."

He releases a heavy breath and looks out of the window. The air is thick in here. My unwillingness to talk has caused an overwhelming silence. We are nearly home when a call comes in.

I glance to see it's from my office. "You're not going to like this," Matrix says, when I answered the phone.

"What?" I grunt.

"Hoover and Spencer, we found them like an hour ago. We were following them, but they split up. There in your neck of the woods," he replies.

My foot has the petal to the metal, before Matrix can get all his words out. When I cut the corner for a short cut home, my brothers are right behind me. I don't have time to tell them what's going on. I need to call Vault and warn him.

CHAPTER THIRTY-SEVEN

Lights Out

Sal

I'd be lying if I said I haven't been watching the door all day. I was surprised when Vault showed up in the middle of the night, dressed in one of his tailor-made suits.

Vault is handsome and hilarious. He's also very smart. It was no surprise when he made his way through Law school and blew right through his bar exams. If I'm right, he passed in multiple states.

Cage was so proud of him when he graduated undergrad with honors. I know Vault stayed committed to his Law practice after we all thought Cage had died, because he wanted to honor Cage's memory.

Now Vault is a partner at L & S. I laugh every time I hear the name of the firm. To the outside world, it looks like Larry and Schultz. That's not true at all. The firm is Lost Souls property.

The Lost Souls have some of the most educated bikers you will ever meet. Cage made sure of that. These dirty boys clean up nice when necessary.

Vault has King by a few years so Cage was a large part of his life. I've always looked up to Vault like another big brother. He would pick me up from school at times.

He sat with me when I built my first computer from spare parts, watching in awe because I couldn't have been older than ten. I'd also only looked at the instructions once. That's all it took for me to memorize the design and replicate the build from the research I did online.

Now he's stands at the kitchen island with his back leaned against it and one ankles crossed on over other. I've just come back from the bathroom. I stop in my tracks as I watch his thoughts play on his face.

"Where'd you get those marks from?" Vault finally asks, pointing his half-eaten apple at my neck.

I knew he was going to. He's been staring at my neck since he got here. I almost blurted it out just so he'd stop staring.

"It's nothing, trust me." I wave him off.

"Nothing… could get someone hurt, baby girl. King will want to know what's going on," he says, with a lifted brow.

"King is going to mind his business. I'm a big girl. I can handle this." I cock my hip to the side and cross my arms over my chest.

Vault holds my gaze. He shakes his head at my determined and defiant glare. Taking another bite of his apple, he narrows his eyes at my neck.

"Did he tell you he sleepwalks?" he says knowingly.

I shake my head. "No."

"I don't think he knows. Shit freaked us the fuck out the first time. King told us not to bother him."

"What?" I lick my dry lips and start again. "What happens when he does?"

"Nothing much really. He comes out of his room and sits on the floor, outside the door. Almost like he's guarding something inside. Weird shit, but you have to be some type of fucked up to be one of us." He winks.

"This is so very true," I tease and wink back.

"Is that from one of his episodes?"

I also knew Vault wasn't going to let this go. I rub at my neck and wince. It's still a little sore.

"Yeah, sort of."

"Yeah, King isn't going to like that." He frowns.

"King isn't going to find out. Gutter and I will handle this when he gets back," I hiss, glaring at him in warning.

Vault watches me for a moment, those honey eyes homing in on me. Not saying a word, he studies me. He finishes his apple and tosses it.

"Gutter doesn't say much to many, but I don't think he's a bad guy. Just be careful," he finally says.

I walk over and throw my arms around his waist. "Thank you for your concern. It will be fine," I reassure him. I look up at Vault. "You want to order something to eat?"

"Nope." He taps the tip of my nose. "You should know by now I plan to cook something up. My other great talent. I could have been a chef, you know?"

I give a genuine heartfelt laugh. It feels good and goes a long way to calm my nerves. I'll feel better when I can see Gutter and we can talk about what happened last night.

Vault moves into the kitchen and I sit on a barstool at the island to watch. He has always loved cooking. Once he gets started, we get lost in conversation about old times and have a few good laughs.

When his phone rings, he smiles and wiggles his brows. He holds it up waving it at me. Gutter's name on the screen. Vault chuckles then puts the phone on speaker.

"Talk to me," Vault says with a smile.

"You with Sal?" Gutter says gruffly.

Something sounds off. I scoot to the edge of my seat. My palms become sweaty. The smile slips from Vault's lips.

"Yeah, she's right here," Vault replies.

"I'm on my way. Hoover and Spencer popped up on grid about an hour ago. The boys lost Hoover. My gut is telling me you're going to have company," Gutter rumbles.

No sooner than he finishes his words, the lights go out. Instantly, something feels off. My blood turns cold and my flight instincts begin to takeover.

"We got company, all right. You boys move your asses," Vault hisses at the phone.

I can see him through the phone's light. He moves quickly to my side, grasping my arm. I try not to panic, but my mind is racing. The generator hasn't kicked in.

"I'm going to need you to stay as quiet as you can," Vault orders, while dragging me to the nearest closet.

He opens the door and pushes me inside. I don't even have time to reply, before the door shuts behind me. I start to hyperventilate.

My hands are shaking, my palms are sweaty. I close my eyes and reel it in. I'm not going out in some closet.

That's when it hits me. This is the hallway closet Gutter showed me when I moved in. There's a secret doorway in here. It leads to a safe room. There are guns and cameras in there.

All of that stuff runs on a backup generator. I scramble to find the knob, running my hand along the back of the closet. I bump into something that tips over and makes a small sound.

I close my eyes and soundlessly stomp my feet in frustration. I go completely still after my quiet tantrum. When I hear nothing outside the closet, I try once more.

Seeing it in my mind from the first time Gutter showed it to me, I feel for the handle. When I find it, I breathe a sigh of relief and push the door in, scurrying inside.

I puff out a relieved breath to find the monitors on and the lights working. They cut on as soon as I enter the room. I run to the screens to see what's going on.

I cover my mouth to keep from screaming, when I see the screen before me. Vault is on his knees. The man from the video of my apartment is standing behind him with a gun to Vault's head. I can't hear what's being said, but I know this can't end like this.

I spring into action, needing to help my friend. Quickly, I run for the lockbox, glad I insisted Gutter show me the weapons to protect myself. I lift my hand to scan my print.

I will not sit here and watch my friend be killed. It's not in me.

Gutter will be pissed, but oh, well.

Gutter

"Drive, drive, drive," I chant in my head, while racing the mustang toward my apartment.

I wish I was on my fucking bike, but this baby will do. I'm only blocks away. I try not to sound panicked when Vault answers my call, but I'm fucking losing it inside.

I swerved hard around a car moving at a snail's pace. There's a red light coming ahead, but I blow right through that shit. A truck nearly clipped my backside, but I fishtailed out of the way, making it through without the blink of an eye.

Terry cringes in his seat, but he doesn't say a word as I barked out information to Vault. All plans of taking Terry to the clubhouse first go up in smoke. Sal and I have so much to talk about. I need her to understand how serious what happened last night was.

However, all of that was forgotten the moment I could feel in my bones my woman needs me. A chill runs through me with Vault's final words back to me over the phone.

"We got company, all right. You boys move your asses."

I shifted gears, blowing right through another light. When my building comes into sight, I can't help saying a prayer. I swerved my car around, hard, literally flying into a parking spot.

"You, stay here," I ordered to a nervous looking Terry.

Me and my crew of four moved swiftly into the building. It's the one time I wish I had a ground level apartment. The anxiety in my chest threatens to kill me before I get to the top floor. Only three floors in this building, but that's two too many.

Now here I stand, outside my apartment door. My own breathing ringing in my ears as I try to calm the fuck down and think rationally. Voices can be heard on the other side of the door.

I nod at Diggs as he flattens against the other side of the door. I can't afford to rush this and get Sal hurt, but I don't want to take too long and risk the same outcome. I place my ear closer to listen for the voices.

"You don't want to do this, man." I recognize that voice as Vault's.

"Where the fuck is the girl?" Someone else snarls in frustration. I hear a bit of fear mixed in his words.

That's enough for me. I shift, haul back and send my boot into the door. I rush in to find Vault on his knees and Hoover or at least what looks like Hoover, standing over him with a gun to his head.

Hoover's face fills with panic at the sight of me and my four brothers around me. He grabs the collar of Vault's dress shirt and presses the gun closer to his head.

Vault looks more annoyed than worried. We lock eyes and he tells me all I need to know with a look. Sal's safe. This motherfucker is about to die.

"Where's your boss?" I ask. The fear in his eyes clues me into the fact that this is indeed the real Hoover. From what I know of that psycho Spencer, he doesn't have enough sense to know fear.

"Fuck you," Hoover snaps. "I came for the girl, hand her over."

I snort. "Do you look like you're in the position to make demands?"

He licks his lips and looks around me again. I know we make an imposing sight. I have at least two other Squad members at my back. Their eyes alone suggest death is near.

"I'll blow—" He gets ready to threaten, but I cut him off.

"Don't even finish that shit. Trust me, that's not what's about to happen." I snort. "Tell me where Spencer is. My patience ran out days ago."

He stands with his lips pursed tightly. There's indecision in his gaze. Something catches his eye that brings confidence back to his face. I chance a look out the corner of my eye and see Sal, holding up a gun with shaky hands.

Her eyes have a glazed over look. She's pointing at Hoover, but something is off. Her lips are parted and sweat is beading on her upper lip.

"Well, hello, sweetheart," Hoover purrs, bringing my attention back to him.

He lifts his gun to point it at Sal and I don't think twice. Vault breaks Hoover's right leg with one swift motion. Simultaneously, I fire two to Hoover's head and two to his chest. In my mind that's two for Sal's mental anguish and two for the damage in her heart.

I don't even wait for the body to fall before I holster my guns and crossing the room. I wrap my arms around a shaking Sal, pulling the gun from her palms and hand it over to Diggs.

I cup her head against my shoulder. "You're safe now," I whisper in her ear.

"I know him, I remember him now," Sal sobs softly. "He was the clerk that I gave my paperwork to for London. He worked in Professor Spencer's office."

"It's okay, it's over," I reassure her.

She wraps her arms around me tightly. It's as if we're anchoring each other in this moment. I close my eyes and just breathe her in.

"I love you, Salalia. It will all be fine," I promise.

She pulls away to look up into my eyes. The trust and love there are like the warm blanket I remember my mother wrapping me in when she sang to me at night. It was always filled with warmth and love.

"Oh, my God. Are you guys okay?" Terry's voice comes from behind me, breaking the moment.

I stiffen, knowing I told him to stay in the fucking car. I turn my head to find him frowning at the body on the floor. He runs a hand through his long dark hair.

"Pier, the police are coming," Terry warns.

"It'll be fine." I grimace. "Welcome to my city, Ter."

Time to Heal

Gutter

I step into the clubhouse with my arm around Sal. I kiss her temple and give her a smile. She's clearly still shaken up. If I could put four more bullets in that motherfucker I would.

"Terry, I planned to give you my room here. Since Sal and I need a place to stay, I'm going to need you to give me a minute to talk to the Prez to get you set up," I say to my wide-eyed cousin.

"He can stay in my room," Sal says. "Or we can, and he can have your room."

"You sure about that?" I lift a brow.

"Yeah, if he doesn't mind that I was boy band poster crazy in my teens and the evidence is still in there."

I choke out a laugh and peek over at Terry. "He'll love it."

Terry gives me a small grin. I shrug it off and wave for him to follow us. Sal laces her fingers through mine and leads the way to her old room. I notice it's in the opposite direction of our room.

"Not for nothing, this place is a lot nicer than I expected it to be," Terry moves closer to me and whispers.

"Stop watching TV," I snort and say over my shoulder.

Sal opens the door to her room and we all step in. She wasn't joking about the posters. She looks to me and stifles a laugh.

"I know, I know. It was bad."

"Okay, we would have been besties," Terry says as he takes his duffle bag from over his shoulder as he looks around the room.

"Still can be," she says, looking back and forth between us. "You guys really do look alike."

I ignore both of her comments. One, they can't be besties because Terry ruins everything he touches. Second, yeah, we look a lot alike and that shit has never been good for me.

"If you need anything. Text me," I say to Terry.

"Are you sure your prez will be okay with me being here? I mean, are all these guys cool with my queer ass being in their club?" he asks, running a nervous hand through his hair.

"Lost Souls aren't like that," Sal replies. "I mean, some of the guys will murmur and have questions, but no one will give you shit, and my brother welcomes family. You're Pierson's family, so you're ours."

He looks at me through his lashes. I would rather talk my shit out with Sal, but I see I need to handle this shit with Terry. This is getting awkward and I know I'm being an ass to him.

However, I know what I have here and I can't afford for him to fuck it all up. So we're going to talk and make some things very clear. I turn to Sal and pull her in my arms for a hug.

I kiss the top of her head. "Do you mind giving us a few? I promise to come right to you."

"Of course, take your time. I'm sure Eva and King want to see me. I'll be fine. Don't worry about me," she says and lift on her toes to kiss my lips.

I watch as she leaves the room. As soon as she pulls the door shut behind her, I spin on Terry and glare at him. His shoulders slump and he moves to sit on the bed.

"There's a bathroom in here. If you don't want to come out of this room, you really don't have to. But if you chose to... this is my family. Those are my brothers out there. They are taking you in, so you be real fucking careful you don't start some shit that threatens my family and the life I've built," I warn.

He stands again. "Pier, I'm not here to cause you any trouble. I'm so regretful for what you've done for me. I promise, as soon as I can get out of your hair I will."

I look him over from head to toe, while working my jaw. The memories of the past have left a bitter taste in my mouth. With a snarl, I move to get in his face.

"You've made that same promise in the past. The difference is... I ain't have shit to live for. I swear to you Terry. I lose my life here because of you, there will be no more you," I say firmly.

With that, I turn to leave the room. "She's gorgeous. I can see why you're so protective of her," he says to my back, causing me to spin around to face him again.

I narrow my eyes at him and he gives me a weak smile. I fold my arms across my chest and watch him closely. He looks clean. I want to believe he is for good.

"God." He looks up at the ceiling, his throat working as he stares up there. "I've thought a million times of all the things I'd say to you. I went from being angry at you, to missing you, to wishing I didn't fuck up so bad.

"I love you, Pier. You're all I've ever had. I see you're happy. I don't want to ruin that for you. If you will allow me to be apart of your life, I promise to toe the line, but if that chance has passed. I'm not going to fuck shit up for you this time.

"I'll go as soon as it's safe. I swear," he says as tears spill down his face.

I look down at my boots. All the things I know about Terry tell me to turn and never look back. However, I can hear Sal in my ear telling me I've grown and if I can, Terry can too.

I nod and twist my jaw, pulling my hand down my face. "I still need more time to heal, but I'll give you the benefit of the doubt. You were once my best friend."

"I'd like to try to get there again. I'm so sorry, Pier. I'll do anything in my power to show you how sorry I am," he pleads.

I close the distance and tug him into a hug. This is my first step to healing. Maybe if I can heal from this, I can kill the demons haunting me in my sleep. That way, I know Sal will always be safe with me.

Sal

"You sure you're good?" King asks for the million time, kissing the top of my head and hugging me around the shoulders.

"Yeah, I'm fine."

"I can't believe that bastard had the nerve to try to break into your place," King grumbles. "But wait, I'm trying to understand something. I thought you guys said he never got a chance to get a hand on you."

I scrunch up my face and frown up at him. "He didn't."

Kings entire demeanor changes. His face turns dark with anger. It's then I remember the bruises around my neck. I groan to myself.

"Where the fuck did you get the marks on your neck from?" King says in a deathly calm.

"King," I warn and roll my eyes. "Leave it alone."

"Wait, tell me that's not from where I think its from."

"It is. I'm sick to my stomach about it—"

"King," I scream and jump up to grab his arm.

He turns and swags on Gutter so fast my head is spinning and I just barely manage to tug his arm back before he could land the blow. Luckily, Gutter ducked out of the way.

"King," I growl as I jump in front of him. "We have enough problems without you butting in. He was asleep. He didn't know it was me trying to week him. I've done the very same thing to him after a nightmare. Drop it."

"You're telling me you choked his big ass in your sleep?" King asks while narrowing his eyes at me.

"No," I murmur.

"I didn't think so."

"I split his lip. That's about the same."

"It's not," King and Gutter say in unison.

I throw my hands up in the air. This is the last thing we need. I need to talk to Gutter and find out where we are.

"You know what? You and I are going to settle this once and for all, otherwise, I'm going to want to kick your ass every time I see you," King says. "Meet me at Axel's gym in the morning."

Without another word, King turns and storms off. I let my shoulders slump and release a long drawn out breath. When I turn to look at Gutter, he's staring at my neck with a look on his face as if he's going to hurl.

"Please, just come and talk to me," I whisper.

He nods his head. I move to his side and wrap around his waist. This is where I want to be. I feel safe and I need that more than anything right now.

We sit in Gutter's room in complete silent for a long time. I've kicked off my shoes and curled my legs beneath me. I'm not sure where we should start, all I know is that we have to start somewhere.

"I'll go to see someone," Gutter says first. "You have my word on that. For now, I don't know if I can sleep in the same bed as you."

My heart sinks. I nod, but I don't know what else to say. I run my fingers through my growing hair.

"I just give your cousin my room," I say bitterly.

"Hey," he says, reaching for my chin to tip my head back. "I can't sleep on the floor or in the chair or something. Not that I sleep much to begin with."

"Maybe we're not right for each other."

He sucks in an audible breath. I look up into his eyes, trying to fight back tears. The pain in his gaze is clear, but I have to get this out.

"Maybe we rushed things. I want totally different things from you—"

"Wait, what?" he says in confusion.

"Do you even understand why I've been so upset with you?"

"I haven't a clue and the shit is stressing me the fuck out."

"You don't want children, Pierson. You totally shut me down and said no. It's like you blackout and dismissed me."

The blood seems to drain from his face. He turns a white as a sheet. His eyes take on a distant look for a few beats. When they clear and focus again, he drops his gaze to my neck.

"You would want to have children with me after what I did to you. What if I hurt our kid? What if I hurt you while you're pregnant?"

"What if I grow a second head and start to breathe fire?" I shout back at him and huff. "I can't live my life by what ifs. Can't you understand that. I want to move on and be normal. I want to laugh, love, and raise a family."

He looks away from me. I scoot closer to him and this time I reach for his face and turn his gaze back to me. Searching for the man I love within his eyes, I find so muchvulnerability.

"I want all that with you. I trust you with my life, Pier. Can I say that you will never wake and hurt me again? No, I can't. Can I be mindful never to try to wake you like that again? Yes, lesson learned.

"I fell in love with you because you were willing to bare yourself to me. In all our fucked up shit, we found each other. Don't bail on me now," I plead.

"I'm not bailing." He reaches to cup my face in his palm. "A baby? You want to have a baby with me?" He shakes his head. "I'm really going to have to sort my shit out. Give me time.

"This is going to be a hard one for me. Those wounds are deep. I... I don't ever want my child to be left alone without someone to take care of them," he says, sounding so much like lost little boy.

"I get it. But look around us. King is ready to kick your ass over me. Do you think he will be any less protective over a niece or nephew?"

Gutter snort. "You have a point."

"Eva, my mom and dad. Our baby would have so many people to love and protect them. We would never have to worry."

He leans in and captures my lips. When he breaks the passionate kiss, he looks me in the eyes. I smile at him and watch him through my lashes.

"No more blacking out on me when I mention babies in our future."

He runs a hand over my hair and cups the back of my neck. "I truly didn't know. I'll do better."

"I love you. We can do this together."

"I love you too. We'll start looking for a new place. We're not going back to that apartment."

"Thank God," I breathe and collapse into him.

We both start to chuckle. He kisses the top of my head and I know all will be okay. I'm still a bit worried about why Hoover came to the apartment looking for me and something in the back of my mind keeps whispering that Spencer is still out there, that I've had enough drama today to last a lifetime.

I need sleep, hopeful, this man will allow me to do that in his arms. That one we'll definitely have to work on.

CHAPTER THIRTY-NINE

Sal

It's been two months and we still haven't found a house we can both agree on. Terry only makes it worse. He and I have similar taste, so it's like we're ganging up on Gutter.

Today we decided to give house hunting a much needed break. Yes, I want to get our own place and move out of the compound, but I can't take another day of disappointing houses.

No, I'm not picky, but Gutter has this vision on how he wants to set the place up for my safety. Most times he's the one who hates the house and wants to move on.

I sigh and press my face against his shoulder. He leans into the bend of the next turn and I smile at the easy of this ride. He's right, this is just what we needed today.

I place a kiss on his shoulder as he pulls to a stop. We're surrounded by trees. However, we've stopped in the center of a cleaning that bumps up against a lake.

I think back to our time in his truck that one time. It seems like a lifetime ago now. A shiver runs through me and I can't help wondering if he has those types of plans for this time.

"Where are we?" I ask as I pull my helmet off.

He gives me a sexy smile as he reaches for my helmet while tucking his under his arm. I'm so curious now. Gutter's full on smiles are so rare.

"What if I told you this all could be ours?" he says, putting both the helmets on the bike.

I spin in a circle. Suddenly, it hits me what's he's asking and I furrow my brows when I turn back to face him. I don't know what to think or say.

"What do you mean?"

"I was talking to your daddy. He made the suggestion for Eva and Brick to design and build us the home we want. I can help with the labor. So, this lot was the first place I thought of. The lake, the space, it's everything we need and more," he replies.

"You're shitting me, right?"

"This is as real as it gets. What do you think?"

"I think it's absolutely perfect. I can see you doing everything you wanted, and I can have a garage to start building a new bike. That lake is everything, I can totally see drinking coffee and looking out at it," I gush as I look around.

"Then, it's done. We've found our home. Brick has already started on blueprints," Gutter says with a cocky grin.

"And what if I said I hated the idea?"

"Wasn't going to happen."

"But if it did?"

"We would have had a big ass piece of land on our hands and nothing to do with it."

I burst out laughing and throw myself into his arms. The craziness lurking in the background of our lives shrieks and all I can focus on is how much I love this man, flaws and all.

When I look up into his eyes, I see so much love. I also see how tired he is. I cup his face and hold his gaze.

"You have to sleep. There's no way you can keep going like this."

"I'm fine. I get rest in the office. I'll rest when this place is built and you're safe in our home."

"That could be months," I say, worry filling me.

"If we approve the designs and we're not picky about finishings, Brick said he can have it done in three, six max. He's bringing in twice the team for this one," he says with a proud look in his eyes.

"Ugh, you still can't wait that long to get a good night's rest."

"I can and I will," he says firmly. "This isn't about me."

"You're so stubborn and yes, it is."

He nuzzles my neck and shoves his big warm hands into the back of my jean shorts. I can't help moaning when he sucks my flesh into his mouth and begins to knead my ass in his palms.

I'm already aroused from his nearness and his cologne surrounding me and filling my head. Let's not forget having my breasts pressed to his back for the last hour. So when he slides thumb down my crack and toward the front of my shorts, I'm not surprised he finds a slack smooth passage for his thick digit.

I moan and pull back to look at his face. There's a wicked smile on his lips. I peck them softly and cupped his face.

"I have an idea," I say.

"Oh yeah, what's that?"

"Maybe we should spend the weekend at my parents."

He begins to push his fingers in and out of me. "I do this and it makes you think of spending the weekend at your parents?" he asks and lifts a brow.

"No, I was just thinking we could relax and spend some time together and after you can choose any room to sleep in and actually get some rest for a few days."

"If that's what you want," he replies and presses his forehead to mine. Pulling his hand from my shorts, he then lifts his fingers to to his mouth and sucks on them. "Let's get out of here."

With that, we put our helmets back on and get back on the bike headed back for the clubhouse. My heart is so full we'll finally have a place to call home. I haven't even seen the floor plans yet, I know it's going to be perfect. Brick and Eva are sure to design us the perfect home.

I don't think life could get any better. Things are falling into place, which only means something is about to go wrong.

Gutter

I narrow my eyes on Sal and Terry as they sit giggling at the outdoor bar. The two have had their head locked together most of the night. I frown and turn my attention back to my beer.

"You're still waiting for the other shoe to drop."

I turn to Cage as he stops beside me with a beer of his own. I give him a look of confusion wondering what he's talking about. He lifts his beer and gives me a knowing smile nodding his head toward Terry.

"I see it in your face you're waiting for him to disappoint you again. I'm a pretty good judge of character I am usually always right. While it's clear in his eyes he's been through a world of shit. It's also clear that he's doing the best he can to fit in here. There is a whole lot of loss in his depths enough to earn him a patch of his own.

"He's a last soul if I've ever seen one. Your waiting for him to fuck up but all I see is him trying to fit in. I think he's found a home just like you have," Cage explains.

"We'll see I know him better than anyone."

"Finding a safe place isn't easy, sometimes you have to learn when someone has found theirs and when they're not willing to give that up," he replies.

"We've had safe places before and he burned them all down. as long as he's around Sal I'll be keeping an eye out," I say firmly.

"You guys find a place?"

"Yeah, it looks like it. Thanks for the advice."

"Since my track record is proven maybe you'll listen to the advice I just gave you. there's such a thing as pushing too hard and pushing someone away."

I take another pull from my beer and cast my eyes towards Terry and Sal again. they are still in their private world laughing at their own jokes. I should be happy that they're getting along so well but like I said I know Terry. The other shoe will drop.

Explosion

Sal

"You should tell him," Terry says.

"Why it's only gonna cause us to argue and fight? things have been so peaceful."

Terry rolls his eyes at me and crossed his arms over his chest. "Like you guys haven't already come to come close to blows several times today. It's your sister's wedding shouldn't everyone be happy?"

"I'm happy I'm just a little irritable.

"And for how long do you think you'll be able to keep the reason for that irritability away from him. tell him he's going to lose his shit if you don't.

"You don't understand he's not ready for this," I plead. "I promised to tell him just not today like you said it's my sister's wedding. The last thing we need is for him to lose his mind in the middle of the reception.

"Here he comes and he has that look on his face again," Terry sings. I follow his line of sight and find gutter sauntering towards us. there's a scowl on his face and his hair looks disheveled as if he's been running his hand through it repeatedly. "tell him," Terry whispers in my ear.

Gutter

If Terry wasn't gay, I'd be ready to kill him. Every time I look he's hovering around or over Sal. The two are almost inseparable. Somewhere along the line they became besties.

Unfortunately, Sal and I have been locking heads all day. I'm not sure what I did this time, but I plan to find out. I'm under enough stress as it is.

A few of my guys think they have located Spencer they just haven't been able to confirm. If he has resurfaced, then I have a new problem on my hands. I'm gonna put him to ground as soon as I set eyes on him.

I find it awfully convenient that he would appear at a time such as this when we're all busy with the wedding. The report came in about a week ago right around the time we had the house framed out and right when Eva and, Sal, and the girls all started finalizing things for the wedding. Everyone has been super busy.

I plan to confirm things for myself after this wedding is over. Needless to say, we've both been high strung Sal stressed with the wedding and me stressed out with everything else on my plate.

"Can we talk?" I asked as I stop in front of Sal.

She has this weird look on her face it's the same one she's had for the last two weeks. As if she has something she wants to say but doesn't know how to say it. I look over her shoulder at Terry and glare at him. he's helping her keep this secret.

I grab Sal by her elbow and start to walk away putting distance between the three of us. However, she yanks her arm away and glares up at me.

"What's wrong with you?" she says and swats at my arm.

"What's wrong with *me*? what's wrong with you? every time I go to talk to you bite my head off what have I done?"

"I won't bite your head off if you weren't acting like a jerk."

"A jerk *me*? This would be so much easier if you would just talk to me and tell me what's going on."

At this point we're creating a scene in the middle of Eva's wedding. I look around at all my brothers and their old ladies looking on as we argue I noticed king glaring at me from across the yard.

I turn her back to Sal standing before me with her hands on her hips her nose scrunched up as she makes this cute little angry face. I don't know whether to be angry or to laugh. When I do you release a small chuckle as I shake my head, she turns and storms away.

"That could have gone a lot better," I mutter to myself.

Canary

Gutter

When I first got the text, I thought it was King wanting to chew my ass out about his sister acting strange again. In the last five months, we've had our fair share of ups and downs. It hasn't been easy with Terry here as well.

Although, I thought we were in a good place until a few weeks ago. Sal has been clinging to Terry more, and the two seem to have their own secrets.

I've let a lot go by, but Sal flipped her shit on me at the recepiotion. I still don't understand what I did wrong. Hell, everything I do is to make her happy.

Including the new place, I had built after spilling Hoover's brains all over our living room. Salalia couldn't stand to be there. With Spencer still out there, I didn't want to take chances. We've been staying at the clubhouse until I found the perfect location.

I noticed King watching the entire scene Sal made. I had a feeling he was going to call me on it. Shit, it took a month, but King finally called in his pound of flesh from me. I let him beat my ass in the boxing ring at Axel's gym.

However, tonight, when I arrive in the clubhouse basement, I'm surprised to find the entire Squad in the room. Cage standing with a stony look on his face and King looking like he's going to explode as he glares at one of our prospects. Wax, I believe his name is, sits in a chair in the middle of the room.

"Good," King hisses. "Now that your judge and jury are here you can go on and finish singing."

Wax looks around the room nervously. He then looks at his hands, before turning his eyes back up to King. He looks scared as fuck, but determination slips through and he pushes forward.

"A while back, my brother showed up on my doorstep. He had this big plan to take over the club and bring you guys down." He licks his lips and shakes his head.

"I didn't want to help him, but he guilted and manipulated me into it. Trixie has been helping him. She covers so I can snoop around.

"I... I didn't know who Kodak was. I found the file and I thought it would be a little something to shut Pop up for a while. I was sick to my stomach, when I found out I led him to Sal. She's always been like a sister to me." He looks green in the face.

I growl and take a step toward him. King places a hand on my chest to hold me back. I barely contain myself and stay put.

"You guys are my real family. Pop is a fucking lunatic. He's going to get himself and everyone around him killed. At least, this way I'm choosing my death and my family over some crazy ass vendetta.

"He has fucked everything up.

"Cage, you were good to me when I was a little shit. Then, King stepped in where you left off. I'll tell you everything I know and then I'll take my death like a man. I just won't let Pop hurt my family, I can't do this anymore," Wax finishes, dropping his eyes to his lap.

"You're still a little shit," Cage grumbles.

"He's telling the truth," Vault informs the room. Vault is an expert at reading people. It's what he does for King.

"Finally," Reap chirps. "It was getting way too fucking quiet around here."

"Thought it was just me," Diggs mutters.

"Well, if you're gonna tell us every everything start talking," King says.

"Pop is in big trouble. he was supposed to deliver the lost souls operational system to Castro. He thought kidnapping Kodak would deliver that information. now Castro is calling in the debt and pop has nothing to show. He's getting desperate and desperate people mistakes. He's been contacting those weird guys that are obsessed with Sal and.

"what guys," King snarls.

"The two that are stalking her. We've been watching them as they watch her. He reached out to that guy that's looking for his boyfriend. Somehow Pop thinks all these people were going to help him get square with Castro. It's a death trap I tell you they're all gonna get us killed."

I shake my head. Never a dull moment. Never.

"Everyone head back to the wedding and act as if nothing is going on," King commands. "We'll move on this when the wedding is over."

We all file out and do as he says. I'm left with a sinking feeling in my gut. Why has this kid chosen today to sing like a Canary? if you ask me, it's all too convenient.

The Reasons

Gutter

When I get back to the reception my gaze lands on Terry and Sal talking in the corner once again. If Sal I won't talk Terry's about the spill. I March over to them and grab Terry by his forearm dragging him with me.

"What's going on what are you two keeping from me?"

"Pier, this is between you two. Sal should be the one to tell you," he replies.

"I've tried that already. is there something I should be worried about?"

"No, Peir, I think you need to show her it's safe to tell you," he says.

"Why wouldn't she feel safe talking to me?"

"I don't know, but you guys need to figure it out you're both driving me crazy.

I tug at my hair in frustration. I don't know what else to do. Terry taps taps his hand against my chest.

"Listen to me, have you shown her? does she know?" he nodded at the stage where the band had just taken a break.

I groan and roll my eyes. "Yes, she knows. she also knows why I wouldn't do that here."

"Perfect which is exactly why you should. show her you can change take away that fear. If you can do this you can do anything."

I looked from him to the stage and bounced on my toes. For Sal I would, I want to if she needs to know I can change and this will show her I will.

No matter how much it feels like my insides are burning I muster up the courage and start to walk toward the empty stage, I feel Terry following at my back and I already know he's going to do this with me. He runs ahead and sits at the drum set. I step up to the mic trying not to hyperventilate, looking around the club at all my brothers I see a bunch of curious faces but it's not until I see Sal's face and the smile on her lips that I nod my head at myself knowing this is the right thing to do.

If she needs to see change, I'll show her change.

Sal

"What's going on with you guys now?" Eva asks as she Pats the seat beside her.

I take the seat next to my sister and wrapping an arm around her, placing my palm on her protruding belly. "I have something I need to tell him, but I don't think he's ready for it."

"Is it what I think it is?

"Depends on what you're thinking," I say.

Eva turns to me with her mouth gaping open. she reaches a shaky hand out to touch my belly. It's then that I see Gutter step his big frame on the stage. I gasps and cover my mouth.

I'm mesmerized as Terry starts to beat the drums. I know the tune instantly it's "The reason" by Hoobastank.

"Oh my God," Eva exclaims.

My heart fills to the point of exploding. I know he's only doing this for me. He belts out the lyrics and tears spring to my eyes. The man has such a beautiful voice. Terry's not doing bad playing the drums either as his tick dark hair flies about around him. I let the lyrics to the song sink in each one having so much meaning.

"He's so good," Eva gushes.

"I know." I locked eyes with Peirson as his hair falls into his eyes and he belts out the chorus of the song. He's looking at me through his lashes and it's the hottest sight I've ever seen.

I'm mesmerized by the way he points to at me as he really gets into the performance, while singing that I'm the reason. I can't believe he's doing this in front of everyone. Maybe if he can do this, maybe he is ready for me to tell him the truth.

"Go up there go get your man," Eva says as she pushes me from my seat.

I satnd from my seat and start for the stage as I whistle and shout the rest of the brothers and their ladies stand around clapping and cheering as well.

I run for the stage as he steps down I fling myself at him and wrapped my arms and legs around him. He catches me and hold me tight against his chest. I know it's now or never I leaned into his ear and whisper

"I'm pregnant," I breathe and back away to look him in the eyes.

His blue-gray eyes are wide with surprise. He bites down on his bottom lip as he starts to rub my back.

"Did you really think you couldn't tell me that?" he says as he nuzzles the tip of my nose with his. "I'd do anything for you. be a father, stand on a stage in front of all my brothers and sing, anything."

"I love you," I say through my tears

"I love you too and I'm never letting you go."

Over

Sal

"It was such a beautiful wedding," mom says as we wait for them to pull the cages around.

"It was," I say and peek around her to see what's taking so long.

Dad is the first one to pull up. Terry goes to open the door for mom and helps her in.

"Are you guys still coming to the house?" she asks just before he closes the door.

I nod. We planned to spend the night there since the house isn't ready. Mom and dad's has become our home away from home. Mum rolls her window down.

"Use your key we're going to make a stop," she calls out.

I give her and Cage a grin. mom still doesn't remember anything, but at least Cage seems to be getting through to her.

Gutter finally pulls up and tosses the keys to Terry. Terry rounds the car, and they lock their heads together as Gutter whispers something to him. Gutter rounds the car to open the door for me and pulls me into his embrace. I climb into the car as I noticed all the bikes lining up behind us.

When I see reap I noticed she's torn the skirts from her bridesmaids gown and now she has a pistol strapped to each thigh as she straddles her bike. whatever is going on it can't be good.

"What's going on?" I ask as Terry slips in behind the wheel.

"Not sure. I just need to get you home safe."

We pull off in silence the trip to mom and dad is not that far from the clubhouse. Before I can think to turn on the radio we're turning into the driveway of the house. I notice right away something is off. The light in my bedroom is on. I know I turned everything off after Eva and I left the room this morning to head to the church.

Gutter

King wants to move on the intel we have on Pop tonight. all hands on deck. Since Sal will be at the house with her mom, I figured Terry could drive her there while I ride out with my squad.

There will be more than a few brothers at the house to keep an eye on Rose and Sal. They're also there to keep an eye out for Rossi. We still haven't dealt with him, although I know for a fact, he's looking for Terry.

"Let's roll out I'm ready to put it an end to this slippery motherfucker," king says as we all straddle our bikes. I don't miss that even Brick is with us. everyone revs their engine, and we start to roll out in formation.

King pauses and pulls his phone out he then turned to look back at us. It's like someone's poured ice in my veins. I'm frozen in place knowing that whatever he's about to say isn't going to go well. The cold look in his eyes speaks for itself and there's rage rolling off of him. However, when he speaks, I feel like he's put a bullet in my chest.

"Change of plans, we're heading to Dad's. Spencer has made a reappearance.

I pull off without a word heading straight for my woman. he won't be getting away from me this time. I hear the roar of bikes behind me as I drive forward blindly. Once again I'm racing against the clock to make sure I save the most important person to me.

Rose

Cage is such a handsome man. My heart stutters when he turns and winks at me as his tongue follows the swirl of the ice cream on his cone. His charming smile made it impossible to say no when he asked me if I wanted to make a stop for ice cream before heading home.

As I watch him lick the vanilla confection I'm thrown back in time. I still don't remember much but it comes in little spurts here and there like now I'm hit with the memory of cage leaning against his bike with a cone in his hand.

His eyes sparkled as he looked at me. Again licking at his serving of vanilla soft serv. I stand there between his Jean clad legs with my own chocolate cone in my hand as the sweet treat dripped all over my fingers and wrist.

Cage gave me a sexy smile and wink before placing his large hand on my waist. I kept my eyes on his. he reached for my wrists and bent his head to lick the dripping chocolate from my hand. My heart pounded as his tongue glided across my skin. my nipples came to life and started to press against the fabric of my bra.

Humming to himself, he then placed his hand back on my waist and moved his palm down to my backside giving a squeeze.

"Cage," I gasped.

"I've been wanting you for a long time, Rose. When are you going to let me pound that tight little pussy out and show you why I'm meant to be your old man?" he says in a Husky gravelly voice.

"Maybe you should Take Me Home, if the girls are sleeping you can stay the night," I said.

He pulled back giving me a seductive smile and wink. With one hand behind my neck he tugged my face to his and kisses me passionately.

I'm brought back to the present by cage clearing his throat.

"Thought I lost you there, darlin'," he says when my eyes focus.

"Nope I'm right here just remembering how much you like ice cream and how soft your lips are," I reply.

His bright blue eyes go wide, and I can't help but to lean across the seat and peck his lips. He gives me a full out smile that takes over his face.

"Come on let's get home," he says.

We pull out of the parking lot and head for home. Cage has his arm over the back of the seat behind me. We ride to the house in a comfortable silence. As soon as we pulled up, I knew something was off. Cage brings. the car to a slow stop at the front entrance. The front door sits jarred wide open.

"Stay right here," cage commanded.

He stepped from the car and I watch through the front windshield as he enters the house. I waited a few minutes before stepping from the car myself. The house is pitch black except for a rooms upstairs.

Sal

Terry and I let ourselves in the house with the key that mom gave me. We make it as far as the foyer before I froze in place. There is a man standing in my home. I recognized him right away. Ice runs through my veins and I couldn't find my breath. Terry stiffens beside me and reaches out a hand to cover me with and shoves me sme behind him.

My thoughts scrambled to think of where dad keeps his guns I just needed to get to one.

"Who are you and what are you doing here?" Terry asks.

"I'm an old friend of Salialia's. Surely you Remember Me, my dear," he replies.

"You're no friend of mine, Spencer," I say bitterly. "Why are you here?"

"I've come for you, you and I have some unfinished business."

"No, you have a death wish," Terry says.

"The only ones with a death wish are you and that other one that keeps putting his hands on her. How could you betray me like this, sweetheart? after You had to know I was out there watching, that I would see. every time one of them touches you it makes my skin crawl, but it's Okay I'm here now you can make it up to me.

"We'll go far away, and we can start all over no one will be in our way this time," he says, sounding like a madman.

Cage

I send a quick text letting King know something is amiss at the house then slip my phone back into my pocket. When I walk into my home, I see nothing but red. This motherfucker has a lot of nerve. not only is he in my home, he's holding a gun to my baby girl.

He has balls of steel. I look over to a trembling Sal and I completely lose it. I charge the son of a bitch. he doesn't get time to pull the trigger as I slam into him with my elbow to his face. I completely ignore the blood that splatters on my white shirt.

Swiftly, I slam him against the nearest wall and wrap my hands around his neck. I could kill him with my bare hands and that's exactly what I try to do. he reaches out and manages to get his hands around my neck. I barely feel it. Without flinching, I released one hand from around his throat and jabbed him in his ribs.

He gasps from the blow. I go back to choking the wind from his lungs. I grit my teeth in his in his face.

"You you're the one who put your hands on my baby girl. You steal her innonence, I vowed I'd be the one to take your last breathe."

I'm distracted for a moment by the sharp intake of his air that fills the room. turning my head slightly I see Rose has entered the front door. she has her eyes narrowed on a man that I'm choking.

Rose

I get tired of waiting in the car and get out to find out what's going on. I stepped through the front door right on the tail end of Cage's words. this man has touched my daughter. I'm assuming it's during the time that I've lost with Sal which burned me up even more. I moved to the closet where cage said my bat rests. once I have the aluminum bat in my hand, I lift it and stormed forward.

The man is choking cage and they are wrestling back and forth.

"Mom," Sal calls out. I don't turn away from the man wrestling with Cage instead, I bring my bat down on the center of his back and cave his whole shit in. he released his Cage and howls. I keep swinging. I go for his knees and crack him upside his head.

Cage swings with his fists and catches him across the face at the same time I swing for the side of his head the man spins and falls to the ground whimpering. I don't stop swinging I aim for his balls. meeting my target with a satisfied grin.

Sal

I don't think I've ever seen cage so angry. and I've watched him shove the barrel of a gun down a man's throat for calling me the N word. I'm so enraptured in watching my parents fight for justice for me I'm stunned when a man appears through the front door and grabs Terry by the back of his hair.

Terry tries to twist to see who has a hold of him. "Rossi," Terry gasps as fear lights his eyes.

"It looks like my new friend knew what he was talking about," the Rossi guy says.

Terry blue eyes nearly popped from his skull as he as he looks back at the man who's holdings him in his grasp. The guy starts to back towards the door holding Terry at gunpoint, while dragging him by the back of his topknot.

I get the feeling that this guy is bad news, and I can't let him take Pierson's cousin out that door. I reach for a photo frame from the wall of me and my family and turned to swing it at the man's head.

There are two sounds that suck all the energy out of the room the rumbling of bikes in the distance and the shattering of the glass from the frame. Cage and mom stopped tussling with Spencer. When my dad takes in the man trying to back out with Terry he straightens and balls his fists at his side.

"Rossi," Cage says. "You and I both know that's not a good idea. Back away from the kid and leave before you earn a debt you can't pay. To my knowledge you already have one of those."

ROSSI turns his gun on me not releasing Terry as he still moves for the door. Blood drips from his head from where I hit him with the picture frame.

"I'm leaving and I'm taking him with me."

Cage takes a step forward. "Are you sure about that?"

Terry's eyes grow widered and he starts to struggle against Rossi's hold. Roosi starts to look unsure of himself as the rumble of bikes gets closer. He steps outside still holding onto Terry and I follow. A grin as I see the formation driving towards us it's the squad and this guy is a dead man if I ever seen one.

"How did you find me?" Terry asks.

"I got a call from some guy named Pop he had a lot of information in details about all of you."

Terry starts to struggle more to get free, reaching out with his long arm to knock the gun away. Rossi hits him in the back of the head with the butt of the gun. This time Rossi aims at me and pulls the trigger.

"No!" Terry and Gutter scream in unison.

Gutter

The Squad and I are riding up the driveway as figures come into view in front of the house. I noticed right away that's Sal being held at gunpoint. everything seems to move in slow motion.

Terry flails about in the guy's hold. And then the loud sound of gunfire catches my attention. I leap off my bike screaming no.

I watched in horror as Terry runs to shield Sal from the gunshot. his body jerks and slams into Sal's knocking them both to the ground. red spills and begins to cover Terry's white shirt.

Before I can process what's happening, Reap runs past me with her guns drawn. I watch as she puts two in Rossi's chest and then each kneecap.

I run straight to Terry and Sal. I can't believe Terry use his body to shield her. It's the most selfless thing I've ever seen him do.

"Are you OK man? talk to me," I say to my cousin once I run to his side. I take a quick glance at Sal to make sure she and the baby are Okay. she doesn't seem to have any wounds Terry is the one who's bleeding all over the place.

"I'm fine," Terry gasps.

He's not I can hear the blood filling his lungs.

"We need an ambulance. Someone please help me," I scream.

I'm sick to my stomach, I failed him again. Everyone is right he's been trying. and it has felt more like home with him here. Now that all has been changed in the blink of an eye. If he doesn't make it, I don't know what I'm gonna do.

I can't even fully process when rose drags Spencer out of the house by the top of his hair and flings his broken body at King's feet. all I know is help needs to get here to save my cousin, I can't lose him like this.

"Hang in there," I say.

Terry grabs my hand with his trembling one. "I'd do it again," he says. "You're happy and you deserve it. I won't let anything take that away from you."

Pop again

Gutter

I pull my bike up to the office dressed in a suit ready for my morning meetings. When I see Cage, Brick and King's bikes parked out front I pull a face, my meeting this morning don't involve any of them. Pop is still blowing in the wind, so things have been tense around the club and clubhouse.

I swing my leg over my bike a stroll into the office. I can't help the smile that breaks out on my face when I see Terry at the front desk talking away. He's proven to be a big help around here with his attention to detail and organization.

He still has his clothing line as a matter of fact Cage has invested in him to start the lost Souls apparel collection. Terry has designed a full out biker line. When he's not entertaining buyers in our backroom as if it's a showroom he's at our reception desk helping to book clients with the new system Sal built.

Go figure he fits right in with the Lost Souls family. Sal is super protective of him, and it was her idea for him to come and work for me that way she would know I always have an eye on him. after a month of recovery in the hospital Terry was ready to get on with his life, he'd spent nearly six months hiding out with us and neglecting his real life, I couldn't blame him for wanting to find a place of his own so he could start the healing process and start his life over again.

"Your nine o'clock is here and you have a few visitors in your office," Terry informs me as I walked past his desk.

I head to my office first, when I stepped through the door I find king sitting behind my desk with his feet up cage sits across from him as Brick staring at his phone looking like his head is about to explode.

"You're gonna want to see this," he says to King and hands over the phone.

"Has she lost her fucking mind?" king roars and jumps up from my seat.

He pats Brick on the back. "Dad, let's roll out looks like you're gonna get to put an end to Pop today."

They stormed from my office, and I get the feeling that this isn't going to be a quiet day. Whatever Brick showed king with that phone was only the start to more drama I can feel it in my bones. One thing I know you can never say it's quiet around the Lost souls there's always something lurking right around the corner.

ACKNOWLEDGMENTS

This has been an interesting ride with this book. Heck, this series. Because of the way it was started, I had to figure out somethings to make it all work for me in my head. Phew, I got it.

I thank you all for your patience, as I've gone through some ups and downs this year. You hung in there with me and that means a lot. I thank you for your trust in me as an author. I refuse to give less than my best.

I thank those that are Blue members. I hope this is a happy addition to your collection. Thank you to all that supported me in learning new ways to look at the writing purpose and who listened as I talked my way around my thoughts and ideas.

I watch His Grace on a daily. Uncommon favor is a thing to behold and I'm grateful to receive it. Boy, do I have a testimony. Thank you, Lord. You are my Source, may they see your Glory and walk in it.

On to the next! KING! No, for real this time. LOL

ABOUT THE AUTHOR

Blue Saffire is a housewife with too much time to think and not enough time to herself. By some miracle, she has found the time to write books. Blue represents the secret author inside that some of us are too scared to let out.

Blue is a loving wife, who is itching to make her way back to city life. The burbs are not enough background music to the story of her life. Life throws Blue challenges daily and since her diary is no longer enough, she has decided it is time for a new outlet. Thus, you are gaining access to the mind of Blue Saffire.

So here in lays the thoughts of Blue Saffire, the author, the wife, and the woman. Enjoy.

Wait there is more to come! You can stay updated with my latest releases by subscribing to my newsletter at

www.BlueSaffire.com

If you enjoyed Never, I'd love to hear

your thoughts and please feel free to leave a

review on my webpage by clicking here. And when you do, please let me know by emailing me

TheBlueSaffire@gmail.com

or leave a comment on Facebook https://www.facebook.com/BlueSaffireDiaries or Twitter

@TheBlueSaffire

Other books in the Blue Saffire Membership

Always: Lost Souls MC Book 3 Coming Soon…

Other books by Blue Saffire

Placed in Best Read Order of Legally Bound and the connected Spinoff Series

Also available….

Legally Bound

Legally Bound 2: Against the Law

Legally Bound 3: His Law

Perfect for Me

Hush 1: Family Secrets

Ballers: His Game

Brothers Black1: Wyatt the Heartbreaker

Legally Bound 4: Allegations of Love

Hush 2: Slow Burn

Legally Bound 5.0: Sam

Yours: Losing My Innocence 1

Yours 2: Experience Gained

Yours 3: Life Mastered

Ballers 2: His Final Play

Legally Bound 5.1: Tasha Illegal Dealings

Brothers Black 2: Noah

Blue Saffire Coming Soon…

Other books by Evei Collection Books by Blue Saffire